A DETECTIVE INSPECTOR DECLAN WALSH NOVEL

LETTER FROM THE DEAD

NEW YORK TIMES #1 BESTSELLER **TONY LEE** WRITING AS

JACK GATLAND

Hooded Man
MEDIA

Published by Hooded Man Media.

First Edition: November 2020
Second Edition: September 2022

PRAISE FOR JACK GATLAND

'This is one of those books that will keep you up past your bedtime, as each chapter lures you into reading just one more.'

'This book was excellent! A great plot which kept you guessing until the end.'

'Couldn't put it down, fast paced with twists and turns.'

'The story was captivating, good plot, twists you never saw and really likeable characters. Can't wait for the next one!'

'I got sucked into this book from the very first page, thoroughly enjoyed it, can't wait for the next one.'

'Totally addictive. Thoroughly recommend.'

'Moves at a fast pace and carries you along with it.'

'Just couldn't put this book down, from the first page to the last one it kept you wondering what would happen next.'

Before LETTER FROM THE DEAD...
There was

LIQUIDATE
THE PROFITS

Also by Jack Gatland

COVERT ACTION

COUNTER ATTACK

STEALTH STRIKE

DAMIAN LUCAS BOOKS

THE LIONHEART CURSE

STANDALONE BOOKS

THE BOARDROOM

For Mum, who inspired me to write.

For Tracy, who inspires me to write.

CONTENTS

PROLOGUE

THE NEW YEAR'S EVE PARTY WAS IN FULL SWING AS MICHAEL Davies made his way through the ballroom; his face a mask of murderous fury.

'Hey,' he said, as he passed one of the waiting staff; a young Indian girl in white shirt and black skirt, currently with a tray of champagne flutes balanced precariously on her hand. 'You know my wife, right? The woman in the green dress who hired you?'

'Sorry.' The girl shook her head and carried on serving drinks as Michael looked around once more.

'Well, do me a favour. If you see her, come find me. I'll make it worth your while.'

Walking on from the girl, Michael continuously scanned the partygoers for any sign of his wife, but it was too crowded to gain any kind of view from this level. He needed height of some kind. Men in tuxedos and women in evening gowns were visible as far as the eye could see, and all of them were in his way right now. Indeed, Michael himself was wearing a tailored tuxedo that was worth most people's salaries, his thinning hair swept to the side. He looked like *James Bond*, even if he didn't currently feel like him.

Pulling at his collar, he wished he could loosen it, even for a moment. Michael wasn't really a fan of collars, especially tight ones; a throwback from his years of political activism on the far left of the party. But apparently under Blair's 'New Labour' title, Labour MPs wore tuxedos now.

That said, Michael could see that only half of the men attending the party had bothered to wear bow ties, instead preferring the newer trend of wearing black silk ties with their suits. Michael hated people who did that. Almost as much as he currently hated his wife.

Still, at least the party was going better than the previous year's one. The looming threat of 'Y2K' and 'The Millennium Bug' had half the guests staring nervously at their phones for most of the night, waiting for calls while the other half loudly complained at not being invited to North Greenwich and the newly opened 'Millennium Dome', where they could have stood with ten thousand other people, including Tony Blair and the Queen, watching Mick Hucknall and The Corrs.

Personally, Michael couldn't think of anything worse, and he was secretly overjoyed that the whole bloody thing had become an expensive albatross around Blair's neck.

Maybe Blair didn't come this year because Blair knew he would take the piss. Yes, that was probably it.

But secretly Michael suspected that Blair wasn't showing up. He wasn't taking Michael's calls because he'd heard the rumours, and more importantly where Michael's funding money was going from now on. And Blair was probably chewing off advisors' heads over it. Devington Industries was a major donor to the party right now and to have them pull support could create a wave of similar decisions, possibly fatal in an election year.

A man in one of these godforsaken tuxedo-tie combos staggered over to Michael, weaving his way through the crowd with what seemed to be either expert special awareness, or more likely drunken obliviousness.

'Michael!' he cried out, as he fell against his newly found friend. 'Excellent party! Tons of totty! Love it!'

Michael forced a smile and ever so slightly nudged the drunken man away from him. Thirty years old and with a full mane of lustrous blond hair, Charles Baker looked more like a movie star than a Member of Parliament. But a Labour MP he was, having won the Lower Denham seat from the Conservatives in the '97 election.

In fact, he was one of Blair's 'golden boys', allegedly earmarked for top things down the line. If it wasn't for the fact that one of those rumoured top things could be Leader of the Party and therefore possibly Prime Minister if Blair failed to unite the party before next year's General Election, Michael would have told the hideous bore to piss off and annoy someone else.

'Thank you, you're so kind,' Michael replied behind a plastered-on fake smile.

Charles leaned in, rubbing some tell-tale white powder from his nose. 'A little birdy says that this is the last of your bashes. That you're pulling your support. Is this the case?'

Michael shrugged. 'Depends what Blair decides the manifesto is going to be. You know, if he keeps to his promise at the conference.'

'Aw come on, don't be a bore!' Charles loudly exclaimed to the room. 'We're in power! That's what matters!'

'You don't think Socialists should have a voice?' Michael

asked, getting seriously irritated with the drunken idiot in front of him.

'I don't talk politics at parties like this,' Charles mumbled, spying a young brunette across the room. 'I talk totty. Shame they're all stick thin though, you know? I prefer them a bit stockier. Like your sister-in-law.'

Michael tried to move away again, but even though Charles had locked onto a new, more feminine target, he seemed to be focused on currently making Michael's night a living hell.

'You could fund me,' he whispered. 'Screw Blair. We could change the narrative together.'

'But surely if I'm as far left as you seem to think, you're a little too Centrist for me,' Michael replied, his tone almost mocking in nature.

'You'd be surprised,' Charles said, tapping the side of his cocaine-covered nose. 'I'm more a *Bennite* than a Blairite.' He was referring to the elder statesman, Tony Benn, who, although supportive of the current Government, was critical of some of their acts – the bombing of Iraq three years earlier causing him to be very outspoken. There was talk around that he was so unimpressed with the current state of the party that he'd be stepping down as MP at the next election.

Michael looked at Charles, trying to work out how much of this was spoken in jest, or whether drugs and alcohol, most likely supplied by one of his fellow MPs, were loosening Charles Baker's usually well-locked-down lips.

'I hear you're openly funding Shaun Donnal,' Charles said softly.

'Don't believe the rumours,' Michael replied.

'First rule of politics, dear boy,' Charles said, irritating

Michael. He wasn't Charles' *boy*. They were the same bloody age. 'Buy the rumour, sell the truth.'

'You're giving me motivational sales quotes?'

'Same bloody thing.' Charles tried to smile, but it came out more as a leer. 'Anyone who thinks that politicians aren't salesmen doesn't understand how politics work. Anyway, I'm not sure that Shaun's your boy. His morals are ... questionable.'

'I know exactly how moral or immoral Donnal is.'

'Yes,' Charles mused. 'You probably know that better than us right now.'

Michael forced himself to bite back his first response to this. *Of course, Charles knew. They all shared the same bloody office.* 'Maybe I'll pick Andrew instead.'

'MacIntyre? Sure, I suppose that could work,' Charles mocked. 'I could get him right now for you if you want. He's currently in the cloakroom ramming as much gak up his nose as he can before the fireworks go off.'

Michael indicated Charles' face. 'You seem to have been joining him.'

Charles rubbed at his nose. 'Oh, just keeping him loyal, that's all. This stuff does nothing for me. I was born with a natural high.'

'Well, we can always discuss my plans for candidate funding in the New Year,' Michael said, looking around again as he changed the subject. 'I don't suppose you've seen Victoria, have you?'

Charles waved vaguely towards the stairs at the back end of the ballroom.

'I think I saw her going upstairs about ten minutes back. Staring at her phone like it was about to go off. *Boom!*' He made an expansive 'explosion' gesture with his hands, accidentally knocking into the Secretary of State for Social Security.

"Sorry, darling,' he slurred, placing a hand around the shoulder of his bemused new companion while waving his other hand. 'I was talking to ...'

But his words trailed off as Charles looked around to see that Michael had gone.

Michael was in fact already at the stairs, making his way up them two at a time. He wasn't the fittest of men and there were a lot of stairs in this double-height ballroom, but his anger spurred him on right now, almost barging past the security guard at the top of the stairs.

'Sorry, sir,' the guard said. 'Only cabinet members and major donors past here.'

Michael looked at the guard, as if examining something under his nail. He was big built, but this looked more due to the repetitive nature of pasties rather than pull-ups.

'Have you seen any cabinet members here?' he asked. 'I mean, apart from the low-level ones that nobody gives a damn about?'

The guard took a moment to look back at the party before turning back to Michael, as if actually looking for some. 'Well, that's as maybe, sir. But unless you're ...'

'I'll tell you who I am,' Michael hissed, as he leaned in closer. 'I'm the man who paid for this whole bloody thing. You standing here? I paid for you. You work for me.'

The security guard shifted a little in his stance now, as if unsure of the steps to take next. Calming slightly, Michael looked around.

It wasn't this poor sod's fault that he was angry.

'Look mate, I'm sorry for snapping. It's been a very long day,' he apologised. 'I'm just looking for my wife.'

The guard shook his head. 'I don't know your wife,' he replied. 'Maybe if you had a photo of her I could look at?'

Michael was already pulling his wallet out and opening it up, showing the guard the photo behind the small, plastic screen in it. A red-haired woman, slim and pretty, laughing in a garden. An obviously happier time.

'Her,' Michael snapped. 'Victoria Davies.'

The guard studied the photo, nodding. 'Yeah, I saw her. She went past about ten minutes back,' he said. 'Her and a man.'

'Which man?' Michael was starting to anger again. The guard shook his head.

'Don't remember the name, sir. Think she said it was Shaun someone.'

'Shaun Donnal?'

'That could be it.'

Michael looked past the guard. There were a multitude of places that Shaun bloody Donnal and Vickie could have gone.

'Did you see where they went?' he asked.

The guard nodded as he pointed to a side door. 'The lady went to the roof,' he replied. 'Said she needed a smoke where nobody would see her, as the press are all outside the front and she'd told everyone she'd quit.'

'And Shaun went with her?'

'No, I think he returned down there.' The guard pointed back down to the ballroom where, in the middle of the dance floor, Michael could see a balding, bespectacled man in his early thirties.

Shaun Donnal. Another of Blair's bloody Golden Boys.

'Thank you,' Michael said, pulling a twenty pound note out of his still open wallet and passing it to the guard. 'Don't let any of the guests past until I return, right?'

'But the toilets—'

'They can piss in the car park.' Michael's voice was filled with venom as he stormed past the guard and towards the side door leading to the roof. Nothing today had gone as planned. He'd agreed with Labour HQ back in September, during the party conference, that he would hold the Labour New Year's party here at Devington House. Blair himself had confirmed this, but Prescott, *bloody Prescott*, had convinced him that perhaps seeing their representatives living it up like Toffs wouldn't go down well with the proletariat and so Blair, Brown and all of their little hangers on had decided to hold a far smaller event at Number 10 instead, with that guitarist from Oasis and some of the cast of Eastenders.

Michael hated Prescott too. That was a man who was pissed off that Michael was planning a movement within the Labour Party that wouldn't have him in it.

He pulled out his phone, dialling a number on it.

'Sir?' The voice of Francine Pearce, his PA, spoke through the speaker.

'Where are you?' he asked.

'To be honest, I'm not sure,' Francine admitted. 'There are so many bloody rooms here.'

'When did you get here? I've not seen you.'

'Well maybe because that's because you've been too busy shouting at the kitchen staff and not looking,' Francine's voice was terse. 'I was here before the guests turned up. What's happened now?'

'She's missing again,' Michael hissed. 'Find her before I do because I'm gonna bloody well kill her.' And before

Francine could reply he disconnected the call, slamming the phone into his jacket and continuing towards the roof.

If Michael had paused and actually looked around, he'd admit that it wasn't all bad. There were a large amount of Labour MPs and donors here, but the problem he had was that none of the important ones had attended. And with rumours flying of a General Election in less than five months and Labour doing badly in the polls, Michael had wanted to at least be seen to have the ear of the Prime Minister before Blair was booted out of office by the Tories, and Michael had to start the same damn dance all over again, building someone new to face *William sodding Hague* of all people.

Instead, he was hunting around the building for his adulterous slut of a wife.

VICTORIA DAVIES WAS STANDING ON THE SQUARE, FLAT ROOF OF the eastern wing of Devington House, staring down over the parapet edge at the multitude of expensive cars parked alongside each other on the gravel drive. Stunningly beautiful in an emerald-green dress, her long, red hair complementing both the clothing and the expensive emerald necklace that she wore around her neck, she looked no older than twenty, although she was rapidly approaching thirty; a landmark that filled her with dread.

It was a cold, clear night but she didn't feel it as she kept glancing repeatedly down to the phone in her hand. A Nokia 8890, it was a slim plastic brick, a sliding cover hiding the buttons of the keypad. She had wanted one ever since she'd seen Keanu Reeves use one in *The Matrix*. Sometimes she'd even look out of the window, wondering whether she was in the Matrix right now; wondering if there was any way to escape this mess that she'd got herself into.

She looked down at the phone again. The text message was still there.

I know everything. Meet me where we made the pact.

Victoria had assumed the message meant the roof; it was where Shaun had first expressed his love for her. But now she was starting to worry that she'd picked the wrong location. There had been so many stolen moments in so many locations.

The door to the stairs opened, and Victoria turned to see Michael emerge, letting the door slam behind him as he walked slowly towards her.

No, not now. Please not now.

'There you are, I've been hunting everywhere for you,' he said, as he approached. 'Needed some air?'

Nervously, Victoria nodded.

'Felt a little sick,' she replied. 'Probably the caviar.'

Michael nodded slowly, as if considering this. He pulled out a cigarette, lighting it and taking a couple of puffs, allowing the silence to stretch.

'You've had that happen to you before, and caviar can be a rich food,' Michael replied matter-of-factly. 'But it's probably more the morning sickness. I mean, I've heard that can be a bastard.'

Victoria's face paled as she tried to mentally backtrack towards a new conversational path before realising it was too late to bluff this one out as Michael continued.

'I hope you're not high again, *darling*. Playing with benzos and K would be a real bad thing to do in your state.'

'I'm not. I'm clean. Who told you?' she eventually asked.

Michael shrugged. 'Does it matter?'

Victoria forced a smile.

'Well, I'm glad you know our news now,' she said, moving towards him. 'I wanted to tell you after the party. You've been so busy, and ...'

'Is it mine?' Michael asked, cutting her off.

'Of course, it's yours!' Victoria replied, the indignance in her voice rising. 'Who else did you think it could be?'

'With you? I never know.' Michael looked around the roof, tears now building. Whether they were tears of joy, sadness or anger, Victoria couldn't make out. 'But if it was me, it'd be a bloody miracle. Like a *Jesus Christ* level miracle.'

'What do you mean?'

Michael looked back to Victoria, holding her gaze for a long moment before he spoke again. 'Because I had the snip eight months ago.'

Now it was Victoria's turn to look angry.

'You what?' she said, her tone as icy as the wind that was building. 'You did that without telling me?'

'My balls, my rules,' Michael said. 'And I've never been quiet about not wanting kids.'

'And I've never been quiet about my need to have a family,' Victoria replied harshly.

'Well, it looks like you got your wish,' Michael snapped. 'It's a Christmas miracle.' He stopped, looking out across the roof, out towards the gardens behind the house and the night that lay beyond.

'Is it ... is it *his?*' he asked, his voice no more than a whisper.

Victoria went to reply, but then shook her head sadly.

'I don't know,' she answered truthfully.

Michael started to chuckle.

'You don't know,' he muttered. 'Jesus, Vickie. Did you do all three of them before—'

He didn't get a chance to finish before Victoria slapped him hard across the face.

'Don't you dare play the victim here!' she cried out. 'You don't think I know about you and Francine? I have my own spies you know!'

She stepped back, staring at Michael now with hatred in her eyes.

'You'd be nothing without me,' she hissed.

'I'm CEO of one of the largest industrial firms in the UK!' Michael yelled back. 'I think I'm doing pretty good so far!'

'My *father's* company!' Victoria replied. 'Who hired you because of me!' She waved around, taking in the house, the drive, the guests.

'Without me by your side, you'd be nothing more than a failed estate agent with a degree in Sociology! I should have listened to Susan. She always said you'd bring me down. That you'd bring *us* down!'

Michael stood stock still, reining in his anger. He stared at Victoria standing so close to the edge. It would be so easy right now, to push her, to force her over the edge. He could even see the quote he'd give to the press.

'My wife, she was unwell, dizzy ... She slipped ... And on a day of such joy too ...'

He shook his head as he pulled himself out of this delightful fantasy.

'Screw you,' he said, as he tossed his half-finished cigarette to the floor, crushing it beneath the heel of his shoe before he turned and walked back towards the door to the stairs. 'You can have the bastard. I'll be contacting my solicitors tomorrow.'

'And I'll be contacting mine!' Victoria shouted, as he slammed the door shut behind him.

Turning back to the night, she wiped the tears from her eyes. Everything would have been fine if he hadn't had a vasectomy. She could have claimed it was his and nothing would have changed. They could have continued on until after the election and then once that was decided they could quietly move on with their lives. Shaun could leave his wife, and she could divorce Michael quietly and be with Shaun finally. If Blair lost, they could even push to become a new power couple ...

The door opened again and Victoria turned to continue her argument, assuming that Michael had returned for round two.

It wasn't Michael.

'I was surprised that you'd text me tonight,' she said. 'I wasn't sure if you meant here, or if you meant where we—'

She stopped speaking, not because she'd run out of words to say, but because a gloved hand had gripped her hard by the throat. The grip was so tight she couldn't even draw breath. She feebly hit on the arm of the hand, as if trying to knock it away but suddenly she was moving backwards fast, dragged to the edge of the roof.

No.

She tried to say it with her eyes.

No. Please. I love you. Don't do this.

But, if the owner of the gloved hand saw the message, they didn't care as they let go of Victoria's throat and pushed hard against her chest, hard against the emerald pendant that went so well with her red hair, snapping it off in their hand as they sent her tumbling over the edge of the roof, her arms scrabbling for purchase but finding nothing but air as, screaming, she fell from the roof of Devington House and slammed through the roof of a convertible BMW parked below.

As the guests ran screaming both from and towards the obviously dead body, the car's alarm system alerting everyone to the event, the murderer stared down over the edge of the roof for a moment before pocketing the necklace and walking back to the door, pausing only to pick up Victoria's mobile phone before leaving both the roof and the scene of the crime.

1

DAY OF THE DEAD

DECLAN WALSH HATED FUNERALS. HE HATED THEM EVEN MORE when it was someone he loved being buried. When it was someone he sort-of knew, he could find reasons to not attend, or to turn up late, hang around near the back, even bypass the whole event and appear at the wake, pretending that he had been there, and that they just hadn't seen him.

But, when it's your *father* that you're burying, it's a little harder to do.

And so, Declan stood by the casket as they lowered it into its hole, surrounded by people who he didn't really know: friends and colleagues from his father's life who saw Declan as nothing more than the screw-up copper, or the grieving mourner, with the sympathy and attitude given as such to each.

Declan wasn't grieving though. Declan was angry.

Patrick Walsh shouldn't be dead.

The coroner had claimed that it was an accident, but Declan had managed to get hold of copies of the case notes from a friend in the pathology office. Patrick Walsh had apparently died when his car, caught in terrible weather and en route to Maidenhead had spun out of control down a winding country lane in the middle of the night, flipping over as it clipped the edge of the road and coming to a rest on its roof, fifteen feet down a slope. Patrick, smashing his head against the steering wheel with enough force to shatter his nose had apparently died instantly as his heart gave way.

There were those that blamed the slippery roads, or maybe the conditions of the day. There were also those that blamed the brakes on the car for not being at their best that night. And then there were the ones that believed Patrick had simply suffered a heart attack while driving. The ones that shrugged, held up their hands and said, 'there's nothing that could have been done.'

Declan Walsh knew that something could be done. The truth would come out. His father wasn't just 'Patrick Walsh from accounting', he was the recently retired *Chief Superintendent Walsh of the Metropolitan Police*. He'd spent several decades putting the worst criminals in the world behind bars and had a hate list that filled several black books. All Declan had to do was work out which of those dark bastards had managed to get to his father's car to do something to it, and then put them away for it.

This was harder to do though when you were under suspension.

As the crowd started to disperse, the funeral over and the warmth of the wake, held in an upstairs function room of The Olde Bell down the road, calling them, Declan stared down at the coffin with a dark, steely determination.

'I'll get them for you, dad,' he muttered to himself.

He looked around the graveyard of St Mary The Virgin. It was quiet. The whole village of Hurley-Upon-Thames was quiet, to be honest. It always had been. It was one of the reasons he'd run away at eighteen to join the army. Since then, he'd only really returned for marriages, birthdays, Christmases and funerals.

Like this one.

Across the hole stood two mourners: the first, a woman in her late thirties, her blonde hair pulled back into a ponytail, stared into the grave with tears running down her face. The other mourner was a teenage girl no older than fifteen. Her hair was currently cut short and blue, her black glasses chunky and unneeded. She smiled at Declan; a sympathetic smile that didn't quite reach her eyes.

He made his way over to them.

'Thanks for coming,' he said softly.

Elizabeth Walsh looked up from the grave, wiping her eyes with a handkerchief.

'Of course, we came, you idiot,' she replied. 'I loved the old sod. And I wasn't going to stop Jess saying goodbye to her grandfather.'

Jessica Walsh gave her father a hug.

'You doing okay?' she asked.

'I've been better,' Declan replied honestly. 'You guys going to the wake?'

Elizabeth shook her head. 'I don't think so,' she said, looking back to the leaving mourners. 'Most of them are police. Your world. Not mine anymore.' She looked to her daughter. 'Besides, Jess has a test tomorrow.'

She looked back to Declan placing a hand on his shoulder.

'You should go,' she finished. 'It might be good for you.'

Declan shrugged. 'I'll see.'

Elizabeth nodded and, looking to Jessica, the two

mourners turned from the grave and started back towards the church.

'Hey,' Declan called out, pausing them. 'Maybe I could see Jess on Saturday?'

Elizabeth frowned at this. 'It's not scheduled.'

'I know.' Declan looked to the grave. 'I could just … well, I could really use something right now.'

Elizabeth looked to her daughter who nodded eagerly.

'Email me about it,' she replied, and the two continued on.

Declan was about to follow them back to the car park when he saw that he still wasn't alone. A young man, no more than eighteen or nineteen years old was standing the other side of the hole, as if waiting to speak. He wore his police constable uniform but couldn't have been long out of Hendon Training College.

'You okay?' Declan asked.

'I just wanted to say, sir, that I'm sorry,' the young policeman replied. 'Your father spoke to us at training school. He was an inspiration.'

'First off, it's a funeral. I'm just Declan. Secondly, I'm not a Detective Inspector while I'm on suspension.' As he said the line, Declan felt the twinge of anger rise. He relaxed, letting the anger flow out. He didn't need that today.

The young copper shook his head. 'Crying shame what happened,' he said.

'It'll be sorted in the end,' Declan gave a smile, 'but thanks.'

'I didn't mean for you,' the policeman said, his tone changing. 'I meant for the department. You're nothing but a *grass*.' And with that, he left the graveside, walking off with the stiff gait of someone who had spoken their piece and was very much aware that they were likely to be punched for it.

Declan chuckled as he looked back to the hole. This wasn't the first time he'd had someone say something similar to him. The future career of Declan Walsh seemed to be a polarising debate right now. Picking up a rose from one of the folding stands beside the grave, Declan tossed it into the hole, letting it join the others scattered across his father's coffin. Then, without another word, he turned and walked towards the village high street with a quickened pace. The last thing he wanted to do right now was attend the wake, especially one filled with police superintendents who were as pissed at him as the young policeman had been, or village friends who all knew the 'stories', usually told to them by his dad in the same pub. Declan Walsh was the black sheep of a long and proud tradition of policemen, and right now he didn't need any more lectures.

Best to get in the car and drive home before the dirt was shovelled.

It seemed, however, that he was likely to get one final lecture, for as he approached his car in the car park beside Monk's Barn he could see there was a man standing beside it.

In the black suit of a mourner and slim with a runner's frame, the man straightened as he saw Declan approach. White hair, thinning at the parting, framed a face with clear, blue eyes, ones that pierced through when they turned their gaze to you. There was a well-cropped white beard under them.

That's new, Declan thought to himself as he approached. The white-haired man nodded to him.

'Aye Declan, you look like shite,' he said, his voice showing the slightest edge of a Glaswegian twang, as if the man had once lived there, but had spent so long away that the accent was barely hanging on. Which was true, because Detective Chief Inspector Alexander Monroe had left Scotland more than thirty years back.

'DCI Monroe,' Declan replied, nodding politely.

'Oh, so it's DCI today?' Monroe said, a small smile on the edge of his lips. 'Good to know.' He looked Declan up and down. 'You've put on weight,' he said. 'And shaved the beard off.'

Declan looked down at himself. He wasn't large, but he was stocky; years of playing rugby did that to him. But since his suspension, he'd wallowed in self-pity and pizza. As for his beard, he'd shaved it off when Liz left him. Although his auburn hair was clear of any white hairs, his beard was a traitor to his looks, the salt and pepper within it coming through since he turned forty last year.

He smiled at Monroe's words though. He knew that the DCI already knew all of this.

'I had to,' he said, pointing at Monroe's neat white beard. 'Couldn't have both of us bearded at the same time.'

'Well, yes,' Monroe nodded. 'It would, in fact, destroy the very fabric of the universe.' He looked to Declan's car. 'You're not going to drive to the wake, are you? It's only five minutes' walk down the road.'

'Wasn't intending to go, sir.'

'Dec, it was your father.'

Declan stiffened at the name. He had only ever been called *Dec* by Monroe and his father.

'Do you have a reason for me to be there?' he asked slowly. The DCI was usually a straight-talking man, and Declan knew that if something was going on, Monroe would tell him rather than delay it. Monroe in turn nodded.

'I do, laddie,' he said.

'Then say it now,' Declan continued to his car, opening the driver's door. 'Because I've had my fill of people telling me I'm a thug, a traitor or a grass for doing what I did.'

'As you should. But I'm not here to say any of those things, unless you wanted me to,' Monroe smiled. It was one of those smiles that is made to try to give ease and, just like Jessica's earlier, it was one that didn't quite reach the eyes. 'Trust me, I'm only saying that you should come to the pub and have a drink with me, because you'll probably bloody well need one when I tell you what I have to say.'

Well, that doesn't sound ominous at all, Declan thought to himself.

'Fine,' he sighed, as he closed the door and locked the car once more. 'But you're buying.'

'You don't even have money behind the bar at your father's wake?' Monroe tutted, as he turned and walked down the country lane, away from Declan. 'Bad form, laddie.'

Sighing audibly and staring up at the sky, as if looking for the spectre of his father to be staring down from the heavens laughing uproariously at this, Declan swore under his breath and then trotted off to catch up with Monroe.

Because it seemed that DI Declan Walsh was going to his father's wake after all.

2

A SECOND CHANCE

Although they'd arrived at The Olde Bell around the same time as the mourners, Monroe took Declan to a booth in the downstairs bar rather than joining them upstairs. Placing a pint of Guinness in front of Declan, his own drink a clear liquid with ice and tonic – either a vodka, or more likely one of the many varieties of gin that the bar stocked, placed on the other side – he sat down facing Declan.

There was a moment of silence.

'Good to see Lizzie and Jessie there,' Monroe eventually said.

Declan nodded. 'She's fifteen now. Can you believe it?'

Monroe chuckled. 'You're getting old,' he said. 'Soon you'll be a grandfather.'

'Christ no,' Declan laughed. 'She's going to a nunnery when she's sixteen.'

'And Lizzie? You're still talking?'

'We're doing okay. But it's cordial and distanced, you know? Not like it used to be.'

'She forgive you yet?' Monroe sipped at his drink. 'For picking the Force over her?'

'It wasn't like that,' Declan replied into his own drink.

'It never is,' Monroe replied calmly.

'She's angry with me again,' Declan leaned back, almost laughing at this. 'She's pissed because her book group banned her.'

'Because of you?'

'It's a Catholic group.'

'Oh.' Monroe began to chuckle now. 'Yes, I can see that.'

There was a pause. Declan didn't know whether it was his time to speak or not.

'You know what they call you?' Monroe eventually asked. 'In New Scotland Yard?'

'I've heard a few of the nicknames,' Declan replied.

'The favourite is *The Priest Puncher*,' Monroe continued, sipping at his drink. 'I mean Jesus, Declan. A priest?'

'He deserved it,' Declan muttered. 'He was dog trafficking.'

'Don't you mean drug trafficking?'

Declan shook his head. 'No sir, dogs. Father Corden was head priest in Hampstead. Very affluent area.'

'I'm aware of the house prices in London.' Monroe nodded. 'Millionaire's Row's near there, I believe.'

'It is, sir,' Declan nodded. Millionaire's Row was the unofficial name given to a street of houses; all so expensive that the entire road was filled with high walls and electric gates. Premiere League footballers, rock stars, foreign dignitaries and movie stars lived there, behind those gates. 'And that's the problem. Many of the congregation were rich. Super rich, even. Which meant any Catholics in that group had a lot of guilt.'

'A lot to confess?'

'Yes sir. They'd come to the church for confession, but the dogs would have to be left outside.'

'And let me guess,' Monroe said. 'While famous Miss Catholic confessed her sins inside, her dear, darling, expensive doggie was taken from outside?'

Declan nodded. 'They kept claiming that the dogs ran away. That maybe there were kids having fun. The church was right next to Hampstead Heath, so to start with they assumed that the dogs were escaping, running around the scrublands. Some were found, too.'

Monroe considered this for a moment. 'The ones that were chipped and neutered?'

'Exactly.' Declan took a sip of his Guinness. 'No point stealing a thoroughbred dog that can't give you thoroughbred puppies.'

'And you worked out that it was the priest because of the confessional schedule.'

Declan nodded. 'Caught him red-handed. But he tried to get away, pulled the whole "I am the voice of God and you will let me go" act. He struggled.' Declan shrugged. 'And I punched him.'

'On live TV.'

'Well, yes, sir. It was problematic that there was a TV crew filming at the time. Our sting dog was owned by an Instagram influencer. She saw this as an opportunity for exposure.'

'Well, that wasn't the only thing exposed. From what I saw, you knocked him spark out on the six o'clock news,' Monroe said, leaning back on his seat and taking a better look at Declan. 'Catholic Church weren't happy?'

'No, sir. And neither was my commander, DCI Farrow.'

'Catholic?'

'Yup.'

'And that's why you were suspended,' Monroe mused, absently scratching at his chin with his index finger. 'For doing your job. Well, until the punching a priest part. And that's why Lizzie's having trouble.'

'And Jessie,' Declan added. 'She's in a Catholic school. But that wasn't why I was properly suspended, sir.'

Monroe nodded at this. 'The wonderful DCI Ford.'

'The fallout from that, a couple of days after Hampstead ... Well, let's just say it was a lot of the wrong exposure in a short amount of time,' Declan replied.

'I heard you made a right royal mess of things in Mile End,' Monroe mused. 'And you were only there two days.'

'I solved the case.'

'While suspended.'

'I had a note saying I was under Ford's remit.'

'You had a note? A *note* for Christ's sake.' Monroe was chuckling into his drink. 'Och, that makes everything fine then. And there I was, thinking you'd just made everything worse for yourself whilst dismantling the Mile End crime unit.'

'Wasn't my fault that happened.' Declan's expression was darkening.

'Calm down, I read the SCO19 report,' Monroe said. 'You did the right thing. In a cack-handed way, of course.'

'Thank you, sir.'

'So, what now? For you, that is?'

'I dunno,' Declan stared down at his pint. He'd been asking himself the same question recently. 'Depends who'd take me. It's been suggested that I could take a demotion and look at a more provincial post than London. Maybe somewhere that hasn't heard of me. Or I can sit it out, wait for the dust to settle, if it even does.' Declan wasn't hopeful on that. The Catholic issue was a PR nightmare, but could be sorted. The problems in Mile End immediately afterwards weren't so easy.

'Bollocks to that,' Monroe huffed. 'You're too good a copper to stay benched.' There was a pause, as if Monroe was making a decision. 'Come join my team.'

Declan looked up at this. It was well known in the force that DCI Monroe headed a cold-case-orientated team off Fleet Street; all from some antiquated offices in Temple Inn. People called it by a different name, though.

'I'm sorry sir, but I don't think I'd be a fit for the *Last Chance Saloon*,' Declan said carefully.

'Ah, so you've heard of us, then?' Monroe smiled. 'The place where the screw ups and the no-hires are dumped when nobody else wants them?'

Declan squirmed slightly in his seat. 'I didn't mean to imply that.'

'Do you know what happens when a police officer, even one in CID, massively screws up?' Monroe asked, leaning forwards. 'They get fired. Boom. Gone, just like that.'

He took a long sip of his drink, as if working out what to say next. Eventually he replaced the glass on the table, looking back to Declan.

'But sometimes, just sometimes there are detectives of a higher calibre. Ones that are vital, useful even, the future of the police force. To lose them would be a disgrace.'

'And so, you take them.'

'Aye, so *I* take them,' Monroe smiled. 'Some of the greatest analytical minds in the force. The best lateral thinkers out there, all under my roof. Does that sound like a joke department to you?'

'Not when you put it like that.' Declan returned the smile, but it faded quickly. 'But I'm probably leaving the force, sir.'

'Why in god's name would you do that?'

Declan shrugged. 'Maybe because I solved a politically explosive murder, uncovered police corruption and solved a dog trafficking ring in the space of a week and got shafted for it.'

'No,' Monroe replied. 'That's not why. You're thinking of abandoning ship because you don't have faith in us anymore.'

Declan paused, his half-finished Guinness up to his mouth. Monroe was correct. After his father's death had been classed as accidental, the last straw had been broken. Declan had lost faith in the judicial process, and by default, the police.

'Your father would be disappointed if you left,' Monroe chided.

Declan nodded. 'I know.'

'So why not do something different?' Monroe asked. 'Why not make him proud of you?'

'Let me guess,' Declan faced the older man. 'You just so happen to have something on you that does just that?'

Monroe reached into his inside jacket pocket, pulling out a manilla envelope. Placing it on the table, he looked to Declan.

'In that envelope is a possible piece of evidence to an old case,' he said.

'A cold case?'

Monroe shook his head. 'No, actually. It's one that your father closed almost twenty years back. This new evidence might change that outcome, however.'

Declan didn't reach for the envelope.

'What sort of evidence?' he asked.

'Have you ever heard of a dead letter?' Monroe replied. Declan shook his head, so the older man continued. 'It's an undeliverable letter. One where the address is wrong, or the person the letter was sent to doesn't live there anymore and it's sent back, or if it's stolen, lost, a whole load of things. How many times have you received a letter for the wrong address, or maybe one that's your street, but it's a different town?'

'A few times, I suppose.'

'Well then, that's a dead letter. Didn't get to where it was supposed to go. Most of the time they're tossed away. Sometimes people write things like 'not at this address' and post them back, even though there's no original address on there. More than a million letters a month go missing like this.'

Monroe tapped the envelope.

'In there is an envelope that never reached its target. Not because of the Royal Mail, but because it simply got lost in the mix. Was found a couple of weeks back in a Derby police station and passed to me.'

'Why you?'

'Because it was to do with a case I worked on twenty years ago,' Monroe continued. 'When I was with your father.'

Declan tried to recall his father's cases. He didn't know that many of them, but there was one from around that time that fit.

'The Victoria Davies murder,' he said.

Monroe nodded. 'Start of 2001. Few months before the General Election. Victoria Davies, pushed off the roof of her family's manor house on New Year's Eve by her husband, Michael Davies.'

'I remember this one,' Declan said. 'I'd just finished Army

training at Pirbright and was at home for the holidays before I moved on.'

'Redcaps, wasn't it?' Monroe was referring to the Royal Military Police, named 'redcaps' due to the scarlet covers of their peaked berets.

'Yeah. Shipped out to Northern Ireland later that year, so I don't remember what happened in the end, but I do recall dad being convinced there was something more going on.'

Monroe sipped at his drink, watching Declan.

'Go on,' he encouraged.

'Michael claimed he didn't do it, even though it came out in the trial that she was pregnant with someone else's child, he was having an affair with his PA and he was overheard at the party saying that he was going to kill her,' Declan continued. 'That and the forensics found a cigarette with his DNA on that placed him at the scene of the crime at the correct time, and a guard that watched him follow Victoria to the roof after giving him specific instructions to stop anyone else from following.' He looked back at the envelope.

'Do I need gloves to touch it?'

'Christ no, it's been manhandled by dozens of people over the years. We'd never get a solid print from it.'

'He was a Labour Party donor, wasn't he? Tried and convicted before the election, the government desperate to keep it out of the press.'

'Aye, he was,' Monroe said, finishing the drink and rising from the chair. 'It was a simple cut-and-dried case. But in that envelope is a letter that changes everything. Possibly even exonerates Michael Davies.'

'Jesus. Has he been told?' Declan finally picked up the manilla envelope as Monroe shook his head.

'Michael Davies died of bowel cancer five years ago,' he

replied. 'And if we were wrong then, well then a good man lost his life in prison, and I owe it to your father to find the right person and put them behind bars. We could do it together if you felt like it.'

He pointed at the envelope.

'My card's also in there,' he said, already turning and walking from the seat. 'If you decide you do want a last chance at being a copper, come to the address on it tomorrow at 9am.'

And with that DCI Monroe left the bar.

Declan turned the manilla envelope in his hands. Inside it was a letter that possibly proved that his father had been wrong on one of the most high-profile cases of his career. He looked at the fireplace against the back wall of the bar. There was a fire burning low in it; one toss of the wrist and the manilla envelope, the evidence and the business card would all disappear. He could quit the force and the Last Chance Saloon could find another loser to hire.

Declan finished his Guinness, staring down into the glass, the foam sliding down the sides. *He* was the loser. Nobody was going to hire him; the Catholic Church wanted him dead, half the police didn't trust him, the other half thought he was a hero, and either way his career was probably over. At least Monroe was a known evil.

And more importantly, if the people Monroe had working for him were half as good as he believed, then these people would be top notch investigators.

And that's what he needed if he was going to prove his father's murder.

Rising from the table, Declan nodded to the landlord behind the bar.

'Thanks for everything, Dave,' he said, nodding up the stairs.

The landlord nodded. 'Not joining them?' he asked.

Declan shook his head. 'My father's not up there,' he replied sadly.

And with that Declan Walsh tucked the manilla envelope into his inside pocket and quickly walked out of the pub.

3

THE HOMELESS AND THE
AMBITIOUS

THE STREETS OF LONDON WERE COLD AND WET THAT
afternoon. It wasn't raining, but it was that awful halfway
point between has rained and is dry; too wet to sit down
without soaking yourself, and too dry to be allowed into the
warm foyers of buildings for a moment or two of brief
normality.

The homeless man walked the streets alone and silent.
He wore dirty jeans that looked like they were once expensive, worn over black and battered Dr Marten boots. His overcoat and scarf covered the top half of his body, the torso of
which seemed unnaturally bigger than his head and hands,
giving the impression of a man wearing many layers of
clothing underneath it, bulking it out.

On his balding head was a woollen cap, as grubby and
dishevelled as the rest of him, pulled down low over his forehead, almost touching his battered, black-rimmed NHS
prescription glasses. A fuzzy wisp of brown beard peeked out
between nose and scarf as he kept his head down, shifting
the large and heavy looking rucksack over his shoulder with

one hand while his other rooted through his overcoat pocket, pulling out a small, cheap bottle of whisky, shaped in that 'hip flask' style of bottle. Taking a swig from it, he looked around, gathering his bearings. Across the street was a small queue of equally homeless men and women, all waiting in turn for a paper bowl worth of food and a wooden spoon to eat it, these items provided by a lady who stood under a gazebo, a table in front of her; one of the many pop-up soup kitchens that had appeared lately.

Seeing the soup kitchen reminded the homeless man that he was hungry so slowly and carefully he walked across to the line, standing at the end, being careful not to make eye contact with anyone.

There was a small TV on behind the woman as she plated some kind of casserole into the bowls. An afternoon television programme was playing, but the sound had been turned too low for the homeless man to hear. That was fine though. He didn't watch much television these days, anyway. And he recognised the show; *Peter Morris in the pm*, a title that, with the initials of Peter Morris spelling 'pm' and with the show being broadcast in the afternoon, must have made some marketing team at ITV scream with excitement.

In front, an older man was staring at him strangely. Stick thin and in what looked to be a well out of date track suit, worn once more seemingly over every other item of clothing he owned, the man was trying to gain a better look at the homeless man's face.

'Hey,' the older man said. 'I know you.'

'Don't think so,' the homeless man looked away from the older man, back to the TV set, where Peter Morris, casual in pink shirt and black trousers, the sleeves down, his hair a greying black, was now talking to a white-haired man in a pinstripe suit.

The homeless man looked harder at the television.

It couldn't be.

It was.

With that bloody quiff and mane of hair, there couldn't be anyone else.

'Yeah, I do,' the older man replied, breaking the homeless man's concentration. 'Where do I know you from?'

'I come here sometimes on Tuesdays,' the homeless man offered, hoping that this would end the conversation. The older man shook his head.

'No,' he said. 'That's not it ...'

The homeless man looked at the queue building behind him, at the television showing the familiar face and then the older man who believed he'd found his own familiar face in turn. He sighed, shifting his rucksack. He wasn't going to get anything to eat right now. He couldn't risk the older man remembering who he truly was. And besides, if he had to keep looking at that face on TV, he'd end up breaking it.

And so, turning towards the road, the homeless man started away from the soup kitchen, and food.

The older man stared after him.

'I bloody know you ...' he muttered. And then, all remembrance of the homeless man forgotten, he turned back to the soup kitchen and his next meal.

———

On *Peter Morris in the PM*, the presenter and namesake of the show leaned back into his armchair, his notes held in his hand as he watched the man in the pinstripe suit facing him, sitting on the couch with an expression of what could only be called loathing.

'You okay, Charlie?' Peter asked with a smile.

'I've had better days,' came the reply. Peter looked over to the Floor Manager, now waving to attract their attention.

'Coming back from adverts in three, two ...' the Floor Manager made a motion and the red light on Camera Four lit up. Smiling, Peter looked into the lens, directly at the audience. He'd been told once by someone, probably Phillip Schofield or someone like that to always stare past the lens, to somehow insert yourself into the living room of the audience. Of course, with half the audience now watching this on their smartphones, and probably while sitting on the toilet, Peter wasn't sure if he wanted to go quite that far.

'Welcome back,' he smiled, indicating his guest, now sitting straighter and with as fake a smile as Peter had beaming out through the camera. 'We're here with Charles Baker, the current Secretary of State for the Government.'

Charles kept his smile, even though his eyes twitched at Peter's usage of the term "current".

'Pleasure as always, Peter,' he replied.

Peter looked briefly at his notes before the camera turned back to him. 'So, before the commercial break, we were discussing the recent changes that have been happening since the last election—'

'Which we won with a handsome majority,' Charles interjected, still all smiles. 'The British people put their faith in us, and we have delivered.'

'But have you, though?' Peter asked, his smile fading. 'I mean, with all the problems with Europe, the housing crisis, unemployment at its highest in a decade, you seem to constantly U-turn on yourselves.'

Charles leaned forward, his smile also fading as if he realised that this was a serious question, and this meant that he needed to have a serious face to answer it.

'I know there have been speedbumps along the way,' he replied, 'but the Conservative Government made a promise to steer us through these choppy waters, and that's what we shall do.'

'With a different Captain, perhaps?' Peter pressed on.

Charles paused, gathering his thoughts. He'd been waiting for this. Every time a Prime Minister faltered the media started asking this.

'I have the utmost faith in our leadership,' he said calmly. 'As does the rest of the cabinet.'

Peter looked down at his cards as he responded.

'And the rumours in yesterday's *Daily Mail,* that you're already being spoken of as a contender to the throne?'

'As I said, I have the utmost—'

'Yes, but you said the exact same thing in 2003 about Tony Blair before you jumped ship to the other side of the floor,' Peter interrupted.

Charles looked at Peter, his calm demeanour faltering. *This wasn't one of the pre-arranged questions. The bloody fool was going off script.*

'You have to take the context into account,' Charles said calmly, while desperately thinking of an answer. The last thing he wanted was for people to remember that he used to be a Labour MP. 'We're not in the middle of an unsanctioned invasion, for a start.'

There was a long moment of silence as Peter looked to his notes and nodded, ever so slightly. *Probably getting a bollocking from his Producer in his earpiece,* Charles thought.

'Of course,' Peter simply replied, looking back up. 'We do

indeed live in different times. Thank you for speaking to us today.'

He looked to the camera.

'And now, let's go over to Gail Smith with the weather.'

The Floor Manager looked up to the Director's box, listening into his earpiece as the red light on the camera winked out. 'And ... We're off for ninety seconds,' he said as he turned from the set, walking back to one of the cameramen.

Peter unclipped his mic and leaned over the side of the chair, pulling up an expensive water bottle from behind it. 'Thanks for that, Charles,' he said before taking a sip.

Charles Baker tore his own mic off, tossing it onto the couch in anger.

'You're a prick, Morris,' he snapped. 'What the hell was that? We never discussed that! And the nerve of bringing up bloody Blair?'

Peter smiled. 'You want to be Prime Minister, you need to expect curveballs,' he said. 'And also, you need to gain the hearts and minds of people. My people. Currently, you're just a miserable elitist who thinks that he's better than everyone else.'

Charles smiled, but there was no humour in it. 'Who's to say I'm not?'

Peter leaned in. 'Has the 1922 Committee spoken to you yet?' he asked.

Charles, already rising from the couch stopped. 'Have you heard anything?' he asked.

Peter looked over to the crew as the Floor Manager returned. Reclipping his mic onto his shirt, he hid the bottle once more behind the chair.

'Just that you have many skeletons, and your choice of

friends and alliances in the past has been questionable,' he said with a fake smile. 'Better keep them hidden, eh? Oh, and if you could get off my set that'd be great. We're about to go to Coventry for a bake sale.'

Charles Baker stormed off the studio set in absolute fury and embarrassment, making a silent deal with himself that when he was Prime Minister, he'd do whatever it took to ensure that Peter sodding Morris was blacklisted from all television.

4

HOMECOMING

It had been about five years since Declan had visited his father in Hurley, but the doorstep he stood in front of was one of the most familiar sights he had ever seen. He'd grown up on this doorstep. He'd thrown up on this doorstep. He'd stormed out across this doorstep and had returned in both humility and triumph, although at separate times, over this doorstep.

And now, key in hand, Declan was about to cross over it once more, although this time it was technically his doorstep.

This was the part he couldn't get his head around yet. The fact that the house he lived in for most of his childhood, that he watched his father grow old in, was now his. That said, as the only child of a widower, unless some kind of long-lost brother or sister appeared out of nowhere, he was always going to inherit it.

Declan paused, looking around briefly, as if expecting one to turn up. Then, key now in the lock, he opened the door and walked in.

There was a pile of letters on the floor, all addressed to
MR PATRICK WALSH, as if none of the companies posting
to him even knew that he was dead. Declan had an irrational
flash of anger before he realised that of course they wouldn't
know, and that it would now be his job to contact each and
every one of these to inform them of this. He'd likely be
contacting a lot of people to tell them.

Thanks, dad.

He made his way into the living room now, tossing the
envelopes onto a coffee table as he took off his overcoat and
loosened his black silk tie, unbuttoning the top button of his
shirt, stretching his neck, feeling the little stress clicks in his
neck and shoulders as he manipulated them. Looking at a
clock on the wall, he realised that no more than an hour had
passed since he had said goodbye to his father at the church.
In fact, the wake was probably still going on in the village. He
had no desire to return, though.

There was a smell in the house, a familiar one; a smell of
old leather and musty books that took Declan back to his
childhood. Idly walking over to a cabinet by the wall, Declan
examined the photos in silver frames on the top. A photo of
Declan's parents on their wedding day. A family photo from
five years earlier of Declan, Lizzie and Jess, ten years old here
and with normal coloured hair. He picked it up, staring down
at it, wondering how the last five years had turned so bad.

Shaking himself out of the approaching melancholy, he
opened the doors to a cabinet beneath the shelf, one he knew
well, revealing a small but well curated selection of whisky
bottles. Pulling the first he could see out, he examined it. A
twenty-year-old Balvenie faced him.

'You'll do,' he said, grabbing a tumbler and walking back
to the coffee table. Placing tumbler and bottle onto the table,

he looked around for somewhere to throw his jacket. It was then that he noticed the pile of A4 papers next to an old iMac, the desk that they were both on hidden in the alcove under the staircase. Walking over to it, he picked up the top sheet, staring at the words on it, his expression slowly darkening.

'Oh, you stupid sod,' he muttered as he picked up the other pages.

It was a manuscript. A memoir, in matter of fact. His *father's* memoir. Even from a cursory glance, he could see enough stories from his father's time on the force to piss off half of the criminal underworld, not to mention a few top brass at New Scotland Yard. Placing the pile of papers back onto the desk, he returned to the coffee table and poured himself a generous Balvenie. Taking a sip of the whisky he let it slide down his throat; warming it as he looked around the room.

If anyone knew that this was being written, they'd have a reason to kill my father, he thought to himself. The motive was obvious now. All he needed to do was find the means and opportunity.

But that would take research; something more than he could do alone in a Starbucks with a laptop and Google.

With the tumbler in his hand, Declan took a stroll around the house, breathing in the memories from his childhood; the banister that he would always slide down, until the time he slipped and cracked his head open; the small room that to a young Declan was the biggest bedroom in the world, the racing car wallpaper long covered by a more sensible green pattern; his parents room – more recently just his father's room – the double bed and wardrobe still giving the impression that Declan's mother, dead four years now, was still living there; and finally the upstairs study, where Patrick Walsh worked when he was at home. This was now a junk room, with boxes strewn around the floor, and a variety of unused exercise equipment balanced against the walls.

Declan went to leave, but something stopped him.

Why would his father work in an alcove under the stairs when he had a study?

Declan could understand not using the spare bedroom, but Patrick wasn't the sort of man who would dump things just to keep them out of the way.

There was something else wrong with the room – Declan remembered it being the longest room in the house, almost running the length of the house itself; but here it seemed to be no longer than the bedroom next door.

Making his way through the boxes of seemingly junk, Declan realised that there was a kind of path that went to the back wall. And against the wall was a ceiling-high empty bookcase, one that used to be filled with books and placed against a different wall when Declan was last in here.

Positioning the tumbler of whisky precariously on one of the boxes, Declan investigated the base of the empty bookcase. To the side of it he could see that the carpet had also been flattened, as if something heavy and bookcase-shaped had been on it. Walking to the other side, Declan placed his hands on the wood and pushed at the bookcase.

Slowly it slid across the carpet revealing an opening within the wall.

Looking at the makeshift entrance, Declan could now see that this wall was a new addition; quickly made, plastered and painted to look like the room, but hiding a small space behind it.

Walking through the doorway into the secret room,

Declan saw his father's old desk against one wall, a tall filing cabinet next to it and a leather office chair discarded to the side. Piles of papers were on the desk; old case files and mugshots were strewn everywhere.

But it was the other wall that paused Declan. A giant whiteboard had been screwed into it; the type that detectives just like Patrick would stick photos to when creating a crime board. Currently it held a mish mash of pictures, notes and threads linking faces together. Some of the faces Declan recognised: Johnny Lucas, one of the crime 'twins' of the East End stared out at him beside images of car accidents and gunshot victims. However, some of the others were unknown to him, random images and faces from years of detective work. There were even photos of Hurley itself mixed in: the lock across the Thames, a local campsite, the church ... It made no sense to anyone except the person who put it together.

Who was now gone.

On the desk in the secret room was a single post-it note. All that was written on it was a name and a mobile phone number. Declan recognised both. It was the personal number of Kendis Taylor, currently a political reporter for *The Guardian*. Declan knew this because twenty years ago Kendis Taylor had been his girlfriend. And, in that way that you do, he'd found himself bumping into her several times over the years.

'Ah, dad,' he muttered. 'Why the hell did you contact her of all people?'

Carefully and reverently Declan exited the room, sliding the bookcase back over the door and picking up the whisky before it fell. He assumed this secret crime room was filled with research for his father's memoirs, but why Patrick had gone to all this secrecy was beyond him. And, as he walked back down the stairs, he decided that this was a mystery for another time. He had another, more time-sensitive mystery in his overcoat.

Returning to the armchair beside the coffee table, he sat for a moment, trying to process what he had just seen before reaching over to his coat and pulling out the manilla envelope. Finally opening it, he pulled out the small white business card, examining it in his hand. Monroe's Last Chance Saloon.

A thin envelope slipped out with the card, and Declan picked it up from where it had landed on the floor. It wasn't postmarked, but the first-class stamp was a picture of an eye, wide open with *Millennium 2000 / Year of the Artist* written up the side. The address was unknown to him, a suburb in Birmingham, but the name was familiar.

Susan Galloway. The name which the younger sister of Victoria Davies used to be known by; before she had inherited Devington Industries.

Opening the envelope, Declan pulled out the single sheet of paper. It felt expensive and high quality to the touch. At the top in green was a small logo: a portcullis, chains either side of it and a crown on top. Declan knew immediately what this was, and the text underneath confirmed this. It was a sheet of headed paper from the Houses of Parliament.

Looking back to the envelope, Declan saw that he'd missed the tiny portcullis on that too; stationery that could only have come from Westminster. Unfolding the letter again, he started to read. It was dated 24th December, 2000.

Dear Susan, it started. *By the time you read this, I'll be dead.*

Declan paused, reaching for the whisky. Victoria Davies knew that Michael was going to kill her. She wrote this a week earlier, but somehow it was never sent. Or maybe it was lost on its journey. Finishing off the tumbler, Declan placed it back onto the coffee table and started from the top again.

24th December, 2000.

Dear Susan. By the time you read this, I'll be dead. I can't speak to Michael about this, he doesn't know about the baby yet and he'll know it's not his when he does. We've barely slept together since the incident in March, and thanks to you, I know he's been sleeping with his PA, that bitch Francine.

I was hoping I could keep it from him until at least mid-Jan, but it looks like that won't happen now.

The problem is that if he found out the truth, he'd confront the real father, maybe take it higher up the chain, and then they'll remove him, maybe in an 'accident' like that bitch Sarah. They might remove me, too. But I'm rambling.

I'm sorry. I'm so scared right now. I love him so much, and now they're coming for me. I can't have him involved; I need to finish this myself.

If I don't make it, tell Michael that even though he's a cheating ratbag, I do still love him. And tell him I'm sorry.

Love Vicky xx

The handwriting was written by pen, and near the end it

started to waver, as if the person writing was shaking, possibly crying as they finished the letter.

Declan stared at the letter for a good few minutes, half a dozen questions running through his head. If Victoria Davies knew her killer, and if it was Michael, then why would she write this? Was it even her handwriting? And more importantly, who was this mysterious 'they', and the *bitch Sarah* that was spoken of? Was Patrick Walsh wrong to have arrested Michael Davies? Did an innocent man die in prison?

One thing was certain. Either way, Declan Walsh was going back to work tomorrow.

IT WAS GETTING DARK WHEN THE HOMELESS MAN MADE HIS WAY back to the street where the soup kitchen had been. As he expected it had gone for the day. Sighing to himself, he walked over to a NatWest Bank, pausing by one of the ATM machines. He looked around to see if anyone was watching him, but nobody paid him the slightest attention.

Good.

Slowly, and without drawing any further attention, the homeless man reached into his trousers, pulling out a traveller's wallet: the thin, skin-coloured pouch that you wore under your clothing to ensure that when or if you were mugged on holiday your valuables weren't taken. Unzipping the pouch, the homeless man reached in and pulled out a debit card, the name on it reading SALLY DONNAL. The homeless man was definitely not a 'Sally', but he placed the card into the ATM anyway and tapped in the four-number pin with the speed of a man who not only knew the number by heart but had also tapped it in many times before.

Checking the balance, he saw there was £50 available. There was always £50 available. She always made sure of that. She was a good girl, was Sally.

Tapping on the screen, the homeless man withdrew the £50, tucking it carefully into the traveller's wallet with the card. That would get him into a hostel for the night. After that, he could maybe—

'Oi! You!'

The voice from behind was confrontational and unfortunately familiar. The homeless man turned around to find himself once more facing the older man from earlier that day.

'What you doing with the machine?' the older man asked. The homeless man stayed silent. Unperturbed, the older man smiled a dark, triumphant smile.

'I knew I'd seen you,' he said. 'Took me a while but I don't forget a face. It's the eyes. I always get the eyes.'

The homeless man went to move, but the older man stepped in front, blocking his way.

'You're Shaun Donnal, aren't you,' he said as more of a statement than a question. 'You used to be my MP.'

'You're mistaken,' the homeless man replied, trying once more with no success to leave the scene.

'What a joke,' the older man spat on the floor. 'The Welfare Minister now on sodding welfare. Good riddance too.'

'Look, I have some money. We could share it.' The homeless man started to reach back to his pockets. The older man shook his head.

'I don't want a handout from you,' he spat. 'I lost my house because of you.'

The older man looked around the street now, still empty.

And even if it had been busy, most of the people of Central London would ignore two homeless men having an argument.

'How much would *The Sun* give me for this?' he hissed. '*The Mirror,* perhaps? Ex Government Minister on the skids? I reckon—'

He didn't get to carry on as Shaun, pulling out a small flat-head screwdriver moved in quickly, ramming it repeatedly into the older man's gut.

Shunk. Shunk. Shunk.

Grabbing his bleeding gut and staring at the homeless man in shock, the older man staggered back to the wall of the NatWest, his legs giving out on him as he slumped to the floor.

The homeless man, his face a mask of pure anger knelt down beside him. 'When the police come, you'll tell them that kids did this to you,' he hissed, looking around to see if anyone had noticed the exchange. 'You never saw me. You never met me. Understand?'

The older man, now terrified, nodded.

The homeless man held up the flat-head screwdriver, showing that the flat end had been sharpened to a razor-sharp edge. 'You ever speak to anyone about this, no matter who it is, or if you even find yourself on the same patch as me, or if I see even a whiff of this in a paper, I'll find you. I'll find you and slit your throat and laugh as you bleed out.' He wiped the screwdriver clean on the older man's jacket. 'Got it?' he asked.

Once more the older man nodded silently.

The homeless man smiled: an actual warm, friendly grin as if talking to an old friend. 'Good talk,' he said, rising. 'And, you know, sorry about the house and all that.'

And with that said, swiftly and with great care not to draw any more attention to himself, Shaun Donnal slipped his screwdriver away, slung his rucksack over his shoulder and walked off down the street, leaving the gut-wounded older man to scream for help.

5

THE LAST TEMPTATION

ANDY MAC'S EXPRESSION WAS SOMBRE AS HE STARED DEEP INTO the camera's lens. Just shy of fifty years of age, he wore a deep blue Ted Baker jacket over a pastel tee shirt and jeans, his jet-black hair slicked back in the latest fashion and framing his suntanned face.

'Our show was saddened this week to learn of the death of one of our most valued members,' he said as the camera-man, standing behind a tripod and with a small but expensive SLR camera recording pulled back on Andy, bringing the studio set into clarity behind him, the LEDs lighting up a sign that read *God's Will Television – with Andy Mac.* 'A very sad loss indeed. For this week, we lost *Someone else.* Someone's passing creates a vacancy that will be difficult to fill.'

The cameraman gave a silent thumbs up as Andy made his way to the set, sitting on a trendy pastel-coloured chair as he turned and continued.

'Whenever there was a job to do, a class to teach, or even a meeting to attend, one name was on everyone's lips,' he said calmly as he leaned slightly closer, lowering his voice. 'Let

"Someone Else do it", people would say. Whenever leadership was mentioned, they would say "Someone Else can work with that group" and go on with their business.'

Andy held for a moment, letting the last line sink in. he knew that around the world, thanks to his YouTube channel, people would be hanging on his every word as he live streamed the message out.

It made him feel like God.

'Someone Else left a wonderful example to follow, but who out there will follow it?' he asked. 'Who's going to do the things Someone Else did? When you're asked to help out this year, no matter for what or for whom, just remember ... We can't depend on Someone Else anymore.'

Andy stopped for a moment, letting the camera move in once more. Then, in the calmest, softest voice he could muster, he finished his sermon.

'I'm Andy Mac, and this has been God's Will,' he said, allowing the screen showing the feed to fade to black. 'Like, follow and subscribe.'

With the camera now off, the fake smile disappeared as Andy slumped back into the chair.

'Christ, I need a croissant,' he said to nobody in particular as a young man looking no older than twenty ran over to unclip his microphone. Andy watched him hungrily as the man's hands brushed against his tee shirt, stroking his chest unintentionally. He was called Sebastian; a trainee runner and intern on the show and he was beautiful. An Adonis, slim and muscled, his youthful innocence shining on his face.

He was temptation, sent from the Devil himself to torment Andy.

Sebastian took the mic and smiled at Andy as he pulled away.

'That was great today,' he said with what seemed like utter conviction. He wasn't a sycophant. He was a believer. 'I truly felt the power of the Holy Ghost pass through me as you spoke.'

Andy fought down the urge to mention what he really wanted to pass through Sebastian and forced a smile.

'As ever, Sebastian, it's not me,' he said. 'I am but a vessel for the Lord.'

Nodding, his smile brightening the whole room Sebastian left with the cameraman, heading downstairs to the main office and leaving Andy alone. Getting up off the cheap studio chair, Andy made his way over to a side table on the hunt for some uneaten pastries. The show over for the day, the studio was already emptying as the crew, mostly students and wannabe YouTubers were already making their way to their next event. Andy envied their youth. Their innocence. Their trust that everything would be all right when the whole world was screwed and their whole existence would amount to nothing.

Grabbing a glass, he poured some sparkling water into it, and sat drinking at the table. There was a newspaper beside him, so he turned it over absentmindedly, to see what the header was for the day. It was a *Daily Mail*.

MEET THE NEW BOSS?

The headline was plastered over a photo of Charles Baker; taken on one of the many times that he had left Number 10 Downing Street since becoming a member of the Cabinet. The puff piece below spoke of how respect was dropping in the Conservative Party for the current Prime

Minister, and that Baker was one of three possible options for replacement.

Andy's eyes expressed a complete lack of emotion as he read the article, but his body *wasn't* as composed, as the glass in his hand shattered with the pressure of his tightening grip, the shards slicing his hand's flesh as Andy rose with a start, swearing as he dropped the broken glass and ran to the sink, washing the now bleeding hand under the cold tap, ensuring that all the glass shards had been washed free and (more importantly) that he didn't bleed onto his Ted Baker jacket.

As he was doing this, Sebastian walked back into the room. Seeing the blood, he ran over to Andy.

'Mister Macintyre!' he exclaimed. 'Are you okay?'

'Yes ... a shoddy glass broke,' Andy lied. 'Could you get the first aid kit ...'

'Sebastian.'

'I know,' Andy wrapped a towel around the still bleeding hand. 'I just need a plaster or something.'

'Let's see about that,' Sebastian fussed, taking the bleeding hand in his own, pulling the towel off it and turning it over as he examined the small wounds.

'You're lucky,' he said with a smile. 'I think we can wipe this down with an antiseptic wipe and then wrap it up. No stitches needed.'

He moved across the kitchenette area, rummaging around in cupboards as he searched for the first aid box. Finding it, he returned.

'I don't think we've really met before today?' Andy said.

'I'm usually in the main office,' Sebastian replied, gently wiping down the wounds.

'Ah,' Andy looked away, wincing as the pain from the antiseptic wipe bit into him. 'You're doing this very well,' Andy encouraged. 'Did you learn this from school? Or maybe from your parents?'

Finishing the cleaning, Sebastian was already grabbing some gauze from the first aid box. 'First aid course at school,' Sebastian replied modestly. 'I never knew my mum. She died when I was a baby. An accident. And my dad ... I was adopted.'

'I'm so sorry,' Andy replied with mock sincerity, internally moaning as Sebastian's fingers caressed his own. Sebastian shrugged.

'I was a baby,' he replied. 'And besides, Moses had a similar start, and look at him.'

Andy genuinely smiled at this. Such resilience in the face of uncertainty. It made Andy want him even more.

'Can I ask you something?' Sebastian said.

'Sure,' Andy replied.

Sebastian smiled, but it was a nervous, unsure one. 'When did you know?' he asked. 'I mean, know that God wanted you to do all of this?'

'You having some kind of crisis of faith?' Andy asked. It wasn't uncommon. Christ, even he had his moments over the years.

'No. Yes ... I'm not sure. I was hoping you could ... Well, help.'

Andy nodded, grateful for anything to take his mind off the sensation of Sebastian's fingers stroking his injured hand.

'I remember the moment well,' he said. 'It was in the House of Commons. I can't remember what session it was. Brown was Prime Minister then, and I remember watching him and thinking that I was lying to myself, that I wasn't happy there anymore.' He winced as Sebastian started to tightly wind a bandage around his hand. 'That night, I found myself in the chapel in Westminster, asking God for help.'

'What happened?'

Andy chuckled. 'Two weeks later I lost my seat in the General Election. Took it as the sign I'd asked for and started preaching God's will.' He waved around the studio. 'Best decision that I ever made.'

Sebastian finished tying off the bandage and stepped back. 'Thanks,' he said. 'That helps a lot.'

He didn't however move away from Andy, who was very conscious of the closeness of the intern. Licking his now dry lips, Andy placed his bandaged hand on Sebastian's.

'God will help you with any ...' he paused for a moment, '... *desires* that you may have. Just speak them aloud.'

Sebastian looked around, as if expecting others to be watching.

'But what if I can't?' he asked. 'What if I'm ashamed?'

'There is no shame here,' Andy smiled.

Sebastian looked to the floor.

'It's silly,' he replied. 'Nothing more than a dream.'

They were moving closer now.

'God speaks to us in dreams,' Andy said, almost too scared to continue, in case he'd misread the situation here. If he said the wrong thing, attempted the wrong thing and it came out in the press, he could lose everything. 'So, what is your greatest desire?'

Sebastian moved in quickly, kissing Andy on the lips. And, once he realised that Andy wasn't protesting he moved in again, kissing harder.

His bandaged hand forgotten, Andy pulled Sebastian closer, kissing hard.

He didn't notice Sebastian's hand reach into his pocket,

pulling out a small Bluetooth clicker from it, holding it in his hand as he ran his other through Andy's hair.

Andy certainly didn't notice the smartphone, placed to the side of the counter, arranged quickly when Sebastian had gone for the first aid kit, now aimed directly at them, the camera app silently clicking continuously while Sebastian took picture after picture through the Bluetooth device ...

———

6

THE LAST CHANCE SALOON

DECLAN HADN'T MEANT TO STAY THE NIGHT IN HURLEY, BUT half a bottle of your late father's best whisky will change many a plan. And so, it was a hung over and slightly dishevelled DI Walsh who entered Inner Temple through a large, black wooden door at the junction of Fleet Street and The Strand the following morning.

Its full name was *The Honourable Society of the Inner Temple* and it was one of the four 'Inns of Court' in London; the four professional associations for Barristers and Judges in the city, and it had been around since the Knights Templar had set it up almost a thousand years earlier. Surrounded by walls and gated security, Inner Temple (and Middle Temple, situated beside it) contained some of the safest streets in London. Shakespeare had performed *Twelfth Night* for Queen Elizabeth in Middle Temple Hall; the legendary 'picking of the sides' in the War of the Roses was supposedly held in the garden outside. Much of both Inner and Middle Temple had been destroyed in the Blitz, but thanks to a large number of donations, they were both completely rebuilt in 1959.

It was also around then that the City of London Police had taken up offices there as part of a reciprocal deal for police security. The deal was long forgotten now but the premises, grandfathered into the deeds, meant that in this maze of barrister chambers and dinner halls, of courtyards and of pillared walkways there were two floors of a small, red-bricked building off King's Bench Walk that were City of London Police property. It had almost been overlooked; used as nothing more than file storage for the last fifteen years. There were no upgrades to the networks or the wiring there and the furniture was two decades out of date, but when Alexander Monroe had created his crime unit nicknamed the "Last Chance Saloon", this seemed to be the perfect place for them.

As Declan walked through the car park that led to the doorway to his new home, he saw that Monroe was already at the door, waiting for him.

'Jesus, lad, I thought you looked like shite yesterday, but today you've reached a new low,' Monroe said as he shook Declan's hand warmly. 'Is that your father's tie?'

'I ended up staying the night at the house,' Declan admitted. 'Too much whisky imbibed.'

'At the wake, or alone?'

Declan shrugged. 'I don't like to drink with strangers.' He looked around. 'How did you know I was coming?'

Monroe smiled. 'Each entrance to the Inns of Court has gate guards to keep an eye on the miscreants and ne'er do wells who come in and out. I gave them your photo when I came in this morning and told them that if they called me when you arrived, I'd buy them a drink.'

'So, I'm a miscreant or a ne'er do well now?'

Monroe smiled. 'Aye, laddie, you act like that's new to you.' He pointed off east, to another entrance. 'I thought you'd be driving in, though.'

'No car,' Declan said. 'I took a cab to Maidenhead station, changed at Ealing and took the District Line to Temple.'

He looked at the car park.

'I assumed you had a pool of cars I could borrow from.'

'You're confusing us with a wealthy department,' Monroe grinned. 'We're less expense cards and more *Oyster* cards. But surely you won't need a car, unless you're considering staying in your father's house?'

'Lizzie kept my actual house, so for the last year I've been in a studio apartment in Tottenham,' Declan replied. 'Nice area, but still a bugger to get anywhere. Even without driving, dad's place is just over an hour train journey. It's slightly longer and more expensive, but I wouldn't be paying an extortionate amount of rent anymore.'

'So, you're considering it?'

'I don't know what I'm considering. I wasn't even considering this until twelve hours ago,' Declan replied honestly.

'Well, either way, I'll sort you a car out later today,' Monroe said, leading Declan into the building. 'It might even have all four wheels. And you'd better keep some of the good whisky aside for when you invite me to your house-warming.'

The building was divided into sub sections; the lower floor was primarily held aside for forensics, the overwhelming smells of formaldehyde and bleach striking Declan as he passed a door leading to a wiped-down examination table. There seemed to be nobody in right now but as there didn't seem to be anything to examine, Declan assumed the forensics team were somewhere else, probably seconded to another case.

Declan had a momentary flashback to Mile End and pushed it to the back of his mind as he started up the stairs to the next floor.

The upstairs floor was open-plan, with three closed-off glass offices on one end, each with solid walls dividing them. The first was obviously Monroe's office, the middle was a briefing room and the third had a single desk with two chairs, probably an interview room of some kind. All the rooms had ceiling to floor blinds that could open or close when needed.

The remaining open space was set in rows of desks: seven in total, with an eighth desk loaded with printers. But although there was space for six detectives, only three other people – two women and a man – sat in the room.

'Not up to full quota yet?' Declan asked.

Monroe snorted. 'I'm picky with who I choose,' he replied, leading Declan into the room, 'and forensics are on a course. Come on everyone, gather closer for the new freak-show! Meet Declan Walsh! He's joining us today!'

The elder of the two women nodded at Declan. She was Indian and in her thirties; her dark hair cut into a trendy bob, while her suit was charcoal-grey and off the peg. She seemed every inch the professional female officer that wanted to *not* stand out in a man's world.

'Alright,' she said.

'Declan meet Detective Sergeant Anjli Kapoor,' Monroe said, indicating the woman. 'Straight from Mile End.'

Declan froze. He'd had enough issues with Mile End police recently.

'You worked for Ford?' he asked.

Anjli nodded.

'You like Ford?' Declan continued.

Anjli smiled. 'Until I realised what a lying bitch she was. You'll get no issues from me on what you did there.'

'Then it's a pleasure to meet you,' Declan said, finally warming up.

'And next to her is Detective Constable Billy Fitzwarren,' Monroe continued, motioning towards the male officer, who didn't look a day over twenty. He had pale blond hair cut into a hipster style and wore a well-tailored three-piece suit, most likely from somewhere like Savile Row.

'William Fitzwarren, sir,' Billy replied to Declan. 'Guv likes to call me Billy, to apparently mock my heritage.'

Declan thought for a moment. 'Fitzwarren ... Are you one of the—'

'Yes, he's one of those Fitzwarrens,' Monroe interrupted.

Declan understood the tailored suit now. Billy was probably a Viscount or something.

'And no, he's not here as a favour to someone high up,' Monroe continued as if reading Declan's mind. 'He's a good copper. They both are. Billy's our resident cybercrime whizz. Sits at a computer all day; scared of doing the real work.'

'Cybercrime *is* the real work,' Billy grinned.

'I have issues with cyber experts,' Declan said, remembering Mile End again. Billy's smile simply widened.

'Everyone does,' he said.

'But we don't talk about our pasts here. We start here with a fresh slate,' Monroe finished.

'And who are you?' Declan indicated to the third member of the team; a girl no older than nineteen, in jeans and a hoodie, currently flicking through Instagram on her phone.

'That's Trixibelle—' Monroe started.

'Trix.' the young girl corrected, her eyes glued to the screen.

'That's Trix,' Monroe continued. 'She's here on work placement. Don't expect much from her.'

He clapped his hands.

'Right then,' he started. 'Now we're mostly here, shall we get on with it? Dump your stuff on that desk, Declan. Good lad. Now! With me!'

And with that he walked into one of the rooms at the back of the open plan. Following him, Declan saw that most of the plasterboard wall was a plasma screen rather than a whiteboard. Monroe followed his gaze, smiling.

'You see, laddie, we do get some toys here,' he said as he moved to the front of the room, standing beside the whiteboard as Billy, Anjli and Declan sat in chairs facing him.

'So,' Monroe said, tapping the plasma screen. A photo of Victoria Davies appeared. 'I'm guessing you read the note, DI Walsh?'

Declan nodded, noting the formality of the name. Monroe was all business in this room.

'I did, sir.'

'Good. Then you're as up to speed as the rest of us,' Monroe replied, pointing to the image on the screen. 'Victoria Davies. Maiden name Victoria Devington, and heir to the Devington Industries trading fortune.'

Tap. The image changed to a tabloid photo of a young Victoria and Michael, out on the town.

'Met Michael Davies while at Cambridge; they were both studying Sociology. Both joined the local Socialist movement in 1990, becoming more active in the Labour Party during the Kinnock years, culminating in the Labour defeat of 1992.'

'So, Victoria was a Left Winger? I bet that didn't sit well with daddy,' Anjli muttered. Monroe nodded.

'Devington Senior wasn't a fan of this, but at the same time she was his eldest daughter. And first-born daughters always get a little more leeway in things.'

'I've always found that,' Billy replied. Monroe paused.

'You'll always be my prettiest princess, DC Fitzwarren,' he said in a mock serious manner. 'Can I continue now?'

'Yes, sir. Sorry, sir.'

Monroe looked to the digital board. Now Declan could see a paparazzi wedding photo.

'They married in 1995,' he continued. 'Shortly before that, Michael was working in the Devington Industries sales office. He was promoted to CEO that year, right after Devington senior passes away.'

'Pays to marry high,' Declan said as he looked out of the door into the office. Trix was still on her phone, her finger swiping upwards with incredible speed.

'Now, things start to fall around about now,' Monroe tapped the screen as a series of images popped up on it. Photos of Michael and Victoria arguing, attending galas with stone faces or even attending alone. 'We don't know what it was, but around 1998, their relationship started to fracture. Perhaps it was because Michael was a major donor to Tony Blair's 'New Labour', while Victoria still kept to her Socialist beliefs. Maybe it was because he snored. All we know is that by 2000 he was sleeping with his PA, Francine Pearce, while Victoria was ...' He sighed. 'Actually, that's the problem we have here. We don't know what she was doing. When questioned, Michael Davies claimed that Victoria was pregnant with someone else's baby, and that his vasectomy from a few months earlier invalidated her claim that it was his.'

'Vasectomies have been known to fail, sir,' Anjli replied.

Monroe nodded. 'Aye, but we'll never know. The night she told Michael about it she fell from the roof of Devington House.'

'And Michael was charged with her murder,' Declan finished.

'It was pretty much an open and shut case at the time, we felt.' Monroe stared at the photo of Victoria now on the screen. 'They're seen fighting, husband goes onto the roof, nobody else is allowed to follow, she falls ... But now it seems more like one of those bloody "closed room" mysteries, because of this.'

The screen now showed a scan of the letter and the envelope.

'Okay then, chaps, we've all seen the evidence now, some more recently than others. What do we know?' Monroe asked, leaning against a table.

'Letter was sent to Susan, her younger sister, but under a fake surname,' Anjli read from her notes. 'In late 2000, Susan Devington was more of an activist than Victoria ever was.'

'Little sisters always like to outdo their elders,' Declan mused. 'So what, she used a fake name so they didn't know she was a rich girl slumming with the proles?'

'Most likely,' Billy continued. 'The address the letter was sent to was on a watch list for road protestors back then. Bit of an "anyone can stay" squat locale.'

'So, Susan was a road protestor?' Declan wrote this in his notepad.

'Oh yes. She was arrested at the Newbury Bypass protest in '96, and again in '97. Carried on until 2001.'

'What happened then?' Declan asked.

'She started using her surname again and took over Devington Industries when Michael was convicted.'

'Poacher turned Gatekeeper,' Monroe mused. 'What about the letter itself?'

'House of Commons stationery,' Billy started.

'Which proves that Victoria was either in Parliament, or was able to gain access to the paper,' Anjli continued.

'Could have been Portcullis House,' Declan suggested. 'Many of the MPs have offices there.'

Monroe shook his head. 'Portcullis House wasn't opened until early 2001, a few months later,' he replied. 'This has to be elsewhere. But where ...?'

Declan leaned closer to the screen, looking at the scanned image.

Something was missing.

'It's not there,' he said suddenly, getting up and walking out of the office.

'What's not there?' Monroe shouted as outside the office Declan went to his jacket, pulling out the envelope and pulling the letter out of it as he returned.

'This,' Declan said as he held the letter to the light. 'The scan doesn't show it, but there's a watermark. It's very small.'

He was right. In the bottom right-hand corner and easy to miss were a small series of incredibly small, watermarked numbers.

9845.76

'What is it?' Anjli asked.

Monroe started to pace as he thought. 'It couldn't be that simple,' he whispered to himself.

'What couldn't be that simple?' Declan said as he put away the letter.

Monroe looked back; his eyes bright. 'Back in 1994, John Major's Conservative Government were getting hammered from all angles,' he explained. 'Cash for questions, about half a dozen affairs in his Cabinet all coming out ... All from leaks that were emanating from Parliament.'

'MPs getting some pretty public kicks in to their rivals?' asked Billy.

Monroe nodded as he looked back at the scan of the letter on the screen. 'This was before emails, remember. When these things were sent to journalists, it was often through leaked memos. Headed paper.'

'Paper just like this.'

Monroe nodded. 'It came out later that Major had managed to stop this by secretly tagging the stationery of each office. If I'm right, then that number there gives the location and the room where the letter came from. So, when a leak came out, they could back trace it.'

'And fire whoever sent it, I assume,' Billy nodded. 'Vicious.'

'When Blair took over, it seemed pointless to change the stationery, so they kept using the watermarked supply.' Monroe was already walking to a desk phone, picking it up and dialling. 'And they didn't change it until, as DI Walsh there correctly surmised, Portcullis House was opened. After that, emails took over.'

'So, the code says whose office Victoria took the paper from?' Declan asked. 'It'll tell us who was in it?'

'Sort of. Remember that Portcullis House was built because of MP overcrowding and many MPs shared the same office,' Monroe replied. 'Yes, hello?' Now he was talking into the phone. 'Can you put me through to Anthony Farringdon? Tell him it's Detective Chief Inspector Monroe. He knows me.'

Now on hold, he looked back to Declan.

'Luckily, I know someone who can tell us exactly who was in that office when Victoria wrote the letter,' he said. 'And I'm going to send you and DS Kapoor to speak with him today.' He grinned. 'Welcome to the Last Chance Saloon.'

7

DEALS AND CONSEQUENCES

CHARLES BAKER HAD NEVER BEEN A FAN OF THE PUGIN ROOM.

There were thirty bars in the Palace of Westminster; throwbacks to the days when "Gentlemen's Clubs" were all the rage. These days, however, the bars were as different from each other as they could be; from the stately rooms of the House of Lords bars all the way down to the Sports and Social Club in the basement by the bins.

They played darts there.

Charles Baker had never been a fan of *darts*, either.

But here he was, smiling at his two dining colleagues as he sipped expensive tea and pretended to give a damn about what they said. The Pugin Room wasn't busy right now; probably something more exciting happening on the members' terrace. And there was a distinct lack of journalists in the room right now; probably more by choice and arrangement than accident.

As Walter Symonds, current Chairperson of the Conservative Party's *1922 Committee* talked about some West End musical that he'd recently been to see, waffling on about how opera was still a very underrated art form, Charles let his attention wander, looking around the room while trying to look invested in the conversation. It was papered with a hideous gothic red/gold wallpaper known as Gothic Tapestry, based on the Italian red velvet tapestries of the Renaissance, leading up to the ornate stencil-patterned roses of the ceiling. A giant gilt brass and crystal chandelier hung in the middle. It had once hung in the Earl of Shrewsbury's house, Alton Towers, but of course these days people knew the place for a far different reason, as Alton Towers was now the UK's biggest theme park.

Charles noted that Tom Wylde, SNP Member of Parliament for Strathclyde North was currently sitting under the chandelier, and a wistful desire to see it fall crossed Charles's mind.

Augustus Welby Northmore Pugin was one of the builders of the new Palace of Westminster, more known as the Houses of Parliament, in the 1840s. He was an accomplished architect and a visionary of his time, but what wasn't mentioned as much was that Pugin was quite mad. In fact, he was committed to Bedlam Asylum at the age of forty. If you visited the Houses of Parliament, you'd find a lot of Latin carved into the wood, the same saying time and time again. It was even written around each of the four faces of Big Ben. *Domine Salvam Fac Reginam Nostram Victoriam Primam.* It meant *O Lord, keep safe our Queen Victoria the First;* a prayer to his patron Queen Victoria, Pugin apparently believed that by the simple act of seeing these words, of MPs and dignitaries walking under them, through them hundreds of times a day, they would give power to the prayer, effectively deifying Queen Victoria.

Charles wondered if it actually worked, whether Victoria was watching down on him right now.

But which Victoria?

Pushing back the sudden macabre thought, Charles forced himself to sip at his tea as he looked to Walter, still going on about some Military Tattoo that he'd been to the other day. Overweight and sweating, and as much a dyed-in-the-wool "old guard" Tory as you'd ever see, Symonds looked like he'd run a marathon rather than walked the few steps from the members' canteen where he'd had his second lunch of the day. Wiping his hand through his thinning, grey hair, Symonds carried on with whatever new, boring anecdote had crossed his mind.

The second man at the table was Malcolm Gladwell. Known for being the "trouble-shooter" of the Conservative Party, Gladwell was a weasel of a man that you really didn't want to have appear in your office doorway. Stick thin and with curly ginger hair, Gladwell was in his late forties, but looked a decade younger. Gladwell was a biohacker and ate more weight in supplements and pills in a day than Charles had in the last year. He was also sickeningly fit, too. Often, Charles had heard Gladwell talk about his hobby of ultra-running, his holidays spent effectively running alone across deserts.

He must be a joy at parties, Charles thought to himself.

Walter was reaching to a pile of scones in the middle of the table. He used a butter knife to open one, spreading clotted cream on one of the sides before taking a large mouthful.

'Anyway, I suppose we should get down to business,' he said, the half-eaten scone in his mouth visible to the world.

Charles straightened in his seat.

'Yes, please,' he replied.

Symonds looked to Gladwell.

'Charlie, you know what they're going to say,' Gladwell began. 'They're going to point at your past allegiances as to why you shouldn't be considered.'

'I left the Labour Party fifteen years ago Malcolm,' Charles replied. 'I've been here longer than pretty much every other candidate on the list.'

'But Labour is Labour,' Symonds added.

'Blair's Labour!' Charles snapped, bringing his voice back down so as not to draw attention to the meeting. 'Come on, Walter, the man was practically a Tory. His father even tried to run as a Conservative MP in Durham.'

'The 1922 Committee hasn't made any choices on this as yet,' Symonds continued.

'After all, we still have complete faith in our leader,' Gladwell added.

'Of course, you do,' Charles smiled. 'As do we all.'

Gladwell leaned closer to Charles, looking around to ensure that he couldn't be heard.

'Look, Charlie,' he whispered. 'Even though you definitely kept that old red flag flying back in the day, you're a popular choice amongst the backbenchers. We see that. We really do.'

'But?'

'But hypothetically, if you did go for the brass ring, we'd need to ensure that you're squeaky clean.' Gladwell replied.

'You know, any issues in the past that could come out and bite us, cause us some problems,' Symonds said through another half-eaten scone.

'Such as?' Charles sat back up now. Gladwell mirrored him.

'You know the sort of thing we mean,' he said. 'Affairs, illegitimate children, sticking your todger in a dead pig's mouth, a certain "liking" for kiddies ...'

'Selling guns to the Ugandans, you know the rules.' Symonds chimed in.

Charles thought for a moment. It was true that some of their more recent choices for Prime Minister had been less than stellar, only kept in power by the Left's inordinate ability to place someone as equally dismal in opposition.

'Then let me say this as straight as I can,' he started. 'Since joining the Conservative Party, I've been sure to keep my nose clean. There are no skeletons in my closet.'

'And when you were one of Blair's golden boys?' Gladwell asked.

Charles didn't say anything. A single moment, a memory hidden for decades flashed up.

Holding a broken necklace, Victoria's necklace in his hands.

'I said—' began Gladwell.

'I heard what you said,' Charles interrupted angrily. 'There's nothing.'

Gladwell nodded, looking back to Symonds who, stuffing the last of his cream scone into his mouth like it was a race nodded and rose from the table, shaking both Charles and Gladwell's hands in turn.

'Then we'll be talking soon, Minister,' he said. Or at least that's what Charles thought he said. His mouth was so full, he could have been talking about another of his god-awful West End musicals again.

And then Symonds left, leaving Charles and Gladwell alone at the table.

'You know it's going to be a no,' Gladwell said matter-of-factly.

'You're kidding me,' Charles replied. 'Have you seen who's on the list? Nigel Dickinson!'

'Doesn't matter,' Gladwell picked up his glass of wine, sipping at it as he gathered his next words. 'They'll want someone younger to gain the youth market. Maybe the Chancellor after the next budget if he does a nice one. And let's be honest, your loyalties are still a concern.'

'Oh, for Christ's sake,' Charles muttered. 'I'm further to the right than half of them.'

'I might be able to turn them around,' Gladwell said. It was such a simple statement that Charles almost didn't realise what Gladwell was offering.

'You can?' he asked. 'Why?'

'Honestly? Because I think you could be the man to get us back to where we need to be,' Gladwell replied. 'And, because I think you understand how things truly work around here.'

'What, you scratch my back and I scratch yours?'

Gladwell laughed. 'Oh Charlie,' he said, 'if I scratched your back on this, I'd expect you to get down on your knees and take my entire bloody load.'

He rose from the chair, throwing his napkin to the table.

'The only question you'd need to ask is whether you're prepared to spit or swallow.'

'Oh, I think the committee would learn that I'm a very considerate lover,' Charles said, forcing a smile.

Gladwell nodded. 'Then I'll be in touch.' And with that Gladwell too was gone, leaving Charles alone.

'You pricks,' he muttered. God he needed a drink right now. Somewhere that he wouldn't bump into any more Gladwell sycophants.

The Sports and Social Club it was, then.

———

ANDY MAC LIVED IN WILTSHIRE, NEAR AVEBURY, BUT DUE TO the long hours he worked in the *God's Will TV* studio, he'd bought a small one-bedroom apartment off Teddington Lock, literally around the corner from the studios for the nights he simply couldn't get home to his wife and daughter. And as the workload grew, so did the amount of time he stayed there.

It was minimalistic. Andy used it mainly as a base to sleep in so the walls were still the original white with a couple of prints on the wall, and his living room was basically a sofa, a TV with a YouTube Creator Award made of gold-plated brass – given for one million subscribers next to it – an expensive spinning bike with a monitor screen attached and a coffee table. But it was the bedroom that really mattered. Egyptian sheets and pure cotton pillows on a king-sized bed under a duvet filled with 100% Siberian Goose Down; this was a place for kings to sleep.

But Andy Mac wasn't sleeping. Currently he was sitting on the edge of the bed, naked and with his head in his hands, unable to believe the stupidity with which he had excelled today.

It was true that Sebastian had been worth it; the muscled torso and ruffled hair of the sleeping man were visible on the bed, the duvet mercifully hiding the rest. But at the same time this was career killing. This was marriage ending.

This was so good.

Rising, Andy walked back into the living room, picking up the strewn clothes as he did so, a force of habit more than anything else. However, as he picked up Sebastian's black denim 502s, he felt a slight vibration in the pocket. A phone, on silent mode, most likely.

He couldn't help himself. With a small pang of jealousy, he pulled the phone out to see who was sending Sebastian messages. Was it a boyfriend? A girlfriend? Had Sebastian lied too?

It turned out that he had.

The message was a reply to a thread, one that showed up when Andy tapped on the screen. Only two messages, but enough to freeze Andy's blood.

So what do you think? Can we do this?

Hell, yeah. Send me the best ones and we'll finish the bastard once and for all.

Andy pressed the 'pictures' icon on the screen and it flooded into life with photos of Sebastian and Andy: kissing by the first aid kit, kissing in the apartment's elevator, even intimate photos of Andy, his head between Sebastian's legs as they sat on the sofa in the living room, Sebastian holding the phone up like a selfie.

Andy felt physically sick as he deleted the photos. *Were they on the cloud? What had Sebastian already sent?*

'What the hell?' said Sebastian, walking into the living area. 'That's my phone.'

Andy threw the smartphone at Sebastian, watching it clatter to the floor as it bounced off the intern's bare chest.

'This was all a lie?' he exclaimed. 'You did this for photos and money?'

'All of this is a lie!' Sebastian snapped back, waving

around the apartment. 'I don't see any photos of your family here! You're a character made for television!'

He didn't manage to say anything else as Andy had quickly crossed the room, ramming Sebastian against a wall, his forearm at his throat.

'What did you send?' he hissed.

'Nothing!' Sebastian replied, now starting to get scared. He might have had age on his side, but Andy was bigger built.

'*Why?*' Andy said, throwing Sebastian across the room, sending him tumbling over the coffee table. 'I thought we had something!'

Sebastian rose, his fear replaced by anger.

'What, you thought that I could be awestruck by the great Andy Mac?' he hissed, pulling on his jeans. 'You're a charlatan. A joke.'

'Then why do this?' Andy waved to the bedroom. 'I mean, Christ, you let me—'

'*I know damn well what I let you do!*' Sebastian shouted back. 'And for those photos it was worth it! They'll end you!'

'What did I ever do to you?' Andy asked softly.

'You killed my mother,' Sebastian replied. 'Or at least you were one of the people that did.'

'You said she died in an accident?'

'An accident that you orchestrated!'

Andy stared in confusion at the young, naked man. 'I don't even know your mother,' he said. 'My assistant hired you—'

'*This* was my mother,' Sebastian said, pulling a folded old photo out of his jeans pocket and tossing it over to Andy. Picking it up off the hardwood floor, Andy opened the photo, staring at the image.

'Oh my God,' he said, understanding everything now.

'Good,' Sebastian replied. 'Now you can tell me what really happened that night, or else I'll take these photos and—'

He wasn't able to finish the sentence as Andy grabbed the YouTube award and with a scream slammed it down onto Sebastian's head, the thin edge of the heavy award shattering the skull as it rammed through into the brain.

Sebastian stared in stunned shock at Andy, unable to speak, his mouth opening and shutting as the blood from the ragged hole in his head streamed down his face. And then, with an almost hurt expression, Sebastian fell to the floor, his eyes glazed and lifeless.

There was a frozen moment of silence in the room. Andy looked around it, trying to see where the phone fell. Spying it, he picked it up. It was locked, the impact with the hardwood floor causing it to restart and relock in the process. Luckily, it didn't need a password, as it had face recognition. Forcing himself not to vomit, Andy held the screen up to the glazed-eyed corpse. It unlocked, and slowly and methodically Andy deleted every single picture on the phone, ensuring that the deleted items folder was also emptied. He then checked to see if there were any cloud provider services linked to the photos and was relieved to see that there weren't. The phone had been the only place the photos had been stored. And the message to whoever had replied had nothing either. It was simply the word of an intern with an infatuation with a star against the literal voice of God.

The voice of God who now had a half-naked, dead man in his apartment.

Grabbing the body and pulling it away from the battered award, Andy wondered if it was even worth getting dressed before he sorted this out; after all, the blood would get everywhere and it was easier to shower it off.

Andy thought about this for a moment.

And then he fell to his knees on the floor, puking violently before collapsing in tears, curling into a foetal position.

Andy Mac hoped that God hadn't been watching this.

But he knew that whatever happened, he was damned.

THE MEMORY MAN

IT WAS RAINING WHEN DECLAN AND ANJLI ARRIVED AT THE National Liberal Club, situated at the junction of Whitehall Place and Whitehall Court. An opulent, white-brick, neogothic building, it merged in with the surrounding constructions seamlessly, with the corner entrance an elaborate arch over a double wood and glass doorway.

Anjli stopped and looked at Declan as he paused at the doorway.

'Well, are you coming in or not?' she said.

Declan nodded. 'Sorry. Bit of a memory. My dad was a member here.'

Anjli nodded back at this, aware of Declan's recent bereavement.

'I don't know if I've said anything yet, but I'm sorry for your loss,' she said. 'I never met Chief Superintendent Walsh, but I heard he was a good man. And Monroe has always spoken of him highly.'

'Thanks,' Declan replied. He didn't know what to say to things like this; usually he found that it was best to simply acknowledge and move on. Entering through the doors, they turned to the left where, in an alcove marked "Enquiries", an ornate clock above it, was the doorman, currently behind a chest-high counter.

'DI Walsh and DS Kapoor,' Declan said, showing his warrant card. 'We're expected.'

'Ah yes, Mister Farringdon,' the doorman nodded. 'He's upstairs in the bar.'

Declan looked to the end of the hallway. 'Up those stairs?' he asked. The doorman nodded and returned to his work. With a look to Anjli, Declan shrugged and continued to the end of the entranceway. There the hallway opened into a large rotunda, a huge spiral staircase that ran along the white marbled wall in front of them, an ornate marble banister circling up alongside as it rose up towards a beautifully designed glass ceiling.

Walking up the stairs, examining the paintings that seemed to watch them as they passed by on the deep red carpet, Declan smiled.

'I came here as a kid, once,' he said. 'I was told off for wearing trainers.'

'I've been here a few times,' Anjli replied. 'The Sherlock Holmes Society have their quarterly meetings in the David Lloyd room.'

They arrived at the door to the first-floor bar, peering through the glass.

'I am genuinely too poor to go in here,' Declan mused as he opened the door.

It was a high-ceilinged room, with red marble pillars running along each side, the space between each one either filled with the green wallpaper of the wall, or revealing a floor to ceiling bay window, complete with green drapery.

Glass fronted mahogany trophy cabinets were beside several of the pillars, but as they walked past Declan wasn't able to see what names were etched on the trophies inside.

Beside a bust of William Gladstone was a low table with three dark-green leather armchairs. In one of these sat an elderly man in a military blazer. His white hair neatly parted to the right, he put aside a copy of *The Guardian* and stood to greet his guests, holding a hand out to shake Declan's with a gait of a man who was once certainly in the military.

'DI Walsh,' he said, shaking Declan's hand, before doing the same with Anjli. 'And DS Kapoor. Alexander told me you'd be arriving.'

'I'm guessing you're Anthony Farringdon?' Declan asked as they took their seats. Farringdon smiled.

'For my sins,' he replied. 'Now, what can I help you with? Alex was a little vague when he spoke to me.'

'Deliberately, I'm afraid,' Anjli said, passing over the letter. 'We wanted you to see this without prior warning.'

'To test the old memory?'

'More like ensuring that word of this didn't get out yet,' Declan replied, and was shocked to see an expression of fury cross Farringdon's face.

'Sir!' the old soldier barked. 'I used to control security for Downing Street itself! I would never reveal—'

'Not you, not you,' Anjli interrupted, waving Farringdon silent. 'It's just ... Well, read the letter.'

His anger now placated, Farringdon opened and slowly read the letter.

He then read it a second time.

'I see now,' he eventually said as he finished reading. 'Yes, I understand. Terrible time.'

'We were told that you might be able to help us with a

number question,' Anjli pointed to the corner of the letter. Farringdon leaned in closer, squinting.

'Ah, that takes me back,' he said, passing the letter back. 'Let's see. Ninety-eight, four five, point seven six. Yes, that would be from the millennium batch. That is, the stationery printed after the start of the 2000 session.'

He leaned back, his eyes glazing.

'So ...' he began before silently staring off into the air. Declan looked to Anjli who shrugged.

'Monroe said he was the best,' she whispered. 'That he had a photographic memory.'

'The term is eidetic,' Farringdon said, still staring off into space. 'And, it's been twenty years with over six hundred MPs in Parliament in any given time, so give me a moment.'

Returning to the present, he looked back at the letter.

'The first part, the nine and the eight? If they were the other way around it'd be opposition, so that means that it's Government. Which for the date on the letter, if it's correct means that this would be Blair's New Labour, near the end of its first term. The second numbers, four and five show that it's not a Westminster Palace office, so backbenchers at best. If not there, it'd be the Norman Shaw building. And the last two numbers mean it's third floor, room ...'

He grinned.

'Just before the 2000 to 2001 New Year ... Then that's Goldenballs.'

'Sorry?' Anjli now looked at Declan.

'Blair's golden boys. We called them Goldenballs. Three of them were in there before the 2001 election. It was a small office, too.'

'Do you remember who they were?' Declan asked, pulling out a notepad.

'Indeed,' Farringdon thought for a moment. 'By the door was Shaun Donnal. He ended up being Junior Welfare Minister or something along those lines. Lost his seat in a 2012 by election. Dabbled in social activism during his time in Parliament, was almost picked to be a kind of grass roots, far left alternative to Blair, but then dropped off the map. Haven't seen him for years.'

'And the others?'

'Hmm. Across from him was Andrew MacIntyre. Never really amounted to much, lost his seat in the 2010 election, Now he's—'

'Andy Mac!' Declan exclaimed. 'Bloody hell. He became a YouTube preacher?'

Anjli looked to Declan. 'You watch his show?'

'Only a bit of one,' Declan replied. 'He mentioned ... Well, he mentioned me last week.' He didn't comment on the fact that it was a denouncement for Declan's public punching of a priest on live TV.

Farringdon nodded. 'That's the one. Takes all sorts, I suppose. Lost his seat on a Thursday, found God by end of play Friday.'

'And the third?'

Farringdon looked over to one of the stewards. 'Peter, be a dear and pass me that *Daily Mail*, will you?' he asked. The steward took a newspaper from the rack and brought it over, placing it on the table, facing upwards.

MEET THE NEW BOSS?

Farringdon tapped the photo of Charles Baker.

'That bugger right there,' he said. 'Swapped teams in 2003, hasn't stopped rising since.'

Declan picked up the paper, staring at the image. So, Victoria Davies was pregnant, scared of her husband finding out that it wasn't his baby and had written her sister a letter from the offices of Britain's most popular Internet TV preacher and the next Prime Minister of the UK, among others.

'Anything else I can do for you?' Farringdon asked. Declan rose, putting the notepad away and shaking Farringdon's hand.

'Believe me,' he said, 'you've helped us out a lot here.'

Turning to leave, Declan stopped as Farringdon spoke again.

'Your father. Good man. Didn't have a heart attack.'

'What do you mean?' Declan turned to face the old man, still in the chair.

'I mean I knew your father, DI Walsh. Patrick was a mainstay here. Fit as an ox. And no matter what they say, he didn't ever drink and drive.'

Declan nodded.

'Thank you,' he said.

'Make it right, boy,' Farringdon continued. 'Your father told me about you. Ex-military speaks to ex-military. Make it right.'

And with that, his point made, Farringdon curtly nodded and went back to his reading.

Leaving Anthony Farringdon to his papers, they made their way back into the rain, standing outside the National Liberal Club as they tried to make sense of this.

'A ghost, a preacher and the next Prime Minister,' Anjli said. 'If we added "walked into a bar" we'd have a cracker of a joke. But one of them had to know Victoria Davies well.'

'Allegedly,' Declan replied. 'She might have found the sheet of paper by other means.'

'Not one of them came forward when she died. I read the notes,' Anjli muttered, frowning at the rain. 'Baker, MacIntyre and Donnal were all at the party. They're on the guest list.'

'Not surprising,' Declan waved for a cab. 'Think about it. Five months before a General Election? The possibility that one of them was about to be outed as an adulterer and a soon to be father. They didn't want this over their heads as they went to the polls.'

'The truth will always come out,' Anjli muttered as the cab pulled up beside them.

'Eventually,' Declan agreed. 'But back then? This was a secret worth keeping silent, whatever the cost.'

'So, you think one of them killed her?' Anjli climbed into the cab as Declan followed. He thought for a moment, then pulled out the envelope as Anjli gave the cab driver the address.

'*And then they'll remove him, maybe in an "accident" like that bitch Sarah,*' he read from it. 'I don't think it was the first time, either. Even decades later, this could be dangerous.'

Anjli grinned. 'As long as there's no priests to punch, we'll be fine,' she said as the cab pulled away from the pavement, en route for Temple Inn.

9

THE CAMERA NEVER LIES

MONROE WAS TALKING TO BILLY AS DECLAN AND ANJLI entered, Billy working on a computer as Monroe leaned over, watching the monitor.

'Ah, excellent,' he said as they walked over. 'So go on, tell me what we have.'

Anjli opened her notebook and gave Monroe an account of the meeting with Farringdon, and the three MPs that shared the room the letterheaded paper had come from. On hearing Shaun Donnal's name, however, Monroe raised an eyebrow.

'Donnal, eh?' he asked. 'He's quite popular these days.'

Declan's face obviously showed confusion so Monroe pointed at Billy's monitor. The face of Shaun Donnal, bearded and dishevelled, taken from what looked like an ATM camera, was on it.

'Seems Mister Donnal was a naughty boy last night,' Monroe explained. 'Got into a fight with another homeless man in Soho when he was recognised.'

'Why do we have Donnal on a screen?' Declan asked. 'We only had his name given to us ten minutes ago.'

'Blame Trix,' Monroe said. 'Call came in, looking for someone to take it on and she accepted it. Only bloody time she's answered the phone. Yet here we are and here he is.'

'Someone recognised him looking like that?' Anjli commented.

'Man by the name of Minty,' Billy said, pulling up an image of another, older homeless man, taken from a hospital bed. 'We've yet to work out his real name. Claims that when Donnal was Welfare Minister, or at least in the department, one of the bills they voted through lost Minty his house.'

'Christ, what a shock that must have been for him,' Declan mused. 'To become homeless and then find the very man you blame sharing the doorway with you.'

'Soup kitchen, actually. Seems that Minty recognised Donnal, but he ran off. Minty then hunted around for him, finding him around eighteen hundred hours on Dean Street, outside the NatWest Bank.'

'Making a deposit?' Anjli joked. Monroe raised an eyebrow.

'Actually, you might be closer than you think,' he said. 'Apparently Minty saw Donnal at an ATM and was convinced that he was withdrawing money with a debit card.'

'Homeless people have those these days?' Declan asked.

'Not usually. But our little Billy here matched the time of the incident with NatWest's ATM CCTV, and we found that Mister Donnal was doing something there. We can't see what it was yet though, and NatWest are being slow in giving us any data.'

He looked to Billy, who was already opening up another folder on the screen.

'Show them the other footage,' he said.

Billy tapped on his keyboard and an image appeared on his monitor screen, a black and white CCTV video of two men arguing. Then one seemed to repeatedly hit the other, letting him slump beside the bank before running off.

'Stabbing?' Declan asked, watching the scene a second time. Monroe nodded.

'Multiple times, all in the stomach,' he said. 'Minty claimed that he held the weapon up afterwards, said that if our man told anyone he saw him, he'd return and finish the job. Apparently it was a long-stem flat-head screwdriver with a sharpened edge. Poor wee sod didn't even feel the injuries until five minutes later. Then he apparently screamed like a bugger until the ambulance arrived.'

Anjli peered at the screen. 'It's blurry,' she said.

'It's a low-resolution image taken from a cheap CCTV from down the street,' Billy replied.

'Can you enhance it? You know, zoom in and clear it up like in the films?'

Billy gave Anjli a withering stare.

'Sure,' he said in a deadpan tone. 'I can zoom in, enhance the image, stick it in photoshop, make them look like Tom Cruise and Bruce Willis, add an alien ship in the sky ...'

Anjli held up a hand. 'Fine,' she said. 'I was just making a suggestion.'

There was a *ping* from Billy's computer and he turned back, tapping on the keyboard. A series of spreadsheets appeared on the screen.

'Looks like NatWest came through with the data,' he said, bringing up a document onto his screen. 'Shaun wasn't using his own card. That's where the issue was. It was a card registered to a Sally Donnal.'

'His wife?'

'Daughter, I think,' Anjli was already searching Google on her phone.

'Interesting thing though, the account is barely used,' Billy said, his screen now filled with account transactions. 'Every now and then she deposits fifty quid in, and then—'

'He removes it by card,' Declan finished, reading the spreadsheets. 'The moment he does, she adds another fifty. She's funding her father. Ensuring he has spending money. This isn't a homeless man we're looking at here; Shaun Donnal's not on the streets because of circumstance, he's hiding from something.' Declan looked back to the crime wall.

'Or someone.'

'We need to get the daughter in,' Monroe said, looking to the doorway. 'Oh, hello.'

Declan turned towards the door to the offices to see a woman standing there, suited men either side of her. She was in her forties; her clothes were expensive, her strawberry-blonde hair pulled back. She looked every inch the business-woman she was known for being.

Susan Devington.

'I hope you don't mind me popping up,' she said to every-one, not focusing on any one person in the room. 'I was told you had some property of mine.'

It took Declan a moment to realise what she meant, but Monroe understood immediately.

'We do, Miss Devington,' he said, walking towards her. 'But currently it's evidence in a murder enquiry.'

'It's *Ms* Devington,' Susan snapped. 'The little things are so important, wouldn't you say?'

'Yes, *Ms* Devington,' Monroe agreed reluctantly. 'And, as I was saying, it's evidence ...'

'In a murder enquiry that was finished up two decades ago, with the murderer being sentenced to life, if I recall correctly,' Susan replied, her tone authoritative, unused to not getting her way. 'Or did I mishear the judge when I sat in the gallery?'

'Michael Davies was indeed charged and sentenced,' Monroe nodded. 'But the letter we recently received gives the impression that other people may have been involved.'

'Show me it,' Susan held her hand out, as if expecting Monroe to have it on his person. Declan didn't move, very aware that he currently held the envelope.

'I'm afraid it's currently at another department, off site, where they're checking for prints,' Monroe lied skilfully. 'We can show you a scan of what it says though, if you and your security guards would like to come through into my office?'

'These aren't security, they're my solicitors,' Susan nodded to the two men at her side. 'I never travel without them these days.'

'In my experience, only guilty people bring solicitors with them to a police station when they haven't been asked to,' Declan said. He didn't mean to speak it aloud but speak it he did.

Susan turned, looking to him. 'Name?' she asked.

'Detective Inspector Walsh.'

'Well, Mister Walsh—'

'*Detective Inspector* Walsh,' Declan interrupted. 'As you said, the little things are important here.'

For the first time since she arrived, Susan smiled. 'Oh, I like this one,' she said to the solicitor on the left. 'We don't need to sue him.'

'There's no need to sue anyone,' Monroe interjected, walking between Susan and Declan. 'As soon as we get the letter back, we'll send it straight to you. I'm the Detective Chief Inspector here, in charge of the case. I'll send it personally.'

Susan thought about this for a moment. 'I want it in progress by the end of the day,' she said.

Monroe nodded. 'I'll ensure the forensics team works as fast as possible.' He looked to the Interview Room. 'Perhaps while you're here, we could have a small chat about that night?'

'I don't dwell on past things, and I wasn't even there,' Susan said, looking to her solicitors and nodding. 'We're done here.'

And with that, she started towards the door.

'Ms Devington?' Declan stepped forwards. 'Please, if you could answer one small thing?'

Susan paused at the doorway. 'What?' she asked, not even turning to face Declan.

'In the letter, your sister claims that she could be murdered, and that it may have happened before,' he said. 'I wondered if you knew anything about this?'

'My sister was known for her histrionics,' Susan said, still looking away. 'And her paranoia knew no bounds. Sarah died in an accident.'

And with that she left, her two solicitors walking out with her.

Monroe looked to Declan. 'Quick thinking,' he said.

'I don't get it,' Billy replied. 'What was quick?'

'Susan turned up expecting a fight,' Declan said. 'She wants the letter and she's willing to throw the full force of the law on it. And I reckon we'll get pressure from elsewhere too.'

'But here's the thing,' Monroe continued. 'We were passed the letter through internal communication. Before us, nobody outside of a couple of desk officers in Derby had even read it.'

'It's one thing knowing that the letter exists,' Declan said with a smile. 'But to know that the name *Sarah* is used in it. We never mentioned that.'

A smile of realisation passed across Billy's face.

'She's read the letter,' he said.

Monroe shrugged. 'Maybe, maybe not,' he replied. 'But one thing's for sure. Even if she hasn't read it, she knows what's in it. And I'm very interested in how she found out.'

Declan looked to Billy, who shook his head.

'Oh no,' he said. 'I know what you're thinking; that Billy and Susan probably move in the same circles, what with his family being, well, stupidly rich. But I'm not part of that circle. I was pretty much kicked off the party invite list when I took down my uncle in a crypto Ponzi scheme.'

'It's why he's Billy and not William,' Anjli added. 'His family also hate him because he's gay.'

Billy looked at Anjli with a hurt expression.

'What?' she replied. 'It's not a secret that you are, and it's certainly not a secret that they hate you because of it.'

Billy shrugged. Monroe looked at the crime board.

'DS Kapoor, go chase up anything you can on these three new suspects. I want to know what they were doing, who they were talking to, who hated them, anything you can find. DI Walsh, go to Teddington Lock Studios. I think you should have a chat with Andy Mac. Once you're done there, go chase down Susan Devington and have a chat with her too.'

'Why me?' Declan asked.

'Because she likes you,' Monroe smiled. 'DC Fitzwarren, find out anything you can on *Holmes 2* about the cold case.'

'I preferred the first one,' Trix said from the canteen area. 'The sequel sucked.'

Everyone turned to look at her.

'What?' she asked.

'Where the hell did you come from?' Monroe asked.

'You told me to make some tea,' Trix replied, pointing at the kettle. 'Tea.'

'That was an hour ago!' Monroe exclaimed, half amused.

Trix shrugged, returning to her phone. 'Well, I'm more used to pods than these bags,' she said. 'You should get a machine in. You could take it out of my wages. You know, if you paid me.'

'She's not wrong,' Monroe replied. 'Well, apart from the film thing. We're not talking about the movie, girl, we're talking about the *Home Office Large Major Enquiry System*. The second one, anyway.'

'Large Major Enquiry?' Trix sniffed. 'Sounds like someone was trying to make the letters fit Sherlock Holmes.'

'Well of course they were,' Billy said. 'That was deliberate. A program and a machine that can work through case files and bring you answers, named after a great detective.'

'So, like Google then.'

Monroe sighed, giving up on the conversation as he looked to the paper on the table. It wasn't a *Daily Mail*, but it still had a picture of Charles Baker on it.

'DS Kapoor,' he said softly. 'When you check into their pasts, look into any connections between Devington and Baker.'

And, with that, he walked back into his office. Declan

followed him in, closing the door. Monroe looked up from his desk

'Did we forget something, laddie?' he asked.

'Sorry sir, but I ... I needed to speak to you,' Declan said. 'It's about my father.'

'Of course,' Monroe sat down, waving for Declan to do the same. Declan stayed where he was, standing in the middle of the office.

'Ah, it's one of those conversations,' Monroe muttered.

'I think my father was murdered,' Declan said. 'And I think I know why.'

'Oh?'

'He was writing a memoir of his time on the force. Had written a memoir, that is. There are pages of it by his desk,' Declan started. He didn't know how much to tell Monroe right now, but this seemed to be a good start.

'The bloody fool,' Monroe sighed. 'He just wouldn't let things lie.' He looked at Declan. 'We put away some murderous bastards in our time, lad. And if he's been writing about them, some of those bastards might take offence. Johnny and Jackie Lucas, for a start. So, what do you want to do about this?'

Declan took a deep breath. He expected to be shot down here, but he had to try.

'I want to find out who killed my father and put them behind bars.'

'Just that? No revenge fantasies?' Monroe watched Declan carefully. 'Because I didn't bring you in here so you could go all *John Wick* on the criminal fraternity.'

'I just want justice,' Declan replied. 'But currently it's just me, and when you're looking at things like this alone you start to feel like a bit of a conspiracy theorist.'

Monroe chuckled. 'I think we have enough conspiracies here right now. But bring me the book, let me have a read through. I'll let you know my thoughts.'

'I'm not sure if the book still exists,' Declan replied. 'I mean, there's a manuscript there but I haven't looked at it fully. And I don't know my father's password to get into his iMac.'

'Try *DeclanSon*, all one word, capital D and the e is a 3 and the o is a zero,' Monroe suggested with a smile. 'It's the one he always used here.'

Declan nodded, a small pang of guilt rising. *DeclanSon.* He'd always felt that his father had been dismissive of him. Now it seemed that he was more proud than he let on.

And Declan would never be able to speak to him about it.

'Now bugger off and find Andy Mac,' Monroe said. 'I want this bloody case off my desk as soon as possible.'

Declan smiled and nodded. 'Thanks, sir.'

'Declan,' Monroe said as Declan was about to leave. 'Thanks for telling me.'

Declan nodded and left the office. He would find his father's killers. He knew it.

But first he had another case that needed attention, and a preacher to interview.

10

THE GUILTY ALWAYS SWEAT

Teddington Lock Studios had once been a series of studio buildings owned by movie giant Pinewood, and in its time had filmed shows for the BBC, ITV, Channel 4 and 5 and even Sky TV. It had started when stockbroker Henry Chinnery had allowed filmmakers to use his greenhouse as a studio at the turn of the century, leading to an actual building being built in 1910. It housed movie sets throughout its life, but in the 1950s it was recommissioned into a television studio, of which it stayed until around 2015 when it was closed and demolished, making way for a new development of homes, apartments and small office studios where architects and designers now worked on the same land where decades earlier stars like Errol Flynn had stood.

Declan stood outside one of these small office and on a small, white painted board outside it read a list of inhabitants: an architect, a designer and God's Will TV.

I suppose YouTube doesn't need much studio space, Declan thought to himself as he pressed the buzzer. After a couple of moments, a bespectacled young woman appeared at the door.

'Can I help?' she asked. Declan flashed his ID.

'DI Walsh, here to speak to Andrew MacIntyre,' he said. The woman frowned.

'What's it about?' she asked.

'Is Andrew here?' Declan replied.

'Is he in trouble?' the woman continued.

Declan sighed. 'Are you Andrew MacIntyre?' he asked.

'Of course not,' the woman sniffed.

'Then why would I talk to you about it?' Declan gave his most serious, police-like expression. The woman's attitude changed. This was obviously something important.

'He's not here right now,' she said, opening the door. 'You're welcome to have a look, but it's only two floors and a large office space that we use to film in.'

'For all the money he makes, I thought this would be bigger,' Declan said as he stood on the doorstep. He didn't need to enter the building if Andy Mac wasn't there.

'The joy of TV,' the woman laughed, now happy to talk about her own world. 'The camera makes all things look exciting. And saying, "Teddington Lock Studios" gives us an air of history.'

'Is that legal though?'

'Well, we're a studio, we're at Teddington Lock and nobody else has that name here, so yeah, pretty much.' The line was spoken with the confidence of someone who had answered the same question many times.

'Do you know where he is?' Declan asked.

'Probably at his apartment, he's always tired after the Holy Ghost comes through him.'

'Yeah, I can see that,' Declan nodded. 'You have an address?'

The woman pointed across the road, to a large block of apartments. 'He has a place in that one there,' she said, writing down a number and passing it to Declan. 'Number fifteen, second floor. That's the gate code. He's not in any trouble, is he?'

'Why would you think that?' Declan asked.

The woman shrugged. 'He's been out of sorts recently,' she said. 'I've worked with him for five years now, but he's been having family issues. Not spending that much time at home. And there's the Baker thing.'

'Baker thing?'

'Charles Baker. The MP. He's going to be the next Prime Minister, and they used to room together. Andy's a little jealous, I think.'

'I don't know why,' Declan said with mock seriousness. 'Baker might be PM, but Andy's besties with God.'

The woman's face brightened at this.

'He is, isn't he?' she gushed. 'Anyway, I must dash, Seb didn't come in today so I'm doing everything right now.'

'Seb?'

'Sebastian Payne. Our intern. To be honest, he's a little bit rubbish. Don't really know why we took him on.'

Declan smiled. 'Yeah, we have someone like that too.'

Nodding a farewell, he walked across to the large, iron gates and tapped the number he'd been given into the door, opening and walking through the gate, entering the complex's cobbled stone courtyard. There was a Land Rover beside the main entrance; it had 'God's Will TV – the voice of the Lord on YouTube' written on it in golden letters. Declan smiled.

Obviously, God loves a four by four as well.

Walking to the main entrance, he buzzed for entry.

ANDY MAC WAS SWEATING WHEN THE BUZZER TO HIS DOOR went, trying to move an industrial 'flight box' to the door. It was a black metal box with aluminium edges, hinged on one side and locked on the other, four wheels on the base to help it spin around. Usually full of LED ring lights, lighting cloths and tripods, Andy had borrowed it from the studio a couple of weeks back to film some 'at home' segments for the show and had left it in a corner of the apartment until he could be bothered to return it. Which was now a blessing as the tripods, lights and cloth were all on the floor now, leaving the box empty.

Well, that wasn't completely true. The bloodied body of Sebastian had been pushed and crumpled inside it, the lid closed and locked.

Andy didn't know what to do with the box; he was working in stages. Stage one was to clear the murder scene up. Stage two was to find a way to remove the body. People saw Andy with these boxes all the time, so it wouldn't raise any concerns. All he had to do was get it into his Land Rover and, while driving home to Avebury find somewhere remote to bury the damn thing.

If it could even be buried.

But now the buzzer had gone.

DECLAN STOOD AT THE DOOR PATIENTLY; HE COULD HEAR movement.

'Hold on!' a voice shouted out. 'I'm just coming!'

There was a clicking of locks and then Andy Mac himself stood in front of Declan, out of breath and in grubby looking gym wear.

'Can I help you?' he asked.

Declan pulled out his ID again, flashing it open. 'I hope so,' he said. 'DI Walsh. I'd like to ask you some questions.'

Andy Mac visibly paled at this. 'What sort of questions?'

'Do you mind if I come inside?' Declan asked.

'Do you have a warrant?'

'Do I need one?'

Andy stepped to the side. 'Of course not, come in,' he smiled.

As Declan entered, he saw that the hand that had opened the door, the one unseen until now was bandaged, blood visible through it.

'Bad wound?' he asked. Andy looked at his hand.

'Oh, just a glass broke. Cut me. All fine,' he said, the smile returning, bringing Declan into the room while indicating an indoor spin bike at the end of it. 'Sorry for the sweatiness. I was on my spin bike.'

'Not a problem,' Declan said, looking around. The place was spotless but there was a strong smell of bleach. It reminded him of the examination room back at Temple Inn.

'Everything alright?' he asked. 'You have an issue with your drains?'

'Oh no, that's me,' Andy laughed. 'I thought I could fix my hand here rather than A&E, bled all over the bloody place. Been cleaning it up for hours.'

Declan noted the case. There was blood on the handle.

'You might want to clean that too,' he said.

Andy saw the marks and immediately ran over, squirting on the blood with a spray and vigorously wiping.

'Sorry, but I'm a bit of a germaphobe when it comes to blood,' he said.

'Really? I thought you'd be okay with blood,' Declan said.

Andy paused. 'What do you mean?' he asked slowly.

'Well, with the whole 'the wine is my blood' and all that,' Declan said, pulling out his notebook and opening it. 'Anyway, I don't want to keep you long. I want to talk about a murder.'

Andy turned, leaning on the case as if his legs had given way.

'Sorry,' he said apologetically. 'Legs like rubber. Spin class can do that.'

'If you need to sit we can sit,' Declan finished. 'I'd like to ask you some quick questions about Victoria Davies.'

'Victoria?' Andy replied, stunned. 'Victoria Davies?'

'Yes,' Declan said, watching Andy carefully. He looked as if he was a drowning man being thrown a lifeline.

'Well, what would you like to know?' Andy replied, all smiles now as he walked over to the sofa, all sign of his rubber leggedness now gone. 'Please, sit.'

Declan did so.

'We have new evidence in her murder,' he said. 'Evidence that shows that Victoria had access to the office that you, Shaun Donnal and Charles Baker shared.'

Andy didn't say anything for a moment, as if his brain simply hadn't caught up to his mouth.

'That's a part of my life I prefer not to talk about,' he said.

'The murder?'

'No, my time in Westminster. Those two men were toxic,

and I was trapped with them for years.' Andy's tone was darkening now, his anger building. 'When Charles back-stabbed us all and jumped ship, Shaun was furious. Never worked out why. Probably all Socialists together.'

'Baker was a Socialist?'

'Closet one, yes,' Andy was warming to this now. 'Those two were always conspiring against the leadership. Shaun even tried to create his own group inside the party. You know, like those people Corbyn had.'

'Momentum?'

'Yeah, just like that. Never worked and Blair cottoned on, so it all fizzled out.'

'Why didn't it work?'

Andy smiled. 'The finances disappeared when Michael Davies found him sleeping with Victoria.'

'And Baker was involved in this too?'

'If he was, he was very good at keeping it out of the news.'

Declan wrote this down in his notebook. *Charles Baker and Michael Davies had been a lot closer than he'd realised.*

'And you knew Victoria?'

'We all knew her,' Andy said. 'And yes, I mean that in a biblical sense. It was before my marriage. I'm not proud of it, but the bloody woman slept her way through half of Parliament.'

'Were you the father of the baby?' Declan asked.

Andy stared at him in horror. 'Christ no! We'd stopped screwing around about a year before her murder. And besides, I always wore a condom.'

'Do you know who the father was?' Declan asked.

Andy shook his head. 'I know it wasn't Michael's. He'd had the chop. Seedless as a Jaffa orange. But, honestly, it could have been anyone's. She put herself around a lot. But if I had to guess, I'd say Shaun's. They were a thing at the end.'

'Thing?'

'An affair in every sense of the word,' Andy said. 'Both claiming that they were going to leave their significant others when there was no way they would.'

'You don't think they could have done that if she'd survived?'

'Not until the election was over,' Andy said, thinking about it. 'And doubtful, considering Shaun and married women.'

'Meaning?'

'Meaning she wasn't his first marital affair, and I'm supposed to be answering questions, not spreading gossip.'

Declan nodded, writing in his notebook.

'Thank you,' he said. 'Just a couple of things and then I'll get out of your hair. Can you think of anyone other than Michael who might have wanted her dead?'

'Only every MP she screwed,' Andy said. 'She was toxic to them.' He thought. 'Oh, and Michael's PA. She bloody hated Vicky. And probably the whole board of Devington Industries. Weirdly, Vicky dying and Michael being convicted was the best thing that happened for them.'

'How so?'

'Because Susan Devington turned out to be a better businesswoman than her sister.'

Declan wrote this down. 'Did you get on with Susan?'

There was a moment of silence, as if Andy was trying to work out what to say, or what to lie about.

'Yes,' he simply replied. Declan knew there was something more here.

'I met her for the first time today,' he said. 'She's intense, but powerful, you know?'

Andy nodded. 'She's a force of nature, that one.'

'You see her much now you're out of Parliament?'

Andy shook his head. 'No, but one thing I will say in an attempt at transparency here, is that Susan was an early backer in *God's Will TV*.'

'Really?' This surprised Declan. 'Any idea why?'

'Because she probably believes in the power of Jesus Christ and the eternal life given by dedication to the Lord's work,' Andy replied. And Declan knew that this was probably the most genuine answer he'd been given this whole interview. He put his notebook away.

'Of course.'

'I recognise you now,' Andy said. 'I spoke about you recently, didn't I?'

Declan nodded. 'The priest in Hampstead.'

'Yes. I was harsh on you,' Andy said. 'Nothing personal. I have to placate my viewers. Personally, anyone who does that to a dog deserves a smack in the mouth.'

'That's appreciated,' Declan smiled. 'I know it was a long time back, but do you remember where you were at the time of the murder?'

Andy was staring off, mumbling softly.

'They showed me it ...' some unintelligible words '... broken necklace ...'

Returning quickly to the present though, Andy shook his head, as if clearing a bad memory.

'What was that?' Declan asked.

Andy looked horrified, as if unaware that he'd spoken out whatever he was thinking aloud.

'Nothing. Sorry. Old sermon came to mind. Where was I?

Oh yes, I said this back when I was interviewed then,' he explained. 'I have a complete blank of the night from about eleven thirty.'

'You were blackout drunk?'

'Probably more pills and pharmaceuticals, but yeah.' Andy looked ashamed. 'They found me in the billiard room, asleep under the table.'

'Sounds like it was a wild party.'

'Back then every day was a wild party for me. It was one of the reasons I had to get out. I mean, I have memories of the night during that time, but they're things that people told me after, you know? My brain just slots them in.'

Declan nodded, taking his notebook back out and writing this down.

'Finally, did you ever know of someone called Sarah?'

'Sarah ...' Andy thought back. 'I mean, it was twenty years ago ... I think there was a Sarah who used to be in the offices. Sarah Hinksman. Was MP for somewhere small and pointless. Was always in the office next to us. Why?'

Declan smiled. 'Just dotting the i's and crossing the t's,' he said, looking at the TV cabinet. Leaning over, he picked up the YouTube award.

'I've seen these before,' he said, looking at it. 'You know, some people show them on their channels. It's impressive.'

'Well, it's no BAFTA, but we don't crave awards when we do God's work,' Andy replied.

Declan nodded, replacing it. 'It's dented. That's a shame.'

'All things break, DI Walsh,' Andy said, turning on his "preacher" voice.

Declan smiled, rising. 'Thank you for your time. Do you need help with that box?' he said, indicating the flight box at the door. 'I mean with your hand and everything—'

'No, it's all fine,' Andy said, walking over to the kitchen counter.

As he did so, Declan saw something poking out from underneath the television cabinet. Snatching it up, he quickly pocketed it before Andy returned, all smiles, a small plastic Jesus in his hands.

'For you,' he said. 'The police do God's work. And maybe looking at it might curb your temper the next time you meet someone of the Clergy.'

Declan took the figure as Andy started ushering him to the door.

'Anyway, must dash, I need to freshen up before my show today. And I still haven't been sent my script yet.'

Declan was about to tell Andy that he'd been told that Sebastian hadn't arrived yet and that this might be the reason for the delayed script, but he found himself already in the corridor, the door closed.

He walked away from the door, ensuring he was out of sight of any peep hole before he pulled out the scrap of paper he'd picked up.

It wasn't paper at all; it was a small photo, old and folded in the middle. A woman with short black hair was on a bike beside a country gate. Declan didn't know if it was important, but Andy Mac had been nervous. About what, Declan had no idea. But he was going to find out.

After he spoke to Susan Devington.

11

TO THE MANOR BOURNE

DECLAN HAD SEEN DEVINGTON HOUSE IN PHOTOS, AND HE remembered it being on the news at the time of the murder but he had never been there, had never witnessed the size of such a building until he pulled up outside it.

It was as stereotypical an "English Stately Home" as you could find: large, sprawling gardens, a circular gravel drive with a decorative fountain in the middle and stone steps leading up to an enormous wooden door under a marble arch, on top of which sat a Lion and a Unicorn. The sun was out, and as Declan climbed out of his car he could see it not only reflecting off the golden stonework, but also off the giant floor-to-ceiling windows that were the mainstay of the façade of the building: twelve windows running along each floor on the front of the house, with easily as many on the rear of the building and along the sides.

The building itself was flat-roofed, and three storeys high; however, the second floor looked to be of a double height, judging from the higher windows along it. Declan assumed that this was probably some kind of ballroom floor. And this also made the building technically the equivalent of four, or even five storeys in height. Added to that, there were two parts of the house, almost like towers, which jutted out slightly from the wall, culminating on another layer of turret at the top, each one with two large windows within. Declan knew from the images he'd seen that there were two identical 'turrets' at the rear of the house making four in total, as if supporting the building within them.

He started towards the main entrance but paused as an old man in a tweed suit came running out, brandishing his walking stick as some kind of weapon, waving it in the air as he approached.

'No no no!' he said angrily. 'Tradesmen enter through the side gate!'

'How do you know I'm a tradesman?' Declan asked, trying to keep the amusement he saw in this wild-haired old man out of his expression.

The man stopped, eyeing Declan up and down. 'And what else would you be?' he almost sneered with arrogance.

Declan looked back to the car Monroe had given him. It was a ten-year-old Audi A4 in a dark, metallic-grey. A functional car. A cost-effective car. Declan could see why the old man had made such a decision.

Reaching into his pocket, Declan pulled out his warrant card, showing it to the man. 'I'm looking for Susan Devington.'

The man leaned in, peering at the warrant card. 'A Detective Inspector?' he asked. Declan nodded. The old man sniffed. 'They could have at least sent a Detective *Chief* Inspector,' he muttered. 'People will talk, you know.'

'Is she in?' Declan ignored the jibe, forcing his face to stay expressionless.

'She's busy,' the old man said, turning away and walking back to the house. 'Come back tomorrow. Or maybe call ahead for an appointment.'

'Tell her it's the one she liked,' Declan shouted out after the man, who now paused in the driveway.

'Christ, I suppose you'd better come in then,' the old man grumbled. 'Wait in the hall and I'll see if she has time for you.'

Declan followed the old man into the house, looking up to the roof just to the right of it. Twenty years ago, Victoria Davies fell to her death from there.

For a moment, he thought he saw a figure standing on the roof, watching him, but then it was gone. Shaking himself to return to the present, Declan straightened his shoulders and entered Devington House.

———

THE HOUSE ITSELF WAS AS BEAUTIFUL INSIDE AS IT WAS outside; the stone walls were overlaid with thick red tapestries, while the floor was a black and white marble checkerboard pattern. Marble busts of Roman emperors stared at Declan as he waited in the hallway, while the old man walked up the stairs that faced Declan as he entered, turning into one of the side rooms to the right. After a couple of moments he returned, reluctantly waving Declan up.

Declan walked past the emperors and climbed the marble staircase, its banisters gilt-edged with gold designs. There was a smell of mustiness, though, as if the giant windows that ran along the side were never opened to allow air into the building.

There was a grunt and a crashing sound in the room that

the old man was pointing to; Declan almost broke into a run, his police instincts kicking in, but as he reached the top of the staircase he saw what the noise was.

Susan Devington had turned part of the ballroom into what looked like a Dojo; a large rubber floor was placed onto the floor to supposedly stop any scratches or marks, and Susan stood in the middle of it, waiting for her opponent to strike.

The opponent was a young man, early twenties, and with the physique of an athlete rather than a bodybuilder. This was someone fast and agile, his brown hair cropped short to match the stubble on his cheeks. He wore a black Gi, the style of clothing worn by martial artists, a black belt tying it together.

But it was Susan that caught Declan's attention.

She wasn't dressed in a Gi, but instead in a two-piece spandex fitness top and pants, the same style that he'd seen so many women wear while working out in the gym. Out of the business suit though, her physical power was easily visible. She was stocky, but toned and muscled, like an MMA fighter or a CrossFit champion. This wasn't a weak woman, in either body or mind. Declan needed to remember that.

The opponent moved in again, a quick snap to take out Susan's leg, but she blocked him and moved in herself, grabbing his arm and flipping him over in what looked like a mixture of Judo and Aikido. Declan was impressed.

Susan helped the opponent up and nodded to him, indicating the session to be over. Grabbing a hand-towel, she wiped her neck, her face glistening as she looked at Declan.

'Detective Inspector Walsh,' she said with a smile. 'I'm afraid my solicitors aren't here right now.'

'That's a shame,' Declan replied. 'They were such fun, talkative people.'

Susan chuckled, and not for the first time Declan could see the beauty in her face.

'What questions do you have?' she asked.

'Just some basic ones,' Declan pulled out his notebook. 'About the time of the murder.'

'Do you have the letter?'

Declan shook his head. 'That's in progress.'

'Then no questions,' Susan said, turning and walking back to the Dojo mat. She paused for a moment, turning back with a dark looking smile. 'Unless you beat me,' she suggested.

'I'm sorry?' Declan asked. Susan indicated the mat.

'Sparring session,' she said. 'You win, I answer anything you want.'

Declan considered this. There wasn't really any way to get Susan to change her mind on this, and he really did have questions to ask. And there was a chance, during the sparring that Susan could drop her guard.

'Done,' he said.

'Good,' Susan replied. 'I want to see the *Priest Puncher* in action.'

Declan groaned inwardly as he walked to a bench, taking off his overcoat, jacket and tie. *Of course,* she'd researched him. She probably had a dossier on each of the Last Chance Saloon before she even walked into the office. Clearing his mind and loosening his shoulders, he rolled his shirt sleeves up, turning to face her.

'You should go shirtless,' she suggested. 'I could rip it by accident.'

'I have others,' Declan replied, unsure whether this was a

rivalry or a strange flirtation that was going on. He couldn't deny that he was attracted to Susan, but then this was probably her plan, placing her in a position of power. Removing his shoes and socks, he walked onto the practise mat.

'So how do we—' he started, finishing with a *whuff* as the air slammed out of his body, crashing to the floor as Susan swept his feet out.

'Like that,' she said, already moving past him, pacing as Declan rose. 'You're not going to be able to ask your questions from the mat.'

Declan wasn't asking questions though; he was already moving in, bringing up his arm to block Susan's anticipated strike. However, the strike never came, and Susan grabbed the arm, hip-tossing Declan to the floor.

As he lay there, Susan looked down at him, unimpressed.

'You're letting me win,' she said. 'Don't do that.'

'Why do you say that?' Declan said, rising. 'You're what, a black belt in God knows how many disciplines, while I'm just a policeman. Of course, you're going to win.'

'No,' Susan said, no longer moving. 'You're hoping that by beating you, I'll let my guard down. That I'll feel superior.'

Declan rose, annoyed now. *She was playing him more than he was playing her.*

'And what if I am letting you win?' he asked.

'This interview is over—'

Susan didn't manage to finish her sentence as Declan suddenly moved in, a high-kick attack that caught her square on the chest, knocking her to the floor.

She rose, smiling. 'Better.'

Shaking off the strike, she threw her own kick at Declan's head, but he ducked, sliding into a leg sweep, knocking Susan's support out as she stood off balance. Landing hard but rising quickly, she suddenly lashed out with a wicked-looking right hook. Caught off guard, Declan stumbled backwards as he barely avoided the strike. He was off balance now, and both he and Susan knew it, Susan now moving in for a second attack.

There was nothing that Declan could do but drop to the mat; while off balance he wouldn't be able to block anything, but Susan was already down too, her full weight on him as she squirmed for purchase. If this had been a different situation Declan might even have enjoyed it, but Susan was trying to wrap an arm around his throat now, trying to legitimately choke him out, to make him tap out in a vicious MMA hold.

Rolling to the side as much as he could, Declan writhed his arm under Susan's, twisting at the elbow and breaking the choke, sending her off him as he staggered to his feet. As Susan rose again, Declan moved forward and leapt into the air, spinning his body around and shooting his foot out, catching Susan in the chest again, dead centre. As he landed on the mat awkwardly, Susan crumpled to the floor, wheezing.

'Are you okay?' Declan asked, moving forward, but he stopped as he realised the wheezing was actually laughter.

'You're no policeman,' she said as Declan helped her to her feet. 'They don't teach that in Hendon.'

'Military Police,' Declan answered. 'Twelve years before joining the force.'

Susan nodded. 'And they teach ninja training there?' she mocked.

Declan walked to a water cooler to the side and poured out two cups, passing one to Susan.

'As a policeman, you need to get into the mind of the person you're hunting,' he said. 'Thieves, muggers, that sort of thing. But in the armed forces, the people you hunt are trained killers, some more so than others. So, if you want to take them down—'

'You have to fight better than them,' Susan said. 'That poor bloody priest got off lucky.' She smiled. 'You ever killed a person?' she asked.

Declan almost lied, but he knew there was no point. Someone like Susan Devington would have the resources to get hold of his army dossier within a couple of hours. If he lied now, she might not trust him later.

'Yes,' he said. 'When I worked for the Special Investigation Branch.'

Susan watched Declan, her eyes flashing.

'Was it hand to hand, or from a distance?'

'Yes.'

'Oh, so more than one,' Susan almost cooed her response. Declan found it a little unnerving. 'Still, a deal is a deal,' she eventually said, returning to business. 'I'll answer your questions. But first I need a shower.'

She raised her eyebrows at Declan.

'You could take one with me,' she said.

Declan grinned.

'On duty, ma'am,' he replied. 'I'll wait for you elsewhere.'

And with that he pulled on his socks and shoes as Susan Devington left the room, already pulling off her top as she did so.

Declan didn't look.

Sometimes being a gentleman was a pain in the neck.

12

PRIEST HOLES AND PROTESTS

THE OLD MAN, WHO DECLAN LEARNED WAS ACTUALLY CALLED Ratcliffe, led him to the Library.

'Not many people can beat the Lady,' he said with a hint of parental pride, 'as she's a formidable foe.'

'I get the impression that she wanted me to win,' Declan said, sitting into an armchair.

'She wanted you to take a shower with her,' Ratcliffe replied irritably. 'I'm glad you were a gentleman and turned her down.'

Declan grinned. 'You are?'

'Of course, sir,' Ratcliffe said with no hint of amusement. 'For if you had, I would have had to cut your knackers off with the garden shears.'

Declan crossed his legs at this. The old man wasn't joking. 'So, you've known her long?'

'Since she was born,' Ratcliffe said, the pride appearing again. 'I been here almost fifty years, man and boy.'

'So, you knew Victoria too?'

'Oh yes, sir.'

'Declan, please.'

Ratcliffe walked over to a bookcase, stroking the wood as if caressing a lover.

'This house was built in the 1500s, you know,' he said. 'Robert Smythson himself built it. The Devingtons back then were very much in with the royal court, but they were also closet Catholics. They used money hidden from the dissolution of the monasteries to build it.'

'Dangerous times,' Declan said.

'When have times never been dangerous?' Ratcliffe replied sadly. 'This house is full of dark secrets. Nicholas Owen himself came here before he was captured and executed.'

'Sorry, I don't know the name,' Declan admitted.

'He was a Jesuit who built secret passages and priest holes in Catholic-friendly houses,' the old man explained. 'That way priests on the run from the authorities had places they could stay and exits they could take.'

'And this house has them?'

'All houses of this time have them, sir,' Ratcliffe said. 'Miss Devington and her sister used to play in them as kiddies.'

'They were close? Susan and Victoria?'

'Oh no, sir,' Ratcliffe smiled. 'You misunderstand me. Miss Victoria would lock Miss Susan into them for hours at a time, just for fun. Why, there was a time she even went down to dinner, telling her parents that Susan had gone to bed for the night, while Susan was trapped in the walls. She couldn't have been older than six back then.'

He went to continue but paused as the door to the library opened, and Susan Devington walked in. No longer in business suit or sportswear, Susan wore a chunky cream jumper over jeans, a pair of riding boots completing the ensemble.

'Christ, you're not boring him with architecture again, are you?' she said, sitting down opposite Declan.

'Can I get you anything, ma'am?' the old man asked. Susan shook her head.

'Just come back in a few minutes and tell me I have a meeting to go to,' she said looking directly at Declan. 'Whatever it takes to get me out of this boring conversation.' She smiled at the end, as if trying to disarm Declan; but not for the first time that day, Declan wondered how much of this had been for his benefit.

As Ratcliffe walked out of the room, Susan pouted.

'I waited in the shower,' she said. 'You didn't come.'

'Your man Ratcliffe was talking about the house,' Declan replied calmly. 'Felt bad to leave him. And there was some kind of underlying garden shears threat.'

Susan nodded, as if understanding this too well.

'Ask your questions then,' she said. Declan pulled out his notebook.

'When did you read the letter?' he asked.

'What makes you think I did?'

'You mentioned a name that's in it without being prompted.'

Susan smiled. 'Sarah. I knew the moment I said it that I'd made an error.'

'So, when did you read it?'

Susan leaned back in the armchair. 'When I received it.'

'It wasn't sent,' Declan replied. 'There was no postmark. How did it end up in your hands?'

'What do you know about me back then, Detective Inspector?'

Declan thought for a moment.

'I know you were an activist under a fake name, living in a

squat in Birmingham and hanging out with road protestors,' he said. 'How am I doing so far?'

Susan clapped her hands, slowly applauding him.

'Good,' she replied. 'But not everything. End of the year, I was on a road protest near Derby. I can't remember who I was with or what road it was for, but there was a scuffle with the police and during it I was arrested.'

'What for?'

'Honestly? Simply being there. Oh, and for kicking a policeman and stealing his helmet.'

Declan couldn't hide the smile as he looked to his notebook. 'And then?'

'Well, that was the weird part,' Susan replied. 'I was kept in for about forty-eight hours, but I was treated very well, all things considered. I think someone had cottoned on that I was that *Devington* girl and they were trying to work out how to get rid of me without causing a massive ruckus. And then right before I was let out, a man came to the cell.'

'What sort of man?'

'The ones that don't exist,' Susan said. 'Nice black suit, bland expression, scared the living hell out of me. Said I needed to fix my sister before she did herself some trouble and passed me the letter. They'd intercepted it before it reached the Westminster post room.'

'You read it in the cell?'

Susan nodded. 'And as I said earlier, it was just Victoria having a meltdown. The man had left by then and the police let me out shortly after, but I gave them back the letter and told them to throw it away.'

And that's how the letter got lost in the Derby police files for twenty years, Declan thought to himself. *Someone forgot to throw it away and it was filed with the wrong folders.*

'Did you see her after? Victoria?'

Susan shook her head. 'I couldn't be done with her histrionics, I went back to the road protests instead,' she replied. 'Next thing I know, she's all over the news.'

'Sorry.'

'We weren't close by then.'

Declan returned to the notebook.

'We know that Victoria was having an affair with one of three people—'

'Shaun Donnal.' The hatred was almost visible in her tone. 'They met at some Labour donor event. She was besotted with him.'

'You weren't a fan?'

'Christ, no.' Susan snapped. 'I was an actual social activist while he was a middle-class prick from Islington playing one. He had Michael and Victoria wrapped around his little finger. Had them believing in "the cause" again after years of New Labour eroding it.'

'I thought Michael was a major donor to New Labour?' Declan asked. 'I mean, the New Year's party was a donor event, wasn't it?'

'The last one,' Susan nodded. 'He'd already started looking at moving on. He didn't believe that Blair was the right man for the job.'

'He thought that Donnal was?'

'Let's just say that Donnal had convinced him that he was.'

'Then what happened?'

'What do you think?' Susan gave out a little laugh. 'Donnal started screwing his wife.'

She leaned forwards, relishing the moment.

'I mean, don't get me wrong. She was no angel. I know

first-hand she slept with MacIntyre and was working her way through the Civil Service, but I also know Baker turned her down.'

'He did?'

'Poor bastard held a torch for me over her, it seems. Unrequited, I'm happy to say.'

'So Shaun?'

'He was different. More serious. But he was a lunatic. Vicky was a Socialist, but he made her look practically Tory by comparison. And he was damaged goods, too.'

'How so?'

'Sarah.' The name hung in the air.

'I suppose you mean Sarah Hinksman?' Declan looked back through the notes, flipping back to Andy Mac's comments.

'You do work fast,' Susan said as if genuinely impressed. She got up, walking over to a cabinet, pouring out a whisky. She offered it to Declan; he shook his head.

'On duty.'

'Shame.' Nursing the glass in her hands, she walked back to the armchair.

'Hinksman was a Lib Dem, one of Paddy Ashdown's team,' she said. 'Married, no kids, looked great on TV. Everyone said she had a future but her assistant, that poor girl did everything for her. And then she met Donnal.'

'They were in adjoining offices to each other, right?'

'Yes and no,' Susan replied. 'You don't mix parties in Westminster. Her husband, Liam was next door. He worked as an advisor for some Labour MP from somewhere in the arse-end of Scotland, and she'd come and visit him from her own offices elsewhere.'

'Was that allowed?'

'What, entering the lion's den, so to speak? People did it all the time. Deals being made all over the place, people trying to swing votes for bills that needed them, all that sort of thing. But there were problems back then; the Lib Dem command, such as it was, felt that their leader Paddy was getting too chummy with Labour, and this caused rifts, in particular with Sarah's marriage.'

'Yeah, I can see how that could cause strain on a relationship.'

'Anyway, Shaun was a shoulder to cry on. And then he became more. She'd send her assistant to arrange "debates" on bills in Queen Anne Chambers. Always under the assistant's name, of course.'

'An affair?'

'The whole nine yards. They were going to elope and everything. She was even pregnant with his child.'

'Bet that went down well.'

'Even better when she quit Parliament and her husband to have the bloody thing.' Susan shook her head. 'Silly cow, thought Donnal was her Prince Charming, and he'd join her once she was settled.'

'But Donnal never went with her.'

Susan took a drink from the glass.

'We'll never know. She had a car accident six months after the birth,' she explained. 'Died. Shaun was convinced that it had been orchestrated by the Labour Party to stop him colluding with the enemy. Made him even more tinfoil-hat-wearing looney than before.'

'What do you think?'

'I think he'd seen too many Princess Diana documentaries. Sometimes a car accident is just a car accident.'

Declan flinched a little at the line. If she saw this or even understood it, Susan didn't comment.

'The baby?'

'Adopted,' Susan said. 'I don't think they even told Shaun it was still alive. The assistant did it; I think it was her last duty before she moved on. Best to be rid of him. Anyway, Shaun grieved for a few months, and during this time Vicky turned up a lot more. She started to hang out with him. She believed his conspiracy theories; I mean Christ, my sister might have been the eldest, but she wasn't the brightest of us. And at the time, Vicky and Michael were destroying the company, using it as their own personal cash dispenser.'

'So, the child was Shaun's? Victoria's, I mean?'

'Who knows,' Susan leaned back, staring at the books on the wall. 'Michael claimed he had the snip, but I know Charles claimed he'd put the kibosh on that too.'

'How so?'

'Do I look like Charles bloody Baker?'

Declan looked back to his notes. So, Michael had wanted to change the Labour Party, and thought that Shaun was the perfect choice, until he learned that Shaun was having an affair with his wife. Meanwhile, Shaun was paranoid about a conspiracy against him, due to the death of his previous partner.

The letter had said that the father didn't know yet.

Had Shaun learned about it the night of Victoria's death?

But that left Andy Mac and Charles Baker, and Andy had lied when he said he didn't really know Sarah. There was no way he *couldn't* have been aware of her if she was having an affair directly in front of him.

'Andy Mac,' Declan said, looking back to Susan. 'He said he didn't know Sarah. Was he lying?'

Susan started laughing.

'God, yes.' she said. 'Not only was he the prick who told her husband about it, Shaun was also convinced that Andy was the one that killed her.'

Declan's pen stopped writing.

'Why would he think that?'

Susan shrugged. 'Because Andy did,' she said.

———

13

NO PLACE LIKE HOME

ONCE HE FINISHED AT DEVINGTON HOUSE, DECLAN DECIDED that although it was easier to drive back to his father's – no, *his* – house from there, he needed to return back to his Tottenham studio apartment instead and change clothes. Although he'd swapped ties with one from his father's supply, he was a different build to him and the shirts and suits would never fit. Besides, it felt a little ghoulish to do this while he had perfectly good clothes back at the apartment.

The problem he had was that he'd never liked the studio apartment. He'd rented it out of necessity rather than choice, being seconded to DCI Farrow and his North London unit at the time, and there was an element of closeness to his late father that he felt in Hurley. But whether he intended to live there or sell the house and buy something closer to London was a conversation with himself that Declan wasn't happy to have right now. And so, after sending Monroe what he'd found out so far by email, he started back to London, dialling Temple Inn from the car.

'Yeah?' the voice of Trix answered.

'Aren't you supposed to say, "Temple Inn Crime Unit" or something when you answer the phone?' Declan asked, more amused than anything.

'Why? It showed it was you on the screen,' Trix replied, obviously bored. 'Do you want me to say it whenever you call? Is that your thing?'

'No, it's fine,' Declan was already regretting this conversation. 'Just tell Monroe I'm on my way home, should be there by about 7pm if he needs to talk and if not, I'll see him tomorrow.'

'Which home?' Trix asked. 'I mean, you've got three now or something, right?'

'Tottenham,' Declan finished, disconnecting the call before the bored intern could ask any more questions. He had no idea what she did at the Unit, or even why she was there. And more importantly, Declan had this nagging feeling that there was something off with her. Something not right. Like a gate crasher at a wedding.

An imposter.

The journey back to Tottenham was uneventful, until the very end. As he arrived, Kendis Taylor was waiting for him, standing outside the entrance to his apartment block.

'Where the hell have you been?' she asked as he approached.

'Well, bloody hell, Kendis, it's been years. How the hell are you?' Declan asked in a monotone, walking past her and opening the door. 'I suppose you want to come in?'

Kendis grinned and followed Declan into the building.

'Have you been waiting all day?' he asked as they walked up the stairs. 'Jesus, you haven't been here since yesterday, have you?'

'No, you idiot,' Kendis replied, matching him step for step.

Her wild black hair was pulled into braids, her black-rimmed glasses accentuating her deep-brown eyes. She wore a vintage German army coat over jeans, the olive colour of it contrasting against her darker skin.

She looked better than he remembered.

Arriving at his door, Kendis looked about.

'Really gone up in the world,' she said sarcastically. Declan turned the key in the lock, opening the door.

'Lizzie and Jess got the house,' he said as he waved her in. 'And besides, I'm probably moving out soon.'

'Yeah? Where?' Kendis stopped herself. 'Ah. Sorry.'

Declan smiled. 'It's okay, even I don't know what to do about it.'

The studio apartment was little more than a bedsit and hadn't really been lived in much since Declan had moved in a couple of months earlier. His clothes were here, a few personal items were strewn around and there was a small TV beside a microwave in the corner, but apart from that, everything was tidied, hidden.

'Nice place, I suppose,' Kendis said.

'And how's your place in Putney?' Declan asked, walking to the sink and filling the kettle.

'We moved to Hackney about a year ago.'

'Nice area,' Declan replied. 'I'm guessing you still take your coffee the same way?'

'Just like me,' she grinned. 'Black and with sugar to the max.'

'You sound like a stereotype,' Declan continued as he found some cups from a shelf.

Kendis shrugged. 'Well to be honest, I prefer a good matcha green tea these days, but saying "just like me, green with a hint of semi-skinned oat milk" spoils the joke.'

Declan turned from the kettle to face her. 'I'm guessing this isn't a social call?'

Kendis shook her head. 'I wanted to say I was sorry about Patrick,' she said, walking to the sofa and sitting on it. 'The guy was a legend.'

'He was that,' Declan agreed. 'He texted me a day or so before he died. It was right after the TV thing. I was waiting for the call from Farrow, expecting to be fired or even suspended, and this text comes through. *You're a bloody idiot, but I'm proud of you.*'

Declan looked back to the kettle, not wanting Kendis to see the emotion in his eyes.

'He was, you know,' Kendis said as Declan brought her drink over to her. 'I know you'd not spoken that much at the end, but he always talked about you.'

'See him much, then?' Declan sat on the other end of the sofa, turning to face her. Kendis's expression flickered for the slightest of moments, as if this was a question she didn't want to answer.

'I did, actually,' she replied eventually. 'He'd asked for my help on a book he was writing.'

Declan nodded. 'I saw it. Bloody idiot. Didn't you tell him not to do it?'

'It was his choice, Declan,' Kendis was getting defensive now. 'He knew what rocks he was overturning. And we both know that some of them needed it.'

Declan felt a pang of anger at this. He'd been almost fired for doing just that at Mile End. If Monroe hadn't appeared, he'd have likely been unemployed by now.

'I'm guessing you'd like to continue with it?' he asked.

'If possible.'

'I'd like to read it first, before making a decision,' he replied. 'I'll come back to you about that, if that's okay?'

'Of course,' Kendis nodded. 'I just wanted to maybe come by the old place, pick up some of the research notes.'

'Which ones?' Declan asked. 'The ones on his iMac, or the ones in the secret room at the back of the study?'

There was a silence as Kendis stared down at her coffee. Declan had known that this was a question that would blind-side her.

'I should have supposed that you would find it,' she said. 'Like father like son. Bloody detectives.' The last part was said almost jokingly, but Declan could tell there was something deeper underneath.

'Why did he build it, Kendis?' he asked. 'He never told me about it, and he went to great lengths to hide it.'

'The problems he had weren't just from his past,' Kendis said carefully, as if picking her words. 'There were some local issues. He'd had someone break into his house and he knew they'd been reading his work. So, he ensured he had some kind of "safe room" to work in.'

Declan considered this. He'd lived in Hurley from childhood. He couldn't think of anywhere that was more *sleepy village*. To think that someone there would break in and go through your things was something he couldn't imagine.

'I'll need to go check that too,' he said. Kendis nodded.

'Of course. I can give you my number—'

'I already have it,' Declan said, a little too quickly. 'Dad had the number on his desk,' he explained hurriedly.

'And yet you never phoned.'

'And yet you never came to his funeral.'

It was a low blow, and it struck. Kendis's eyes flashed.

'Yeah, because that would have been great. Lizzie and I could have had an "all exes together" moment.'

'Yeah, fair point.' Declan hadn't really considered that. 'But you could have still come. She may be my ex-wife, but you were my literal childhood.'

'All people grow up,' Kendis said sadly. 'Anyway, I'd better get on. Peter's taking me out for a curry tonight. Let me know when I can visit the house.'

She rose and walked to the door, Declan following.

'I can find my own way out,' she said.

'I need the fresh air,' Declan replied with a smile as they moved out into the corridor. Walking down the steps to the main door, Declan paused Kendis on the stairs.

'Actually, can I ask a favour?' he said.

'What sort of favour?'

'You work on politics, right?' Declan looked around to ensure they weren't being overheard. 'If you hear anything about Charles Baker over the next few days, can you let me know?'

'You investigating him?' Kendis asked as they carried on to the main entrance. Opening the door to the street, Declan shrugged.

'Let's just say he's a person of interest in a very old case,' he said. 'And one of three people we're looking at.'

'The other two?' Kendis asked before continuing, 'off the record, of course. And if anything big happens, you give me the exclusive.'

'Shaun Donnal and Andy Mac.'

Kendis whistled through her teeth. 'You should leave Andy for the press,' she said. 'We're already gunning for him on some less than savoury things.'

'Just let me know about any of them, please?'

'I'll see what I can find,' she said. 'And Baker will be a pleasure. I hate that bastard.'

'Political or personal reasons?'

'Speak to his wife,' Kendis said, kissing Declan on the cheek and stepping back. 'Ten minutes in her presence and you'll realise what a grade-A shit he is. Stay safe.'

'You know, you were his favourite,' Declan said as she turned to leave. 'He always told me that I was an idiot for losing you, and that you were the best thing that ever happened to me.'

'You were, and I was,' Kendis grinned as she walked off. 'See you later, Detective Inspector.'

But Declan wasn't looking at her anymore. He was concentrating on a man, in a long black overcoat watching him from across the street.

There was something wrong there.

His phone buzzed – he picked it up, answering. It was Monroe.

'Just read your email. Interesting news about Andy Mac,' Monroe's voice was raised, excited. 'Tomorrow we'll nail that little bastard to the wall over Sarah Hinksman.'

'It was just Susan's opinion,' Declan said, his eyes still watching the man. 'And she seemed very opinionated.'

As he spoke the man started to cross the road, walking towards him. The man was middle-aged, with short, dark-brown hair. He wore a pair of rimless glasses and for all intents and purposes looked like an accountant.

'DI Walsh?' the man asked.

Christ, I'm about to be served something, Declan thought to himself. Monroe was already talking about tomorrow's briefing as the man approached.

'Who's asking?' Declan asked to the man. Instead of replying, the man shook his right arm and out of the sleeve a telescopic baton appeared. The man had been holding it out of sight, but now it clicked into its full length.

Declan was familiar with the baton; he'd even used one himself when as an MP and as a uniformed policeman, but before he even registered what it was, the man with the rimless glasses swung up hard with it, clipping Declan's temple, smacking his head back. As pain burst inside his skull and the iron tang of blood was tasted in his mouth, Declan found himself struck again, a rapid backhand blow that snapped his head back again, dropping the phone as the man moved down, clipping the back of Declan's left knee with the baton, taking Declan to the floor.

Fight you bastard fight Declan screamed at himself, but the two strikes to the skull had sent the world spinning; he was off balance and unable to focus. He could feel the blood streaming down the side of his face as in the background he could hear the voice of Monroe, shouting through the phone, demanding to know what was happening.

The man moved in behind Declan, the baton now used across Declan's neck, choking the air out of him.

'You should leave things you don't know about alone,' he hissed into Declan's ear. 'Things that happened in the past should stay in the past.'

And with that the man dropped Declan to the ground, striking the baton rapidly several times across Declan's arms and legs before disappearing.

Declan lay on the floor, a mass of pain, his eyes closed as he heard people running over. Some of the local kids, mainly on the street dealing small time drugs knew who he was and knew to keep a distance. But this was different.

'Call 999!' one of them called. 'He looks seriously battered.'

Declan didn't hear what they said next as blissful unconsciousness took hold of him and he passed out.

———

14

ACCIDENT OR EMERGENCY

It took fifteen minutes for the ambulance to arrive.

By then Declan had been helped to a sitting position, stemming the bleeding from the small wound on his head with a handkerchief while leaning against a tree. A couple of his neighbours were kneeling beside him, ensuring that he wasn't concussed or in shock, and amazingly his fallen phone hadn't been stolen.

However, as the ambulance pulled up a fleet of police cars, lights and sirens blaring also arrived on the scene. The local youths of the estate melted into the shadows; Declan didn't blame them.

Out of one of the cars emerged Monroe, storming over to Declan.

'Who did it?' he asked, a mixture of both fury and concern in his tone.

'Didn't recognise him,' Declan said as the paramedics started to fuss over him. 'But he seemed to know me.'

'Was this case-related or force-related?' Monroe asked, and Declan knew immediately what the older man was suggesting. This could have been someone suggesting that Declan back away from his current line of enquiry; Andy Mac or even Susan Devington could have hired him. Maybe the man was even Government-related, trying to stop the inquiry before it reached Baker. But at the same time, it could have been a friend of one of the Mile End police Declan had recently put behind bars, a devout Catholic with a grudge or even someone concerned that Declan was continuing his father's work.

There was a long list.

Declan allowed the paramedics to lead him to the ambulance, Monroe walking behind him. His body was a mass of aches and pains right now, but not all of these were due to the attacker. Some of them were due to Susan Devington's overzealous sparring.

'Get sorted and we'll discuss this later,' Monroe said as the ambulance doors closed. Declan raised a thumbs up, but was already feeling the shock kicking in.

So much for a quiet night at the old place, he thought to himself. *Should have stayed in Hurley.*

ANDY MAC STOOD ALONE IN THE FOREST CLEARING, HIS CAR side-lights turned on, allowing him to see the ground in a half-lit haze. There was a hastily dug hole there, the shovel on the ground beside a mound of freshly dug dirt.

Across the hole was the flight case.

Getting it here had been nothing short of a nightmare. The flight case was heavy in itself, but adding the body inside made it even heavier, not to mention unwieldy. After the inquisitive policeman had gone Andy had managed to push the box to the elevator, and then out to the *God's Will TV* Land Rover. Getting the bloody thing into the vehicle, especially without drawing notice to it was a problem but Andy was lucky in the fact that this wasn't his first time taking the flight case anywhere. It was often used to carry equipment when doing location shots: *Andy looking pensive as he looks out across the dales, Andy feeling the power of the Lord as he stands outside an old church,* all the "money" shots taken to make the YouTube site feel bigger than just a studio in a business centre.

Because of this, Andy had learned how to lever and pulley the boxes in. Using large ratchet straps, he would attach the flight box to the front seats, wrapping the strap around both and then running the strap out of the back of the Land Rover, securing the base of the flight box. This done, he could use the straps to take the weight off his back as he climbed into the back of the Land Rover and ratcheted them to pull the flight case slowly upwards and into the boot. It wasn't a pretty way to do it, the flight case wasn't upright and the bumper of the Land Rover probably gained a couple more scratches, but the flight box was in, and Andy could leave.

He'd also had the sense to cut the wire on the apartment block's CCTV a few weeks earlier when he'd started to spend more time there. The last thing he wanted was CCTV showing the guests that he brought to his door, so he'd ensured that the feed never reached the recorder. And to be honest there wasn't a security guard in the block who watched the screens, it was a server that deleted over everything after forty-eight hours, and unless something major had happened and someone needed to check the feed, he wasn't going to be found out any time soon. And if it was found out? Then he'd simply deny all knowledge and find a way to change the meetings to elsewhere. It's why he'd felt so secure bringing Sebastian back there.

Sebastian.

Andy steadied himself. Fainting into the hole was not an option.

Finally, he'd wiped mud over his front and back licence plates; he'd seen on a television show once that the police could use a thing called *Automatic Number Plate Recognition*, or ANPR to follow vehicles on busy roads. The ANPR cameras could read the number and instantly check it against databases of ownership. It was how police could stop drivers without MOTs or insurance. There were around eleven thousand of these cameras, not including the ones in police cars scattered around the country, and the last thing Andy wanted was to leave a trail for anyone to follow. The Land Rover's emblazoned *God's Will TV* marketing was bad enough; if he was stopped for having dirty number plates, he'd be fined a thousand pounds. He could pay that on the spot.

He'd driven home back to Avebury. Usually the quickest route would have been the M4 motorway, but Andy needed the lesser used roads. He needed to find woodland areas that would be perfect for what he had planned. He found such a location in Cadley, just south of Marlborough. There you would find the ancient Savernake Forest, with trees up to a thousand years old, all within seven square miles of ancient woodland.

You could bury a lot of bodies in seven miles of ancient woodland.

It was getting dark when Andy arrived, exactly as he hoped for. The roads weren't lit by streetlights, only cats-eyes in the middle of the road. This was a lane that people drove full beam down late in the night and it was perfect. Pulling onto a side entrance that was more track than tarmac Andy carried on up it, away from the main road for about half a mile. Then, once he was sure that he was in the deepest, darkest, densest part of the wood, he pulled into a clearing, leaving the side lights on to give him light to work in the moonless night.

It was easier to get the flight box out of the Land Rover than in; all he did was open the back, get behind the box and push. Landing on its side, the straps still around it, Andy then used those straps to pull the box through the undergrowth, gaining some distance from the track. He knew he was making another track of his own, but it wasn't too far from the car and he could cover it up when he left.

Then, grabbing a shovel from the back of the car, he started to dig.

The problem he found though, was that the ground wasn't easy to dig into. It was easy to get through the topsoil, but under it was a chalky clay-like substance that fought his shovel every step of the way. In fact, after an hour of digging he'd only managed a hole that was about three-feet deep. It was going to take him all night to dig a hole big enough for the flight case.

Maybe he didn't need to bury the box.

When he'd taken the body and placed it in the box, he'd made sure that he'd cleaned it first, trying to remove any trace of his own DNA on the skin. He'd used a condom during sex, so there were no semen traces either, and he currently wore brand new leather gloves because he'd seen people do that in the movies. But to be sure, he had to go that one step further.

He ran back to the Land Rover, grabbing a small plastic petrol can. Then, with the can in hand, he opened the box.

The smell hit him before he could prepare himself, and he almost vomited onto the ground. He managed to force himself not to; the last thing he wanted to do was remove all traces of his DNA on the body only to puke up a ton of new evidence. Once he was prepared, and the smell had dissipated, he looked back into the box.

Sebastian looked like he was sleeping. The clothes had been dumped into the box with him, but the curled-up body was nude, having been cleaned in a bath before insertion. Andy choked back a tear. He hadn't meant to do this, he'd been scared. Angry. It wasn't his fault. Sebastian should have come clean. Andy was—

He was damned.

Andy stood straighter, filling his heart with steely resolution to the task at hand. He couldn't lose what he'd gained. He'd kept his sexuality secret for decades. He could hold another quiet secret in his heart until Judgement Day.

But to do that meant sacrifice.

Pouring the petrol over the body and clothes, Andy Mac lit a match and tossed it into the case, the petrol instantly catching fire, the flames shooting high. Scared of this being seen, Andy grabbed the shovel, using the haft to bridge an opening in the lid as he closed it, allowing air to get in, and smoke to get out. The last thing that he wanted to do was close the lid, cut off the air and allow the lack of oxygen to snuff the flame out.

He stood alone in the clearing for a short while, allowing the crackle of the flames to lull him into a sense of relaxation, as if standing beside a campfire. But then a crack of a twig, most likely from a deer or suchlike brought him back to the present.

The flames had died down in the box. The body was charred and almost unidentifiable, the clothing equally as such. It smelt strangely like roast pork. The flight box wasn't that hot; the heat mainly concentrating on the body, but Andy was taking no chances and kept his leather gloves on. Shifting the box so that it stood beside the hole, Andy simply pushed it over, allowing the charred body and remains to slide out of the box and into it.

Once done he used the shovel to ensure that the box was empty before turning it back upright. Quickly now, he pulled the now lighter box to the Land Rover, using the straps once more to pull it into the boot. Then, with the lid held open, he started to fill the box with stones and pieces of heavy wood. He'd need to ensure that the box was never found again too, and there were some deep areas of the River Kennet nearby; he could park on a bridge and throw it over. It would never be seen again.

Moving back to the body, he grabbed the shovel as he looked down into the hole. He couldn't recognise Sebastian anymore and that saddened him. The man really had been beautiful. Shaking the thought away, he started to shovel soil on top of the corpse.

He'd almost finished when he saw the light.

It was in the forest, and it was moving towards him. A torch, swinging from side to side as someone approached. Still in the distance, but there was no way that Andy would be able to finish before they were on top of him.

'Who's out there?' A faint voice cried out from the distance.

A Forest Ranger. Shit.

Andy shovelled on as much dirt as he could before eventually giving up and running to the Land Rover. Tossing the shovel in the back, he closed the door quickly, leaping into the driver's seat. Starting the engine, he could see the torch getting closer. He hadn't managed to hide the trail left by the box, but the last thing he wanted was for the advertising on the side of the Land Rover to be seen. Andy slammed the vehicle into drive, bumping over the mound at the edge of the track and quickly spun the steering wheel, now facing back down the track towards the main road. Then, without pausing he slammed his foot down. He didn't care if he damaged the underside of the vehicle on this battered old road.

Cars could be repaired.

He just hoped to God that he'd done enough, hidden the body enough to ensure that his career, or even his life didn't need to be repaired too.

15

PARTY POLITICS

DECLAN HADN'T STAYED THE NIGHT IN HOSPITAL, EVEN THOUGH it had been suggested that he should. He hadn't needed stitches to the cut above his eyebrow, instead, three sterile strips currently held it together, and his other bruises just added to the ones he'd received earlier that day in his sparring session.

That said, with the waiting in the hospital, the health checks and the eventual reluctant release, it was gone midnight before Declan returned to the apartment and collapsed into bed.

The following morning the bruises had started to darken; the cut was now a vicious purple and yellow, and another bruise from when the second blow had struck was starting to blossom up on his cheek. It was a cautious Declan Walsh who dressed that morning, careful not to move too fast, wincing as his bruises and damaged muscles flared up with annoyance as he tried to move them. Even sitting in the car was painful, especially the stop-start driving of the London rush hour. However, even with that, he still managed to arrive at the Temple Inn Command Unit before eight am.

Monroe was waiting at the door for him. Declan assumed the gate guard had alerted him. Or maybe the car he'd loaned Declan had some kind of tracker in it.

'You know, laddie, you're taking this joke a little too far,' Monroe said as Declan approached. 'This is the third day in a row I've seen you, the third day I've said you look like shite, and every day you attempt to better it.'

'Wait, when did you tell me I looked like shite today?'

Monroe grinned. 'Right now, son,' he said, moving to the side, allowing Declan to pass through the doorway. 'You look like shite. Come in and have a cuppa.'

Entering the upstairs office, Declan saw that Anjli was already at her desk working. She looked up at him, her eyes widening slightly. Declan assumed that Monroe had briefed everyone on what had happened the previous night.

'Did you manage any sleep?' was all she asked. Declan appreciated that.

'A little,' Declan replied, painfully and slowly sitting at his own desk as Monroe walked over, a cup of tea in his hand.

'No sitting there, laddie,' he said. 'We need to brief you on some new developments, and from the look of things if you settle there we won't be moving you for a while.'

Declan nodded, rising back out of his chair, looking at the mug. 'Is that for me?'

'Christ no,' Monroe replied, sipping at it. 'What am I, your mother?'

He walked off as Declan looked at Anjli. She smiled.

'That's his way of showing concern,' she said.

'Here,' Trix said, offering Declan a coffee. 'You looked like you needed one.'

'Jesus!' Declan almost fell back against the desk as he spun to face her, wincing as the bruise on his side flared up with the movement. 'Where did you come from? You're a bloody ninja!'

Trix passed Declan the mug and walked off. 'I'm always here,' she said. 'I'm the office fairy.'

She stopped, and for the first time Declan saw something new on her face. Something that looked like actual compassion.

'They shouldn't have done that to you,' she said before turning away once more and continuing to her own desk at the back of the office where she was currently refiling old cases.

'Looks like you have an admirer,' Anjli whispered as she passed Declan. 'That's the most she's said to anyone since I've been here.'

As Anjli entered the briefing room, Declan looked down at his coffee, remembering the previous night.

'You should leave things you don't know about alone,' the man with the rimless glasses hissed into Declan's ear. 'Things that happened in the past should stay in the past.'

Was this a personal attack from a disgruntled policeman? It was possible. It could even have been a religious zealot. But there was one thing that stood out. Two things, really.

First, the man had said that Declan should leave things alone. Not *should have left*, spoken in the past tense, but very much the present. Which meant it was something Declan was currently doing. Mile End and the priest were both very much in his rear-view mirror.

That left Victoria Davies and his dad's death.

Could someone have worked out that Declan was about to investigate it? He hadn't been quiet about it. But at the same time, he hadn't even started. Which brought him to the second thing that stood out.

The man was well trained. Military, even.

He knew how to use the baton efficiently and mercilessly. He knew Declan, and most likely knew that Declan was ex-Military Police. He didn't even pause. He walked straight up and attacked him on a public street. That took a particular mindset. One he'd seen many times while working in the SIB.

Declan walked into the briefing room, sitting down. If that was the case, then who was the message from? Susan Devington didn't seem the type to send a messenger; she could have said this in person. Andy Mac was a possibility, but at the same time seemed a bit too cautious. Shaun Donnal had proven he was quite happy to get his own hands dirty ...

Which left Charles Baker, and the British Government. Had the man been a spook? An MI5 or MI6 agent? Special Branch perhaps?

Monroe tapped the giant screen loudly to grab Declan's attention.

'You okay, boy?' he asked. Declan nodded.

'Just working out who did this,' he said, indicating his face.

'Aye, we'll get to that to be sure,' Monroe replied. 'But first we have some goodies to go through.'

An image appeared on the screen; that of a woman, late twenties at some kind of rally. Her long black hair was pulled back, and she wore a navy-blue suit jacket and skirt. There was a yellow rosette on her lapel, fluttering as she shouted out through a megaphone, the crowd cheering. She wasn't slim, but at the same time she wasn't overweight. The suit hid her curves in the same way that Susan Devington's had. It was also a dated style, possibly from the mid-nineties. Behind her and to the right was another black-haired woman, a woolly hat covering her forehead and shadowing her face.

'Meet Sarah Hinksman,' Monroe started, tapping the screen and by default the image, zooming in slightly. 'Taken during the 1997 General Election.'

'This is who Shaun Donnal was in love with?' Anjli asked, already writing in her notebook. Monroe shrugged.

'We'd have to ask him that,' he said. 'At this point they wouldn't have met, but by the time she died, she would have been hand in glove with him.'

'Who's the other woman?' Declan asked.

'Frankie Wilson,' Monroe replied. 'The long-suffering assistant that Susan spoke to you about.'

A tap of the screen and the image changed to the monochrome reality of a police crime photo. A car crash, late at night. The vehicle was crushed almost beyond recognition.

'October the first, 1999,' Monroe continued. 'Hinksman's car crashes on the A31, just north of Stoney Cross, Dorset. Postmortem showed that she was over six times the legal limit, not to mention the drugs in her system.'

'Do we know which drugs?'

'Ketamine.'

'Christ, she took horse tranquilisers with alcohol and drove? Bloody idiot.'

'Was she a known drinker?' Declan asked. Monroe shook his head.

'The occasional drink, but nothing more. Apparently there was a Labour bash that night in Bournemouth to celebrate the end of the Labour Party Conference. Press reports of the event say that Hinksman was a surprise arrival. By this time, she'd quit politics, left her husband; one of the Labour advisors Liam Hinksman, and had Shaun's baby.'

'So not the best guest you'd want to have there.'

'No. And according to a gossip site at the time, it was believed she was looking for a confrontation with the father of the baby. Apparently he wasn't keeping to his side of the bargain.'

'He hadn't left his own wife,' Anjli said. 'Who was probably there at the conference.' Monroe nodded, tapping the screen. Another image appeared; a younger Shaun Donnal, his wife beside him, waving from the Labour Conference stage. To the right, Declan could see Michael Davies, applauding them.

'She was indeed,' he zoomed in on the image. 'If they were separated, she was a bloody good actress here. But there was a big cabinet shakeup on the horizon, Blair's speech hadn't gone down as well as people had hoped, and he was probably scared that anything that came out then would affect his chances of moving up.'

'And then Shaun's Lib Dem mistress appears at the conference,' Declan considered. 'That couldn't have gone down well.'

'For any of them,' Anjli added. 'The three of them were in the same office. They were probably worried that they'd be tarred with the same brush.'

Declan indicated the image. 'And Michael Davies there would have been screwed, considering that he was starting to prime Donnal as Blair's replacement around now.'

'Indeed. Michael would have had a lot riding on Donnal right then. Sarah Hinksman would have been the end of it all. Which leads us to Andy Mac,' Monroe pointed to Declan. 'And the interesting titbit from Susan Devington.'

'Even though Andy says he barely knew her, Susan Devington's convinced that Andy was the cause of Sarah Hinksman's death that night,' Declan pulled out his notebook, opening it. 'Claims that Andy intercepted Sarah before she could get to Shaun, sat her in a bar and pretty much kept her drinking all night.'

'How does she know this?' Monroe pulled up a photo of the young Andy Macintyre.

'Word of mouth after the case. Apparently Shaun found out about the drinks. Probably the drugs too, as Andy seems to have been a bit of a partygoer back then. And for some reason Shaun blamed Andy for the death,' Declan continued. 'Would have made an interesting dynamic in that office. Around the same time, Victoria turns up; it's possibly then or just before the conference that she slept with Andy Mac, bringing her into contact with the other two. Anyway, at some point Shaun told Victoria his suspicions, who in turn confided in Susan. Meanwhile Andy apparently didn't realise that Sarah was driving back that day, and she left before he could stop her.'

'Or perhaps this was his plan,' Monroe mused. 'The old *Sweeney* manoeuvre.'

'Sir?' Anjli looked from Monroe to Declan in confusion.

'Ach, you haven't seen the *Sweeney*?' Monroe was mortified. 'It's a police classic!'

'It is a bit dated, sir,' Declan admitted.

'Well anyway,' Monroe continued. 'So, John Thaw, that's Regan although you probably know him as Inspector Morse these days, bloody kids that you all are, he's captured and they force whisky down his throat. Entire bottle. And then they give him his car keys.'

'You're thinking that Andy Mac deliberately did this?' Anjli looked horrified.

'Susan Devington definitely thought so. I think we need to continue our chat with him soon.'

Declan looked at the picture of Sarah Hinksman on the screen. There was something familiar.

'Sir,' he said, pulling out the folded photo from his pocket. 'Remember the picture I said I found at Andy Mac's?' He opened it out, comparing the two. The one in his hand was a woman with a far shorter haircut, but it was definitely the same woman.

Sarah Hinksman.

'Maybe when we call him, we can ask him why he had a photo of a woman he barely remembered half hidden under his TV cabinet?'

Monroe grinned. 'Get that downstairs and see if forensics can sort anything from it,' he said. 'Although if it's been in your jacket pocket, it's probably just covered in lint.'

'We have a forensics now?' Declan asked, looking to Anjli. 'I didn't see anyone when I came in.'

'They're in later this morning,' Monroe said. 'Billy's sorting it out now.'

'How exactly is he sorting it?' Declan was getting even more confused. Monroe sighed.

'He's getting them out of a police cell right now,' he explained before looking back to the screen. 'Some kind of misunderstanding, I'm sure.'

'What happened to the baby?' Anjli changed the subject. 'I mean, Susan didn't have anyone with her in the crash, and I can't see her husband taking a bastard on as his own.'

Declan looked at the notes he'd taken from Susan Devington.

'Adopted, I believe.'

'Aye, that's right,' Monroe was looking at his own sheets now. 'She named him Sebastian. When Sarah died, Miss Wilson, that's her assistant placed him into care when nobody claimed him. He was then adopted by another family shortly after.'

Declan felt a cold wind run down his back.

'The adopted family,' he said, checking his notes. 'Was the surname Payne?'

'Why yes,' Monroe looked to Declan now. 'That's a bloody good mind trick. Did that bash to your bonce give you mind powers?'

'When I went to see Andy Mac, his assistant mentioned their intern hadn't shown up. She said his name: Sebastian Payne.' Declan quickly counted on his hands. 'Payne would be about twenty, twenty-one now.'

Monroe didn't speak for a moment.

'Well, that's a rather large coincidence,' he said eventually. 'I think we need to have a chat with Andy again a lot sooner than we first thought. Maybe even bring him in here for questioning.'

'Before or after Baker?' Anjli asked, already rising.

Monroe gathered up his notes. 'Oh, I think we need to interview Charles Baker first. Find out what other secrets are going to appear. Then you can go find Andy Mac, have another chat, maybe see if you can catch this boy of Sarah's too for a wee word.'

'Anything else?' Declan asked, almost jokingly.

Monroe turned his steely blue eyes on him.

'Aye, you can also find and arrest Shaun Donnal, who's

still on the run for assault and attempted murder, if you'd forgotten.'

He waited, watching Declan and Anjli.

'So, what the hell are you both still doing here?' he yelled. 'Go be police!'

16

HALLS OF POWER

WHEN HE WAS A KID, DECLAN HAD VISITED THE PALACE OF Westminster, or as it was more commonly known *The Houses of Parliament* with his school. While there, he'd visited the main chamber, the House of Lords, the Queen's Robing Room (with the wooden friezes of scenes from Arthurian legend) and even spent time in the octagonal entranceway known as the Central Lobby, marvelling at the statues of Prime Ministers past. He'd even learned the origin of "it's cold enough to freeze the balls off a brass monkey" from the kindly tour guide, an ex-military man who happily showed a painting in the hallway, one that stretched the entire wall and depicted a naval battle, explaining that iron cannon balls were placed on "monkeys" back then, made from dimpled brass plates, but when the cold struck the brass would contract and the balls would fall off. Literally frozen off. Declan remembered his teacher not being happy with the old soldier for telling this, pretty much because her class were now shouting "balls" at the top of their voices.

It was weird what things you could remember.

But even now, years later and with the authority of a police warrant card to get him through the strict security at St Stephen's Gate, he still felt like a small child as he stood in Westminster Great Hall, staring up at the high wooden rafters above him.

'Do you need a moment?' Anjli said, a hint of amusement on her face. 'You look like you're about to cry.'

'Don't you find this incredible?' Declan asked as they continued along the hall, away from the main doors and towards a large stone staircase, leading up to a giant stained-glass window.

'Not really,' Anjli admitted. 'I come here every year for the Sherlock Holmes Dinner.'

'Of course, you do,' Declan replied as dead-pan as he could. Anjli's smile grew wider.

'Hey, want to see something cool?' she said, leading Declan away from the main route and towards the side. 'See that spot there?' she asked, pointing at a small brass plaque on the floor. 'That's where King Charles the First stood as he was sentenced to death. And over there?' Another spot on the floor. 'That's where William Wallace was sentenced to death. And it's believed that over there,' again another spot on the floor, this time unmarked,' is where Guy Fawkes, after attempting to blow up Parliament—'

'Was sentenced to death?' Declan asked as they walked up the stairs and towards a guard. 'I'm seeing a pattern emerging here.'

'Come on, Walsh, tell me you're not a little bit excited by that. Monumental moments in history have happened in this room.'

Declan watched Anjli as they showed their IDs again and were sent down a corridor to the left. This was the first time that he'd seen her actively excited by something. It was actually good to see.

'It's alright,' he admitted reluctantly.

———

IN THE CENTRAL LOBBY, AN AIDE, ALREADY ALERTED TO THEIR presence had appeared before they could speak to anyone and asked them to wait there for a brief moment; The Right Honourable Charles Baker was in session with some constituents right now before the day's sessions began, and they were trying to wind this up while finding an appropriate place for the meeting. Declan knew that this was shorthand for *they were trying to find a place where the press wouldn't see that two police detectives wanted to have a word with the Tory heir-apparent*, and Declan and Anjli smiled and politely told the aide that yes, they would wait and yes, they understood that Baker's parliamentary duties took priority right now and yes, if they were mucked around in any way they would quite happily walk over to the BBC camera crew beside the wall and loudly discuss the reasons for their visit while standing next to them.

The aide disappeared swiftly after that.

'I bet you know about this place, too,' Declan said.

'Only a little,' Anjli shrugged. 'Just that this is the core of the Palace of Westminster and was designed by Charles Barry as a place where both houses could meet.'

She pointed off down two of the four corridors that branched off.

'That way's the House of Lords; that way's the House of Commons.'

'I could have guessed that by looking,' Declan said.

Anjli raised an eyebrow. 'Okay then,' she pointed at metal grilles in the windows surrounding the lobby. 'There was a fire in 1834, right? After that they put these grilles in the Ladies Gallery, so that the MPs on the floor of the House weren't distracted by the sight of women watching them work. It stayed like that until around 1908, when two Suffragettes chained themselves to one. After a vote almost ten years later, they were removed from the Ladies Gallery and placed here.'

'Now that's more interesting,' Declan replied, mentally reminding himself to tell Jessica that when he saw her on the weekend. He was going to ask Anjli for more on this when the aide returned, hurriedly guiding them towards the fourth door from the Central Lobby, and the Terrace Cafeteria.

As they entered the cafeteria – well, more exited as the terrace was outside, at the back of the Houses of Parliament and looking out across the Thames – they could see Charles Baker sitting at the furthest possible table from the entrance, almost as if he didn't want people knowing he was there.

An overweight man in a Hugo Boss suit interjected himself between Declan and Baker. He was early thirties perhaps, his hair cut short at the side and left long on top. It was a style that didn't match his shape of head or body, and Declan wondered if this was deliberate, or simply the optimism of a man who hoped to "make it work" somehow.

'The Minister only has a couple of minutes,' the man said. 'So, you need to be quick.'

'I think you'll find we'll be exactly as long as we need to be,' Anjli replied, already irritated with the man. 'And you are?'

'Will Harrison,' the man said, a little put back by Anjli's tone. 'I'm the Minister's advisor.'

'Well then I suggest you advise the Minister to answer whatever bloody questions we ask,' Declan pushed past Harrison and continued towards Charles Baker, 'before we take you in for obstructing justice.'

Charles Baker didn't rise to greet them; instead, he sat almost sullenly, sipping at an espresso as Declan and Anjli joined him at the table.

'This is about Vicky?' he asked. Declan nodded.

'We've got new information in the case—' he started, but Charles waved him shut.

'Just ask the questions and get out of here,' he said as he watched around the terrace. 'Speaking to the police is political suicide around here.'

A waiter walked over to the table. 'Can I get any—'

'They won't be staying,' Charles snapped.

Declan held up a hand. 'Actually, can I get some water?' he asked, looking back to Charles. 'Time for some pain killers. Never been able to take tablets dry.'

Charles just glared at him. Anjli opened up her notebook.

'Let me just make things easier for you,' Charles said. 'Yes, I was there that night. No, I wasn't on the roof. I have witnesses who claim I was on the dance floor copping a feel with Lady Ashton as the fireworks went off. My statement is exactly the same as it was back then.'

'You have witnesses?' Declan frowned. 'That's an interesting way to say it.' A line from Andy Mac's interview popped in his head.

'I have a complete blank of the night from about eleven thirty.'

'Can you remember the party?' he asked. Charles shrugged.

'It was twenty years ago. I might have partied a bit too much.'

'Blackout drunk?'

'More a case of utterly exhausted.'

Declan nodded, writing this down in the notes. 'Did you know that Shaun was the father of Victoria's child?'

'No, but we all guessed it later,' Charles sneered. 'He couldn't keep it in his pants.'

'You didn't think it was Michael's?'

'He couldn't. He'd had the snip.'

Declan read from his notes. 'Susan Devington seemed to think that you might have stopped that from happening.'

Charles Baker's face darkened. 'Susan Devington should mind her own bloody business.'

'Did you know that Shaun was the father of Sarah Hinksman's child too?' Declan asked. Charles didn't speak for a moment, as if thrown by the question.

'What's Sarah got to do with Vicky?' he asked.

'Just answer the question, Minister.' Declan was tired of playing games. 'Did you know?'

'No,' Charles's voice was less assured now. 'I mean, we knew she'd had a kid, but I assumed it was her husband's.'

'Did you see her the night of her death?'

Again, Charles paused. This was definitely a line of questioning that he hadn't expected.

'Yes,' he replied eventually. 'We all did. She appeared like Marley's sodding ghost at the Labour conference.'

'Did you drink with her?' Now it was Anjli who moved in.

'No. She was deep in her cups with Andrew. MacIntyre, that is.'

'Who you shared an office with.'

'I've shared a lot of offices with a lot of people,' Charles was managing to gather back his composure. 'Doesn't mean I was chummy with them all.'

'You didn't like Andrew MacIntyre?'

Charles paused, as if working out how to answer. 'Ah, sod it,' he said. 'Look. Andy was a chancer. He was in by the skin of his teeth. Likely to be voted out in the next by-election if he didn't do anything. So, he hung on our coat tails.'

'You and Shaun Donnal?'

'Yes. But when Shaun went all conspiracy nut on us, he fell out with Andy.'

'Because he believed that Andy killed Sarah?'

Charles nodded. 'Stupid sod. Andy wasn't even alone with her. Bloody Michael and Vicky Davies were hovering around like papa and mama bear, terrified Hinksman would shit all over their leadership plans.'

Declan paused as the waiter returned with his water. *Michael seemed to be more involved with Andy than he'd let on.* Taking a painkiller, he swallowed it with a mouthful of water before looking back to Charles.

'How well do you know Susan Devington?' he asked. Charles shrugged.

'In passing,' he said. 'No, that's not true. I was in love with her back then. She was a firebrand. And I was single, so you know.'

'And she was the daughter of a millionaire,' Anjli added.

'No,' Charles shook his head. 'That is, factually you're right, but what you're implying there is wrong. Susan had no way of getting to the family money, as Michael and Vicky controlled it after their father died. All Susan had was her trust fund, which kept her in money for her protests and activism. Sure, we had a fling, and it was fine while it lasted, but the moment she took over the company, she changed.'

There was a moment of silence as Charles stared off across the Thames, as if remembering something bad.

'I wasn't good enough,' he eventually finished. There was dark anger behind his tone, but as if realising he was giving too much away Charles straightened and smiled once more.

'Anyway, losing her was the best thing that ever happened to me,' he continued. 'I met my wife, Donna, a year later and we're very happy together. Susan and I have only communicated since then in a business manner.'

'You do much business with Devington Industries?' Declan asked, but Will Harrison had already made his way over.

'I'm sorry but the Minister has a busy day,' he said. 'Anything else can be sent in writing.'

'I have a couple more questions,' Declan said.

'In writing.'

'I'm happy to shout them out to you as you leave,' Declan added. Charles, already half rising sat back down.

'Quickly then,' he snapped. Declan looked back to his notes.

'We have a source that says that Michael Davies was pulling his funding for the Labour Party,' he started. 'That he had been putting Shaun forward as a candidate for leader but changed direction when he learned of the affair.'

'So? That's not news. It's been out there for years.'

'What wasn't out there is that you had spoken to Michael too, offering your services as a replacement figurehead,' Declan continued. 'From our source, of course.'

'Michael was a murderer and a liar,' Charles said, standing up again. 'He thought that he could be a player like the Murdochs and their kind, but he was nothing more than a failed estate agent playing with his wife's money. The best thing that ever happened to Devington Industries was her death and his arrest. Just ask Frankie Pearce. Francine, I mean.'

'The PA? I thought she'd be loyal to Michael, what with the alleged affair between them.' Anjli wrote the name down.

'That's what everyone thought,' Charles said with the hint of a smile. 'But everyone has their price. And now I really must go.'

Declan and Anjli rose.

'Thanks for answering our questions,' Declan said, passing Charles a card. 'Anything comes up; if you remember anything—'

'I'll tell my solicitor,' Charles replied. 'And he will tell your superiors if required.'

Declan nodded. He'd taken a dislike to Charles Baker at the start of the conversation, but now he full-on loathed him.

'One last thing,' he said, waving at his battered face. 'When we came in and sat down, when I asked for painkillers, you were looking at my bruises, at my injuries. But you didn't say anything.'

'Wasn't my place to.'

'Yeah, but people always do,' Declan replied. 'It's small talk. "Oh, that must hurt ..." or "What happened ..." But you didn't ask. Almost as if you already knew.'

'Good day, Mister Walsh,' Charles turned and walked away, already talking to Harrison as they left. Declan looked to Anjli.

'When I saw Susan, she said Baker's affection towards her was unrequited. But here he is now, happy to say they were having some kind of fling.'

'To be honest, I think I'd be the same as Susan,' Anjli replied as her phone beeped. 'I mean, would you want people knowing you'd slept with Charles Baker?'

'There's something else,' Declan added. 'Both Charles and Andy claim to be blackout drunk at the time of the murder.'

'Yeah, that's not suspicious in any way,' Anjli pulled the phone out, reading the message as Declan moved to the other side of the table, pulling out a small, clear, Ziplock bag. Quickly, and with the minimum of fuss, he took Charles Baker's now empty coffee cup, slipped it into the bag, sealed it, and placed it into his pocket.

'What are you doing?' Anjli looked up. 'You can get souvenirs in the gift shop.'

'Not with Baker's DNA on,' Declan replied. 'And I don't see him being the type to give us a swab willingly. And this is a public place, he just left it for us. So now what?' Declan looked around the terrace. Even though it was almost empty, there were people still taking coffee there.

And all of them were watching Declan and Anjli.

'We return to base,' Anjli replied. 'Monroe's called us back.'

'Why?'

Anjli showed Declan the message.

'Because Sebastian Payne's body was found in a shallow grave this morning.'

17

GRAVESIDES AND ROADSIDES

'You can go a little faster, laddie. We are a police car, after all.'

Monroe's tone was terse, but at the same time his body language was relaxed as he sat in the passenger seat of Declan's Audi. 'This car is rubbish. Who gave you this car? You deserve a better car.'

'Are you always this talkative while driving?' Declan asked through clenched teeth as he undercut a white van in the middle lane of the M4. It was a two-hour drive from Temple Inn to Marlborough, but currently Declan was aiming to get there in almost half that.

Monroe shrugged. 'I don't get out much,' he said. 'I really should rectify that.'

He'd been waiting for Declan and Anjli when they arrived back at the Command Unit. Anjli was sent with Billy to *God's Will TV* to speak to Andy Mac and the crew who worked there to see what else they could find out while Declan and Monroe drove to the scene of the crime; a small woodland area in the middle of a deserted Wiltshire forest.

'Imagine the poor bastard,' Monroe muttered. 'There you are, gamekeeping a forest, think you see poachers, and the next day when you go to see whether they racked up any pheasants you find this.'

'I don't think there were any gamekeepers or pheasants,' Declan replied. 'I think it was a park ranger who was checking for doggers.'

'Doggers?' Monroe tutted. Dogging was a term used by people who liked to watch others have sex in public places, usually in cars in car parks or deserted clearings. 'That's not as good as my theory.'

'No, Guv,' Declan admitted, pulling the car off the M4 at the Hungerford junction, slowing down to turn left at the roundabout, the siren still blaring as the two blue lights in the car's grill flashed intermittently.

'Either way, it's not a good thing for anyone to see,' Monroe muttered again.

Forest Ranger Marshall Judd had called the police mid-morning with his grisly discovery. The previous evening he'd been night walking, checking some badger dens in Savernake Forest when he'd seen a faint, artificial light through a clearing. Assuming it was someone up to no good, he'd picked up a stout stick and, with his equally as sturdy Maglite torch had made his way through the woods towards it. However, as he'd moved closer the vehicle had pulled away, back out onto the trail that led off to the A346. Unable to see where the vehicle had been before the movement, and a little self-conscious that he was alone in a dense wood at night, Marshall had returned home, deciding instead to return to the clearing the following morning to check over the site.

What he'd found when he did eventually return was the half buried and charred body of Sebastian Payne.

He'd called the police and they'd examined the body, learning the identity through some half-burned credit cards in the clothing. Declan had no idea how Monroe had found out.

The trail itself was nothing more than a cart track, the ground muddy and uneven and after a hundred feet of careful driving, Declan pulled to the side behind two police cars that had obviously had the same issue. Getting out, Declan and Monroe started to walk the rest of the way, picking their way along the muddy track.

'Well, there's one thing we know already,' Monroe said, looking up and down it. 'There's no way in hell they got down here in anything less than a four-by-four or a truck.'

As they approached a clearing to the left, the tell-tale white tent of the forensics team could be seen, most likely over the grave itself to ensure less contamination of the site.

Monroe pulled Declan to the side.

'Now, this will likely be a Newbury region case, and their DCI hates me,' he said. 'And to be honest, I'm not a massive fan of hers, either. Either way, she's going to scream bloody murder when we arrive. So, keep quiet, look tough and trust me, okay?'

Confused, Declan nodded as they made their way over to a bored looking policeman, standing guard at the edge of the track.

'Sorry, nobody past this point,' the policeman said.

'DCI Monroe and DI Walsh. We'd like to see the dead man,' Monroe waved his warrant card.

'You'll have to speak to the Guv'nor,' the policeman replied. 'I can't let anyone through, no matter their rank.'

'Then why don't you get her then?' Monroe raised his

voice. 'I mean, the nerve of this! A uniform barring the way of a Detective Chief Inspector!'

'Excuse me,' a forensics officer in full gear stepped past Declan as she made her way into the site, passing a furious looking battle axe of a woman in a white plastic forensics suit, her boots covered in blue booties that matched her blue latex gloves and her long grey hair only just restrained by a scrunchy, storming her way towards Monroe, now visibly smiling with delight.

'Lenette!' he exclaimed happily. 'They've finally allowed you onto the big boy cases!'

'Get off my crime scene and get out of my patch,' the woman said, glancing at Declan. 'Who's your boyfriend?'

'DI Declan Walsh, meet DCI Lenette Warren,' Monroe said. 'We need to look at Sebastian. Just a little peek, you know. After that, we'll be gone.'

Warren was still looking at Declan. 'Another broken soldier for the box of misfit toys,' she said, more as a statement than a question. 'What's your interest in the victim?'

'Purely personal,' Monroe smiled. 'Working my way through the alphabet.'

Another white-suited detective walked over. He was tall, built like a tree and easily several inches taller than either Declan or Monroe.

'Problems, ma'am?' he asked. Warren shook her head.

'DCI Monroe and DI Walsh were about to leave,' she said.

'Come on, Lennie! We've driven hours to be here,' Monroe said. 'Or are you hiding something? Walsh here is an expert in ferreting out corrupt coppers!'

Declan inwardly groaned at this. And if DCI Warren was angry at the insinuation she kept it hidden well.

The other detective however wasn't so subtle.

'I've heard about you,' he said to Walsh. 'Ratted on your own.'

'I prefer to call it *cleaned a Command Unit of corrupt police*,' Declan said. 'And the only people who seem to have issues with it are ones who are worried that they'll be next.'

The detective moved towards Declan but Warren pulled him back.

'Don't be an idiot, Richard,' she said. 'That's what they want you to do.'

'Yes, Richard, listen to mummy,' Monroe smiled. 'And piss off, yeah?'

'*Get the hell off my crime scene!*' Warren was furious now, screaming the order at Monroe. By now at least half of the officers and forensics on site were approaching. Declan felt incredibly outnumbered.

'All you had to do was ask,' Monroe said, still with his disarming smile fixed on his face. 'Come on, Declan. We'll find a nice café and have a cuppa. I saw a roadside van about a mile north, by Postern Hill.'

And with that Monroe turned and left the crime scene, Declan struggling to keep up.

'What the hell was that?' Declan finally managed as they got back to the car. 'We drive all the way up here so that you can make a scene and then leave?'

'Ah no, son,' Monroe climbed into the passenger side. 'Don't diminish the amazing assistance that you gave as well.'

Declan sighed and climbed into the car.

'So now what?' he asked as he started the engine.

'I told you already,' Monroe said. 'We go to that roadside tea hut a mile north and grab a cuppa.'

'And then?'

Monroe smiled.

'And then we wait, my boy.'

DECLAN SAT ON A PLASTIC CHAIR POSITIONED BY THE SIDE OF the A348, sipping from his Styrofoam cup of coffee as across from him, the other side of a rickety table and on an equally as plastic chair sat Monroe, sighing with pleasure as he drank his tea.

'That's the way to make a brew,' he said. 'You southerners make it too weak.'

'We're literally further south than London here.'

'Well, the man in the van must be a northerner. This is proper builder's tea. You can stick a spoon in it.'

Monroe's phone beeped. He read it.

'It's from Anjli,' he said. 'It looks like Andy Mac went home yesterday.'

'To the flat?'

'No, to his house in Avebury.'

Declan looked up the road to the north. 'That's about ten miles from here,' he said. 'And very convenient for dumping a body if you have a Land Rover, like Andy does.'

'Ah, and there we hit a roadblock. Apparently he drove back in his own car, a Tesla of some kind,' Monroe was still reading from his phone. 'Also, according to the receptionist, *God's Will* made a call to the police this morning. Apparently that very same Land Rover was stolen last night, after he was gone.' He looked up. 'It's a miracle. No, what's the opposite of one?'

'It's convenient,' Declan said as he leaned back on the chair. The day was brisk but dry. Even the sun kept trying to appear through the clouds now and then. 'So should we go and speak to him?'

'Eventually,' Monroe sipped at his tea.

'And what are we doing right now?'

'Waiting,' Monroe said. 'Just like your friend last night. Talking of which ...'

Monroe rose and walked to the Audi, reaching into the passenger side and pulling out an iPad.

'Got something to show you,' he said as he sat back down. 'You might enjoy it.'

He opened up a video on the iPad.

'Billy found this for me last night,' he said, turning the iPad to Declan. On it, he could see the entrance to his Tottenham apartment, taken from a CCTV camera down the road. On the screen Declan saw two people emerge from the doorway: Kendis first, then Declan. They spoke, Kendis left and then Declan put his hand to his ear, most likely when he took the call from Monroe. Then, from the other side of the road a figure walked into view. Declan felt slightly out of body as he watched the man with the rimless glasses flick out his baton and attack Declan, leaning in and whispering before calmly dropping Declan to the ground and walking off.

'Billy followed him for two streets after this, but then he disappeared,' Monroe said. 'Problem with CCTV is you're relying on the subject staying the same. Chances are he took the coat off, or put a hat on, even got into a car in a dead spot. Either way, he arrived at your apartment and stood across the road for about fifteen minutes before you turned up.'

'So why didn't he attack me when I arrived?' Declan asked. 'He didn't know I'd be coming back out.'

Monroe leaned across, tapping the screen, pulling the

slider to the left and reversing back the feed. Declan saw Kendis and Declan talking outside the building before entering.

'Because he didn't want a witness,' Monroe said. 'But more importantly, who's the lassie?'

'Kendis Taylor,' Declan stared at the image. 'She's—'

'I know exactly who Kendis Taylor is,' Monroe replied, sitting back and folding his arms as he glared at Declan. 'And who she works for.'

'She wasn't there as a journalist, she was there as a friend,' Declan said, getting angry. He didn't have to explain to anyone why he kept the friends he did. 'She came to give her condolences.'

'Ah,' Monroe nodded. 'I can see that. They were close back then.'

Declan frowned at this, so Monroe continued.

'Back when you broke up with her, your father was furious at you. He thought she was the best thing that ever happened to you.'

'He wasn't the only one.'

'Well, you were the one who broke it off.' Monroe blew on his tea to cool it.

'She wanted to be a journalist. I wanted to be a soldier. It seemed the right thing to do at the time. It was more of a break than a breakup, but while I was in Northern Ireland she started dating someone else at University. And then I met Lizzie.'

'Interesting that she appears when you're no longer with her.'

Declan snorted. 'I think her husband might have an issue with that.' He stared down at his Styrofoam mug. 'She was working with dad.'

'What do you mean, working?'

Declan shrugged. 'I found her number in his office. She was helping him with his book. Whether she was giving advice or writing it for him, I don't know.'

'Well, that must have been a little awkward for you when you found out. Your lost love working with Patrick?'

'I suppose.'

Declan stopped talking as a black Mercedes pulled to the side of the road, parking up behind the Audi. Emerging from it was a woman, middle-aged with olive skin framed by short, untamed, jet-black hair. She wore a bright-coloured hoodie and jeans, and from the colour scheme Declan wondered if she'd dressed in the dark.

She walked over and sat on the third chair at the table between Declan and Monroe.

'Declan, meet Doctor Rosanna Marcos, the Last Chance Saloon's *Scene Of Crime Officer*,' Monroe said. 'You should have met her in the Command Unit this morning, but things moved quickly.'

'You were the one in the police cell,' Declan realised.

'I was, but it was a misunderstanding,' Rosanna said, her accent European. There was something familiar there to Declan's ear, but he couldn't quite place it.

'It always is,' Monroe smiled as Declan realised where he'd heard her accent before.

'You were at the crime scene!' he exclaimed. 'You passed behind me, but you were in full forensics.' He looked back to Monroe. 'She wasn't one of Warren's.'

'No, she wasn't,' Monroe said. 'And if she'd have said who she was, she wouldn't have been allowed on site. Partly because she works for me, and partly because she's banned from all crime site visitations for the next six months.'

Declan nodded, finally understanding. This was why Monroe had made such a scene at the entrance to the crime scene, one so large that half the officers on site had come to see. It was nothing more than a distraction so that Doctor Marcos could get past the officer on guard and into the tent.

And he'd heard of Doctor Rosanna Marcos, too. The brilliant Forensic Support officer who'd worked out the Tancredi murders. Solving the timeline of how four Liverpudlian crime lords killed each other while sitting around a circular table was something that would usually gain a commendation, but Doctor Marcos had achieved it by removing the bodies from the morgue and taking them back to the crime scene, sitting them in their original seats and recreating the moment.

Four dead, naked crime lords being manipulated like dolls did not go down well with the authorities.

'So, what did you find?' Monroe asked.

'I'll have a more detailed briefing in the morning,' Doctor Marcos replied. 'But the killer was definitely disturbed. Dug a shallow grave and only filled in half of it before running. Payne's body was also incredibly burned, but the burning was postmortem.'

'So, they tried to set fire to the body?' Declan asked. 'Makes sense. Remove the DNA.'

'There are easier ways to do that,' Doctor Marcos said, plugging a dongle into Monroe's iPad and attaching an SD card to it. Images from the crime scene started to appear on it. 'This was sudden, as if the killer realised that they hadn't done a thorough enough job.'

'So, the killer drives here, dumps the body and then sets fire to it,' Monroe mused. Doctor Marcos shook her head.

'No, it's the other way around,' she scrolled through some

images, finishing at a close up of the body in the grave. 'You can see here, the ground isn't scorched, and there's no accelerant. The body was burned elsewhere, but post death.'

'Cause of death?' Declan asked.

'Something flat and heavy, something like ...' she paused. 'Honestly? Something like a bronze-age axe.'

'Great, primitive man drives four-by-fours now,' Monroe muttered.

'I said like, you luddite,' Doctor Marcos replied. 'It was metal, but I couldn't get any of the trace samples before I had to leave.'

She rummaged in her pocket, pulling out a small, clear, plastic bag. Inside it was something small, grey and charred.

'I did get this,' she said with a smile. 'It was attached to the body. I think it was burned with him, or it's a piece of whatever he was burned in. It's synthetic, probably cotton, and looks like the interior lining of something.'

'Well, that's a start,' Monroe said, looking back to Declan. 'I'll go with Doctor Marcos back to the lab and start on that.'

'What do you want me to do?' Declan asked, although he already knew the answer.

'Well as you said, it's only ten miles or so to Andy Mac's house. It'd be a crime to come all this way without one of us saying hello, ensuring he's not bereft over his stolen car, especially with all that pretty gold writing all over it.'

Doctor Marcos nodded at this and rose, pulling the dongle out of the iPad.

'See you back at base then,' she said to Declan before walking over to the car.

'When you said you built a unit of people who were too clever to fire, you weren't kidding,' Declan said. Monroe shrugged.

'A man is only as good as the team he has,' he replied. 'And talking of which, it's time for this team to get moving before DCI Warren works out what we did.'

Rising from his plastic chair, Monroe walked back to the black Mercedes as Declan looked down at the iPad. With the photos now removed, the CCTV footage of Declan and Kendis had returned onto the screen. Picking up the iPad and turning it off, Declan walked back to his own car, stopping as a thought struck.

The assailant had arrived fifteen minutes before Declan had returned to his apartment.

But how had he known when to arrive, or that Declan was even returning there? Declan could have intended to spend another night in Hurley.

Declan had only phoned to inform one person he was going back there, after interviewing Susan Devington. The same person who phoned the exact moment that the assailant attacked.

DCI Monroe.

He looked up at the black Mercedes as it pulled out onto the road, already on its way back to London. Shaking the thought off as madness, Declan returned to the car.

This wasn't the time to start thinking up conspiracies.

First he needed to chat to Andy Mac.

18

THE SHAKEDOWN

DECLAN'S PHONE RANG AS HE PULLED UP OUTSIDE THE GATE TO Andy Mac's house. Looking at the screen, he saw that it was Anjli. He answered, letting the car connect the call to the system.

'Heard you're off to see MacIntyre?' she said through the car's speaker.

'Just got there. What's up?'

'Just so you're in the loop,' Anjli replied. 'Sebastian's phone was last seen yesterday morning in Teddington.'

'Studios or in Andy Mac's apartment?'

'Doesn't say. The cell towers only pick up the area, and they're right next to each other.'

'Fair point. You said last seen.'

'Yes, because it was turned off.'

Declan wasn't surprised by this. If anything, he would have been more surprised if the phone hadn't been turned off. It might even have simply run out of battery.

'Have you managed to get anything from it?'

There was a rustling of sound on the speaker, most likely

by Anjli on the other end of the line as she flipped through her notebook, but it was Billy who spoke next.

'They pulled two messages off it,' he said. 'There was nothing else that they could find, and the phone was apparently only purchased a week earlier.'

'What were the messages?'

'One from Sebastian to an unknown number. We're tracing it down now. It reads *so what do you think? Can we do this?*'

'Interesting but could be taken in several contexts without the previous communication,' Declan replied. 'That could be connected to something on the set, or in the office, maybe he was buying something big. We need to know the recipient of these.'

He quickly wrote the phrase down in his notepad.

'And the second one?'

'A reply from the number he texted to. *Hell yeah. Send me the best ones and we'll finish the bastard once and for all.*'

'Okay, so maybe the context is a little more clear now,' Declan said as he wrote the second message down. 'Looks like Sebastian was working with someone,' he mused. 'But the *send the best one* line is the one we need to follow. What could be sent to finish someone once and for all?'

'Evidence of something?'

Declan nodded. 'Possible, but the message tells us that Sebastian had multiple things that could finish someone off, but that someone, this mysterious other person wanted just one. The best one. Any photos on the phone?'

'No, but that doesn't mean there wasn't any,' Billy said. 'They could have been deleted.'

'Is there any way we can find them? Could they be backed up on the cloud, on some server or something?'

'That's what we're hoping,' Billy replied. 'Working on it.'

Declan sighed. He really didn't want to speak to Andy Mac right now.

'Right then, I'd better have a chat with him.'

'Is Monroe with you?'

'No, he's returning with Doctor Marcos,' Declan said. There was a chuckle down the phone line.

'Yeah, she's something, isn't she,' Anjli said. 'Speak soon.'

'One last thing,' Declan quickly said before the phone went dead. 'Do we have anything on the meetings Shaun and Sarah had at Queen Anne Chambers?'

'Actually yes,' Billy replied. 'It's now a hotel but back then it was a series of short-term rooms and apartments that MPs could grab some sleep in if they'd gone into the night. It was within earshot of the Division Bell, so that MPs staying there could get to Parliament in time to vote. Neither Shaun nor Sarah stayed there, but I've found seven occasions of an F. Wilson booking a room there for a short time between January and June 1998.'

'The assistant booked the getaways,' Declan nodded. This matched what Susan had said. 'Nothing after that?'

'Not that we can see, but she was pregnant around then. Maybe her libido disappeared. And then shortly after that she resigned.'

Declan wrote this down. 'Good work, guys. Keep on it.'

Disconnecting the call, he stared out of the window at the house. It wasn't large compared to many of the houses around here, no more than a five-bedroom, but the driveway and garden was enough for a far bigger estate. And the gate that blocked the way was imposing.

Luckily, Declan had a magical key that opened all gates like this.

Climbing out of the Audi, he walked over to the gate pillar, buzzing it. While he waited, he thought through the information he'd recently received. Sebastian was dead and had been buried ten miles south of here, on a road that only an off-road vehicle could get down. Andy Mac had such a vehicle, but it had allegedly been stolen. Which meant that he couldn't be tied to the murder, as yet. Of course, there was another option; that someone else had killed Sebastian and taken the Land Rover. But, in that case why bury it so close, unless it was a deliberate attempt to frame Andy for this?

Declan wasn't sure. And the uncertainty annoyed him.

'Yes?' A voice on the intercom brought him back to the present.

'DI Walsh, here to speak to Mister MacIntyre,' he said into the video screen of the gate buzzer, showing the warrant card as he did so.

'Mister MacIntyre isn't here,' the voice responded.

'Look, we've spoken to his employees and I know he's here, so let me in,' Declan said irritably. 'Or I'll come in and arrest you for wasting my sodding time.'

There was a pause. Probably the amount of time needed for whoever was operating the buzzer to either find Andy and confirm that it was okay to let the police in or, if the voice had indeed been him, for Andy to eventually decide to press the button himself.

The gates slowly creaked open as Declan walked back to his Audi. Taking a moment to compose himself, he clambered back into the driver's seat, closed the door and drove into the driveway of the house, the gates closing as equally slowly behind him.

19

HOLY GHOSTS

'YOU LOOK TERRIBLE,' ANDY SAID AS HE WALKED DECLAN INTO the sunroom, a small glass-walled conservatory to the side of the house. 'Can I get you anything? Aspirin? Paracetamol?'

'I'm fine,' Declan said, sitting down on one of the chairs. 'And I'm not here to talk about me. I hear you had an eventful night too.'

'You did?' A momentary flash of panic crossed Andy's face before composing back to what Declan believed was mock concern.

'Your car being stolen,' Declan added.

'Oh, that,' Andy nodded. 'Yes, it's a pain, but it happens more than you'd expect. Land Rovers can be broken into quite easily when they have a keyless locking system.'

'I've heard,' Declan opened up his notebook. It was well known that car thieves could buy equipment online that allowed them to "hack" the key system of recently produced cars. For a thirty-pound outlay, you could steal dozens of five or even six figure cars in a night. 'I believe it can be tracked though?'

'Only if the fob isn't in the car when it's stolen,' Andy sighed. 'Unfortunately, one of the crew took it to the shops yesterday and left it in the little divider area between the two seats.'

'That's unfortunate. Still, it's not as if the vehicle doesn't stand out,' Declan opened his notebook. 'I'm sure we'll find it quickly.' He looked up to Andy with a smile. 'And we're very good at finding things people want hidden.'

Andy shifted on his seat.

'Well, I'm guessing that you didn't drive all this way to talk about my stolen car,' he said, forcing a smile. 'What else can I do for you?'

'You lied to me,' Declan carried on staring at Andy, not breaking eye contact as he spoke. 'When we spoke before.'

'I did?'

'You said you barely knew Sarah Hinksman, but you were with her the night she died.'

Relief once more flooded Andy's face, and Declan realised he'd seen the same expression the first time they met. It was almost as if Andy had been expecting a far worse question, and the expression that appeared was a relief that this was a question he could answer.

So, what was the question he was scared of?

'It was a long time ago, and I haven't really thought about it that much. And, when you visited me yesterday, I'd just taken some major pain meds.' Andy waved his hand, professionally rebandaged since they'd spoken. 'I was a little all over the place.'

'How major?'

'Pardon?'

'The meds you took. Are we talking something over the counter or more prescription?'

'They were strong. I have a prescription.'

'For what?'

Andy was starting to get irritated. 'Does it matter?'

'Sure. I mean several hours after we spoke, you popped into your Tesla and drove here. I'd hate to think you would take something strong and try to drive.'

Declan was definitely on the right track. Andy's face was paling as he spoke.

'So would you like to change your answer?' Declan pressed on.

Andy put on his most winning smile and told Declan the exact same story that he'd already heard from Charles Baker: that Sarah had been with Shaun, how she'd appeared at the Party Conference, and how he'd been asked, begged even to keep Sarah out of sight, a task completed by sticking her in the members' bar of the hotel and feeding her bourbon.

'Who asked you to do this?' Declan asked. 'Shaun or Charles?'

'Both, actually,' Andy replied. 'I mean, it was Michael that asked me to do it, but they both had reasons to hide from her. I just guessed that they were too chicken to ask me themselves.'

'Really?' This was a surprise to Declan. 'I know Shaun's reason, but why Charles?'

'Don't know,' Andy said, more careful now with his answers. 'I just felt something was going on, you know? He made a point of disappearing when Sarah appeared in the offices after she resigned.'

'But that was it. You just did the job, fed her alcohol.'

'Yes.'

'And the ketamine?'

Andy looked confused, and this time it felt genuine.

'You didn't know,' Declan continued, 'that she had enough ketamine in her system to down a horse?'

'No.' Andy looked angry now, as if realising something.

'What did you think of?' Declan asked. 'Just then? Who gave her the ketamine? You know, don't you?'

'It was a party conference,' Andy replied, back to his calm manner. 'Hundreds of people could have had some.'

'Did you?'

Andy nodded. 'But the fact that I'm admitting to that should show you that I'm not trying to hide anything. I was an addict while I was in office, true, but even I knew that mixing K and booze was probably fatal.'

'Then who did you think of?'

'It doesn't matter,' Andy replied. 'I won't speak ill of the dead.'

Declan wrote this down. The only currently dead people he could think of that would have been there were Michael and Victoria Davies. He decided to move on, but he wasn't letting Andy Mac off the hook that easily.

'So, there was nothing personal between you?'

'God no. Look, I might not have been a saint back then, but I had my morals.'

Declan pulled out the folded photo of Sarah Hinksman.

'If there was nothing personal going on, why did you have this in your flat?' he asked. Andy took it, his face visibly whitening as he looked at the image.

'Where did you get this?' he asked.

'It was on your floor when I visited,' Declan replied.

'And you took it?'

'I didn't get a chance to return it before you pushed me out of the door.'

Andy swallowed. There was a moment of silence. Then, he looked up to Declan.

'You should give it to its rightful owner,' he said. Declan knew that something had shifted here. Andy Mac seemed to have a new narrative that he was going to follow.

'And who would that be?'

'One of the interns, Sebastian Payne,' Andy replied, calm once more. 'He was Sarah Hinksman's son. I'm guessing that he must have dropped it when visiting.'

'You had him in your apartment?'

'I have a lot of people in my apartment, DI Walsh. Often they'll be bringing or taking away equipment.'

Declan remembered the large case he'd seen the last time he was there.

'Was he there the day before I arrived?'

'Probably.' Andy started to nod, as if remembering something. 'Yes, actually. He brought me a flight case filled with lights. I was going to film some vignettes, but then when I cut my hand I decided to wait.'

'The one you were struggling with.'

'Yes.'

'And what happened with that case?'

'I put it back in the studio. Took a while, one-handed, but I'm quite resourceful.'

'I'll bet. Why didn't you just wait for Sebastian to return, and get him to do it?'

Andy shrugged. 'I am not my brother's keeper, detective. I didn't know when he'd return.'

Declan nodded, writing this down. 'Why did you hire him?' he asked. 'I mean, was it because he was Sarah's son?'

'I didn't know that when we took him on,' Andy admitted. 'The surname was Payne, you see. I only learned when he spoke of his mother. When he ...' he shook a little. 'When he showed me that photo.'

'What prompted it?'

Andy shrugged. 'We were talking about family. Sebastian was asking me ... About faith. As in when you knew that God was calling.'

'Was God calling him?' Declan leaned closer. 'Or was it something else?'

'Like what?' Andy was starting to sweat a little. Reaching to the coffee table between them, he poured a glass of what looked like lemon squash, taking a large sip. Declan waited for him to finish, letting the moment hang.

'Maybe he blamed you for his mother's death,' he suggested.

Andy didn't flinch at this, and Declan wondered whether this was the question that he had been prepared for.

'I didn't kill Sarah,' Andy replied calmly, no emotion visible in his voice. 'It was an accident. She shouldn't have mixed her vices and driven.'

Declan leaned back in the chair and stared at Andy. In his mind, he tried to remember what had been in the room when he visited it. *There was a bike, some lights, a television ...*

'What happened to your award?' he asked. 'The YouTube one?'

'I don't know what you mean,' Andy replied, his voice rising slightly.

'It was dented.'

'It fell.'

'What's usually inside a flight case?' Declan started another line of questioning.

'Equipment.'

'No, I mean the lining. If I was to open one up, what would I see?'

'Foam, maybe some fur lining, I don't know. There's so many.'

'And they're made of metal?'

'Aluminium. Why?'

Declan changed tack again.

'The night of Victoria's murder, you said you couldn't remember anything. Did you know that Charles Baker had the same problem?'

'We never spoke of it.'

'Never? The night a woman died?'

'No. As I said, the place was pretty toxic. Charles was already working out how to use this to his advantage, like he'd done the snip.'

'What do you mean?'

'You should ask Charles that.'

Declan was impressed. That was clever, to try to throw the conversation onto someone else.

'Let's go back to your comment about faith,' he continued. 'Do you believe in God?'

'What kind of stupid question is that?' Andy replied angrily, finally snapping. Declan shrugged.

'You wouldn't be the first preacher to lose faith.'

'I believe in God.'

'And Heaven? And the ten commandments?'

'To believe in one is to believe in all.' Andy was drinking from the glass again, his face flushing slightly.

'Will you go to Heaven or Hell?' Declan asked.

'Only God will decide,' Andy said calmly, as if it was a line he'd used a lot.

'But you have to follow His commandments, right?'

'Of course.'

'So, let's go through them.' Declan had done his time at Sunday School, and he still remembered them from when Jessica had done the same. '*Thou Shalt Not Covet Thy Neighbour's Ox.* That'll be jealousy, right? Be envious of something that someone else had?'

'Man is born with sin. I think God will allow us some envy, as long as we confess it.'

'What about *Thou Shalt Not Commit Adultery?* I mean, you definitely did that with Victoria Davies. You said so the last time I met you.'

'I think you should leave now,' Andy was starting to fidget, to twitch. 'I did that when I was young, and during a time of many vices. I've confessed this to the Lord, and the fact that He came to me years later, setting me on this path—'

'What about *Thou Shalt Not Kill?*' Declan pressed on.

'*I did not kill Sarah Hinksman!*' Andy shot to his feet with fury. 'I am sick of—'

'I wasn't talking about Sarah,' Declan interrupted, rising to face Andy. 'I was talking about Sebastian Payne.'

'What?' Andy stopped, his hand trembling as it held the glass.

'He was found this morning in a half-covered grave, not ten miles from here,' Declan continued. 'The murderer had tried to hide his prints and his DNA by setting the body on fire.'

Andy Mac stared silently at Declan, as if too shocked or scared to reply. Declan carried on, warming to the task now.

'He was killed by a sharp blow to the head. Something sharp, narrow and metal. You know what I think?'

Declan placed his notebook away as he leaned closer.

'I think you honestly didn't know who he was. And that

he joined *God's Will TV* to get revenge on you for a believed sin: that of killing his mother. I think he got something to do this with, too, something he had photos of. Maybe drugs. Maybe something worse. We're looking into that right now. And then I think there was a confrontation in your apartment.'

'This is madness,' Andy was starting to rock now.

'I think then perhaps you fought. Maybe it was self-defence, maybe it was pre-meditated. I think it was a spur of the moment act, though. Maybe he was the one that cut your hand. Either way, I think you grabbed your YouTube award and struck him on the head with it.'

'No ...' Andy shook his head wildly. 'Shut up ...'

'But now what do you do? He's dead and on your floor.' Declan walked around the table now. 'So, you clean up the blood, and stick him somewhere that can be moved. Where he can't bleed on your expensive floor anymore. A flight case, for example. With grey fur lining to soak up all the blood. There's a lot of blood in a body. The same flight case that I saw when I came to see you.' Declan shook his head. 'I'm a fool. The body was next to me all the time and I didn't realise it,' he said. 'And I believed the "blood from your cut hand" story when I smelt the bleach. I even suggested you clean up the blood. Sebastian's blood.'

He leaned in, close to Andy now, so close that he could smell the fear emanating from him.

'If only you'd cleaned up Sebastian's photo. But maybe you were about to do that when I called.'

'I'd like you to leave now,' Andy said, backing out of the conservatory. 'I want you to leave now!' he repeated louder.

'But I haven't finished yet,' Declan continued. 'Nobody says a thing when you stick the flight case in your Land Rover because you do it all the time, and then you drive to a known area, but not *too* known to bury the body. I'm still not sure why you burned it first, or where the flight case is right now, but we'll find it. And we'll find your car.'

Declan was hoping that by constantly pressuring him, he'd convince Andy Mac to let something slip, to break down, but something different happened.

Andy Mac stopped shaking.

Instead, he smiled.

'Prove it,' he said, suddenly calm and collected. 'My Land Rover was stolen. The flight case filled with lights is in the studio with all the others. My award fell on the floor and I cut my hand.'

Now it was Andy's turn to lean in.

'God loves me, Mister Walsh,' he said. 'I speak His word. And neither you nor that bitch can stop me.' And with that Andy turned and walked out of the room. 'Next time you want to talk, we'll do it at your offices and I'll bring my solicitor,' he said from the doorway. 'Until then, *get the hell out of my house.*'

Declan nodded to himself. He knew he was right, but everything was hearsay and circumstantial. At the end Andy had managed to pull himself together. No confession would be coming from Andy Mac any time soon.

But he had let one thing slip.

'And neither you nor that bitch can stop me.'

Who the hell was *that bitch?*

20

RUN FOR YOUR LIFE

SHAUN DONNAL HAD NEVER BEEN A FAN OF KING'S CROSS. IT was smelly and busy and filled with people, and the last thing Shaun wanted was to be around people. He'd spent five years doing his best to avoid that.

If they couldn't see him, they couldn't kill him.

King's Cross was filled with the afternoon crowd as Shaun picked his way through them, trying not to stand out, while at the same time brutally aware that he was standing out: the bearded homeless man with the rucksack on his shoulder. There was a policeman on duty at the entrance to King's Cross Underground, and Shaun turned his face away, quickly walking in the other direction. He didn't know if the older homeless man had told anyone about his attack a couple of days back. If he had, then the police would have no trouble recognising Shaun. He hadn't seen it in the newspapers that he'd scavenged from bins or stolen from pavement tables over the last couple of days, but then a homeless man claiming that he was attacked by an ex-Welfare Minister with a screwdriver probably didn't go that far without more corroborating evidence. That didn't mean that there weren't journalists out there looking for it, however. Or police.

All looking for Shaun Donnal.

Turning down a side road, trying to keep away from Euston Road, Shaun started to walk alongside the red-brick wall of the British Library. He used to love visiting there when things were normal. He'd even applied for a Readers pass, just so he could find rare books that Vicky liked, and show—

Holding a broken necklace, Victoria's necklace in his hands.

Shaun tumbled to the floor at the memory, a small cry escaping from his lips. It had arrived more often now, the memory returning quicker and quicker and staying for longer and longer. He shook his head, as if rattling the brain inside his head would somehow stop the visions and cease the tears that followed. Pulling a bottle out of his coat, he sat down on the pavement and drank from it, oblivious of the people walking past, staring down at the drunk as he cried in long, racking gasps at his suddenly remembered loss. After a few swigs, allowing the cheap whisky to flow down his throat, warming it back up, he rose wobbly to his feet and carried on. He needed to get to Camden. He needed to gain space from Soho before he used an ATM machine again. He'd been a fool. Weak. He'd tried to call Sally, to hear her voice, but *her* voice had answered instead. Somehow they'd intercepted him. They were waiting.

They were always waiting.

Shaun had slammed the phone down and run from the phone box. He knew that they could see him, that they could follow him if he got on a train, or a bus. The CCTV cameras were their eyes and would show them where he went; anywhere they could watch wasn't safe for him. But the

Regent's Canal towpath was just a little further north, there weren't as many CCTV cameras on it as there were outside the shops, and once on the towpath he could make his way quicker to his destination for the night.

There was a black car on the other side of the road, outside the entrance to St Pancras Station, nestled in amongst the black cabs that waited there for fares. It was the only place a car could really park around here, but there was something wrong with it. It felt out of place.

Like it was waiting for him.

He stopped on the pavement, bottle still in his hand, watching the driver as he stared ahead, his hands on the wheel. The back windows of the car were tinted black, and this could have simply been a chauffeur waiting for his ride to arrive from the Eurostar.

But then the driver turned, and looked directly at Shaun, his rimless glasses glinting from the sunlight. Shaun stepped back in fear. It was a face he recognised too well.

They'd found him.

He'd been keeping a low profile in case the police had been looking for him, but now that stopped. He needed to get away and get away fast. His legs shaking, he turned and started to walk quickly down Dangoor Walk, a small pedestrian street beside the Frances Crick Institute. It was a narrow road, more of a pedestrian path and he knew that the car wouldn't be able to make its way down there. They would have to chase him on foot, and that gave him the smallest of advantages. Putting his bottle in it, he tossed the rucksack to the side; it was too heavy and he needed speed. As he looked behind he saw that the man and a friend had left the car and were now running after him, crossing Midland Road with stormy expressions on their faces.

Out onto Ossulston Street now, a tree-lined road with cars parked on either side, Shaun turned right, sprinting north, taking in deep gasping breaths as he ran, knocking aside people as he did so. He hadn't run like this in years, but the adrenaline that flowed through his body gave him speed, pumping his legs, and he knew that he had to outrun his pursuers. He needed to make some kind of distance and find a place to hide.

But the two pursuers were now out onto the street as well, running just as hard and still following him.

At the end of the street he could see an outdoor gym area, but there was nothing that he could use there as a weapon. There was a small path that ran between the park area and a primary school; Shaun knew that if he could get through there, he'd hit a maze of streets. If he could get into those he had a chance, and—

He hadn't seen the car as it drove in from the left, slamming into him and sending him flying across the road, tumbling to the floor. The doors to the car opened and two more suited men clambered out of the front seats, walking over to Shaun as the man with the rimless glasses finally arrived, an extendible baton now in his hand.

'Stay down,' he hissed as he struck at Shaun. 'Don't make me hurt you.'

Shaun did as the man said. He was surrounded now, and seriously outnumbered.

'I didn't say anything!' he cried out. 'I've done what she said!'

The back doors to the car opened and a woman emerged. Shaun almost whimpered in fear. Slim, in her forties and with a black, 1920's bob-cut to her hair, she wore a burgundy dress under a fur overcoat.

'*She* didn't say make a bloody name for yourself,' the woman said irritably as she walked over, looking to the man with the rimless glasses. 'For Christ's sake, get him up. People will call the police.'

The men helped Shaun up as the woman walked closer, wrinkling her nose.

'Christ, you stink,' she said. 'But then you always had a bit of an odour problem, even back then. Do you want to tell us what happened?'

Shaun knew what she meant. 'The man knew me,' he whispered. 'He was going to out me.'

'So, you attacked him with a screwdriver in the middle of Soho,' the woman sighed. 'You're a cretin. For someone who used to amount to so much, you're a bloody imbecile.'

'Please, don't hurt my family,' Shaun begged. 'I did what you said. I became a ghost.'

The woman considered this for a moment.

'The police have reopened the case,' she said. 'Some bloke named Walsh has been sniffing around. Has he spoken to you yet?'

'How could he?' Shaun asked. The man with the rimless glasses grabbed his arm, twisting it back, causing Shaun to yelp in pain.

'That's not what she asked,' he said into Shaun's ear.

'No! No, he hasn't! The last thing I want is the police right now!' Shaun pulled free of the grip, rubbing at his arm as he glared at the man with the rimless glasses, who was smiling, as if amused by the pain he'd caused.

'You need to make sure of that,' the woman said softly. 'He's looking at the wrong people, not going the direction that we want him to. So, if they arrest you for that muppetry you did in Soho, he'll find you. If he does, you demand a lawyer and you stay silent. If you have to say anything, make sure you aim him at the right target. Because if you say anything ...'

'I know, I know,' tears streamed down Shaun's face. 'You'll hurt Sally. I promise. I won't do anything.'

'You'd better not,' the woman said, looking back to the men. 'Remind him why.'

The four men started to kick and attack Shaun at this point, but he'd expected it. He slipped through them, running for the car, as if clambering into the driver's seat and locking the doors would actively help him somehow right now. He's almost managed it when the men caught him by the leg, dragging him back out of the front seats of the car and onto the floor. Shaun held his arms in close as they kicked at him.

'Francine! Please!' he cried to the woman. 'I promise!'

Francine Pearce nodded to the men to stop.

'I never want to see you again, Shaun,' she said. 'We're done here. Just go away somewhere and die.'

And with that she climbed back into the car, the two men that had emerged from it returning to their seats. The car pulled away, driving west as the man with the rimless glasses gave Shaun one more kick before walking with his colleague back to St Pancras Station.

There was a moment of silence as Shaun shuffled back to his feet. He looked around at the buildings, at the park, at the people who had seen this happening in front of their eyes and not done a single bloody thing about it.

And then he started to chuckle.

His hands, hidden in his jacket now emerged, one of them holding a pistol. He'd taken it when he'd clambered into the car. He remembered from the last time he'd been in the vehicle, the last time they'd given him a beating, that there was a backup weapon kept under the passenger seat for emergencies.

And now Shaun Donnal had it.

It was time to stop running. It was time to stop hiding.

It was time to find Walsh and end this.

BY THE TIME DECLAN HAD LEFT AVEBURY IT WAS MID-afternoon and, although he was driving back into London on the M4, he'd already planned a short diversion at Junction 8/9 to visit his father's house.

His house. It was still weird to think of it like that.

Pulling up to the driveway however, his phone rang. Looking at the number as it flashed up, Declan saw that it was Billy.

'What's up?' he asked, putting the call across to the car system.

'Interesting little thing we've found out about Sally Donnal,' Billy said. 'You know how she's been sending her father fifty pounds a shot?'

'The ATM money?' Declan pulled the handbrake and opened up his notebook, pen already in his hand.

'That's the one,' Billy replied. 'So, we managed to get the statements from the bank the debit card is connected to, and there's about six or seven transactions a month.'

Declan whistled. 'His daughter's funding him three or four hundred pounds a month?'

'That's the thing,' Declan could almost hear the smile on Billy's face. 'She hasn't. In fact, she's not spoken to her father for the last four years and pretty much wishes he was dead.'

'Ouch.'

'Apparently some lady turned up a few years ago and suggested that Sally create the account. Said she understood why he had to run, and that she'd fund Shaun due to an old debt. Paid her two hundred pounds to do it.'

'And Sally did it? Just like that?' Declan was surprised.

'She was seventeen years old and it was two hundred pounds.'

'Yeah, fair point.' Declan wrote this down. 'So, what happened with the account?'

'That's the thing. Sally Donnal never heard from this woman again. Never even got her name when they first spoke.'

Declan leaned back in the driver's seat, thinking. 'So, Shaun's been running around for the last four years thinking that his family is funding him, when it's actually some company. Did you show her a photo of Susan Devington?'

'I did, but she said it wasn't her. Hair was black and the woman was skinny, apparently.'

Declan got out of the car now, putting the phone back to his ear as he approached his house.

'Anything else?'

'Yes.' Billy was on a roll now. 'Found a picture from the first week in Parliament back in 1997. One of those shots where all the new MPs and their teams are smiling and laughing for the press.'

'I know the type. What about it?'

'Sarah Hinksman and a Labour MP are in the back of one of them, getting very chummy.'

'I'm guessing because you didn't say the name of the Labour MP it's not Shaun?' Declan opened the door, entering the house.

'No,' Billy replied, a hint of triumph in his voice. 'It was Baker. I've zoomed in on it. It's definitely them.'

'Send it to me,' Declan said. 'I'll be back in a few hours, but I'd like to see that right now.' He picked up some new post that was on the mat. 'Oh, and do me a favour, check whether Michael or Victoria Davies ever had any run ins with vice. Primarily ketamine.'

'You think they killed Hinksman?'

'I think they may have had access to it for sure. Something Andy Mac said. Humour me.'

Billy agreed to send it within the next fifteen minutes and then disconnected. Once more alone in the house, Declan looked around.

No whisky tonight.

Before he could enter properly however, the doorbell to the house rang. Turning, Declan opened the door to find Karl Schnitter at his door. A tall, tanned, robust German in his mid-sixties, Karl had lived in the village as long as Declan could remember. He'd embraced the life of the "country squire" ever since moving to the UK after the fall of the Berlin Wall and was the village's main mechanic. He was also Patrick's neighbour, his garden backing onto the rear section of Patrick's house.

'Declan,' Karl held his hand out, his accent still echoing his past. 'I wanted to give condolences.'

'Thank you Mister Schnitter,' Declan said, shaking the offered hand. 'I didn't see you at the funeral?'

'I do not do funerals,' Karl replied. 'I came later, whispered a prayer for him. I hope you do not think I was being rude.'

'Not at all,' Declan opened the door wider. 'Would you like to come in?'

'No, no,' Karl almost backed away from the door, his German manners almost horrified at the imposition. 'I just wanted to see you, to say that whatever you need, I am just around the back.'

He looked to the Audi in the driveway.

'And when that breaks down, as it looks like it will soon, remember my garage,' he smiled. But it was as polite a smile as you could expect. A salesman's smile.

'I will do,' Declan said. 'Thanks.'

Karl nodded and backed away from the door, turning halfway down the drive. Declan watched him leave. Karl was a lonely man; his wife had died around the same time that Declan's mum had, and both Karl and Patrick became each other's support network. Declan hoped that now alone again, Karl wouldn't retreat into himself. He'd have to take him to the pub some time, get some stories out of him. After all, if Declan stayed in the house, Karl would become his neighbour.

Turning back into the house and closing the front door behind him, Declan didn't wait around; he was here for a reason, and one reason alone. Making his way upstairs, entering the study and pushing the bookshelf to the side, he entered the secret room, his father's modern-day priest hole, turning on the light.

A line from Ratcliffe, spoken about another house the previous day flashed into his head.

'All houses of this time have them, sir.'

If Devington House had a priest hole or two within it, what was to stop someone hiding in one the night of the murder? Maybe the guard at the top of the stairs didn't see them come past, because they found another way? He'd have to speak to Ratcliffe again, see if he could gain a set of plans, although the thought of seeing Susan Devington again both intrigued and scared him.

Walking over to the metal filing cabinet he pulled the top drawer out. Row after row of brown folder files faced him, all neatly labelled at the top, and Declan gave a silent thanks to his father. The one main thing he remembered from being a kid here was that his father always brought his work home. Literally. He would copy the sheets of his case files, sometimes even by hand and bring the duplicates to his study to ensure that he always had backups. And of course, this probably helped immensely when he decided to write his memoirs.

There was a folder in the second drawer that he pulled out marked DAVIES. Removing it from the cabinet, Declan carried it across to the desk and opened it up.

It was the Victoria Davies files. Or at least copies of them. Reports, photos, musings on paper and even three cassette tapes. Picking one up, he saw written on the side was:

MICHAEL DAVIES – INTERVIEW 3,
JANUARY 6TH 2001

Pulling out the tape from the case, he looked around the room. On a shelf was an old tape recorder, the type that had the buttons one end and a small flap where the tape slotted into the middle. Placing the tape in, and praying that the recorder still had batteries, Declan pressed play.

He wasn't ready for what he heard.

'Interview three with Michael Davies, commencing at eight fifty-two am. Detective Inspector Patrick Walsh and Detective Sergeant Alexander Monroe recording.'

Declan paused the tape, tears already welling up as he tried to process what he'd just heard: his father's voice, only a little older than Declan was now, echoing in the study he used to work in. Unsure of what his life would bring; unaware of what would occur down the line.

Declan couldn't do this right now.

Taking the tape out of the recorder, he placed it back in its case and returned it to the rest of the notes. He'd take them back to Temple Inn and work through them there, somewhere that didn't have such a personal connection to his father. Maybe there was something Patrick missed within these pages.

As he went to close the folder, he stopped. A single piece of paper half filled with scrawled notes in his father's handwriting was poking out from behind a divider. One of the scrawls on the page had caught his eye. Pulling it out, he read the line in its entirety.

Necklace broken off. Who has necklace?

Declan placed the note back into the file. When he had first interviewed Andy Mac, Declan was absolutely sure that Andy had mentioned something about a broken necklace.

'They showed me it ... Broken necklace ...'

It was too soft to truly pick up, but he knew there was something here. Someone did have Victoria's necklace. Was it Andy Mac? If so, how did he gain it? Declan knew that if Andy's tale of blacking out was true then even if he did have it, he might not know how it came into his possession.

Unless he was the killer.

There was a faint sound downstairs; his front door was being knocked upon again. Gathering up the file, Declan left the secret room, hiding it once more behind the bookcase. Then, walking down the stairs and placing the file on the coffee table, he walked to the door and went to open it. It was probably Karl again, or one of the other inhabitants of Hurley, wishing the best for the grieving son.

He stopped himself a split second before opening the door.

What if it wasn't a local? What if it was the man with the rimless glasses again, here for a second round?

Declan grabbed a walking stick from beside the door, holding it behind his body, keeping it hidden, but at the same time ready to strike with it as he opened the door.

A bearded wreck of a man stood in the porchway, blinking at the sudden light. Declan recognised him immediately.

Shaun Donnal was at his father's house.

'Who are you?' Shaun asked, confused, his voice slurring, obviously drunk. Declan wasn't sure how to play this; he needed to take his time. For a start, he had to work out how a prime murder suspect knew his current address.

'I'm DI Walsh,' he started. Shaun's eyes widened and he stepped back, pulling out a flat headed screwdriver for protection.

'You're not Walsh!' he exclaimed, waving the screwdriver viciously at Declan. 'You're with them!'

Declan held his hands up, trying to placate the drunken madman. 'I'm not *Patrick* Walsh,' he said quickly. 'I'm his son, Declan.'

'I need to speak to Patrick Walsh,' Shaun said, the urgency obvious in his voice.

'Well then you're shit out of luck,' Declan said, deciding

that tough love was a better option here. 'My dad died just under two weeks back.'

Shaun visibly deflated at the news, as if punched in the gut.

'They said he was sniffing around again,'

'I think "they" probably meant me,' Declan carried on, deciding that "good cop" might be his best option here. 'Why don't you tell me what you wanted to speak to him about? Maybe I can help you?'

Shaun stood silently for a moment, rocking back and forth. Then he stopped, as if making a decision. He looked at Declan as he returned the screwdriver into the folds of his dirty coat.

'My name is Shaun Donnal,' he said, the tears already welling up in his eyes, 'and I killed Victoria Davies.'

Declan was about to reply to this when Shaun's eyes rolled into his skull, and he toppled to the side, collapsing like a puppet with its strings cut to the floor.

Declan stared down at the unconscious drunk. He wanted to know how Shaun had found this address. He wanted to know why Shaun was confessing to his father.

But more importantly, he wanted to know what the hell he was going to do with this unconscious man on his doorstep?

21

THE MANCHURIAN CANDIDATES

IT WAS DARK WHEN SHAUN DONNAL FINALLY WOKE, THE headache already pounding heavy in his skull.

He was lying on a sofa, a pillow placed under his head and a bucket put on the floor beside him. Rising gingerly to a sitting position, his fingers at his temples as if trying to keep his brains held in, he looked across the room to Declan, who was sitting in an armchair, a cup of tea in his hands and watching him silently.

'There's a fresh cup there,' Declan indicated a mug on the coffee table. 'I made it white with two sugars. I didn't know how you'd take it, but I thought the caffeine and sugar would help.'

'I'd prefer a whisky,' Shaun muttered, still confused. 'And what's the bucket for?'

'In case you threw up,' Declan replied. 'And we won't be drinking tonight.' He smiled as Shaun reached to his pocket. 'And I removed your own supply.'

'You had no right,' Shaun snapped, spittle foaming at his

mouth. Then, as if a switch was flicked, he calmed down, reluctantly grabbing the mug and sipping it.

Declan shrugged. 'Well, considering you appeared at my father's door and confessed to a murder I'm currently investigating, you're lucky you didn't wake up in a cell.'

Shaun grudgingly nodded. 'How long was I out?'

'Little over half an hour,' Declan replied. 'I was about to open the windows. You stink.'

'Sorry, I don't get to shower much.'

'Why the screwdriver?'

Shaun looked around. 'Police don't arrest you for carrying one,' he said. 'And the gun's hidden with my stuff.'

Declan wasn't sure if this was some kind of joke so he kept quiet. Shaun looked back to him.

'And sorry for your loss. I only met him a couple of times, but Patrick seemed a decent man, apart from his demons.'

Declan leaned forwards. 'That's the other reason you're not in cuffs,' he said. 'How did you know to come here?'

'I didn't,' Shaun admitted. 'I didn't know where else I could go.' He sipped at the tea, as if taking the moment to frame his response. 'I came here. Back before ... Well, back before. It was about five years back. It wasn't hard to find the address.'

'Why did you come here?'

'To warn your dad.'

'About what?'

'*Why do you care!*' Shaun screamed this, his face a mask of fury. And then, as quickly as it came, it went. Calm once more, Shaun sighed. 'How much do you know about Michael Davies?'

Declan watched Shaun warily before continuing. He knew that Donnal had a temper; he'd seen that on the CCTV footage, but this was different. This was more than the alcohol. This was a man who'd been living on the knife edge of conspiracy and fear for years and had finally slipped off. 'I know he was a socialist, that he was working with you on changing the Labour Party before you slept with his wife. I know he was charged and convicted on her murder, and that five years ago he died of terminal bowel cancer in prison.' Declan stopped, the maths finally catching up. 'That was when you disappeared, wasn't it?'

Shaun nodded. 'He didn't die of bowel cancer,' he said, the anger rising again as he spoke. 'I know that officially he did, and that the papers all said it, but it wasn't terminal. It was stage two. That's an eighty percent survival rate these days.'

'So, you think that he was killed?'

'Of course, he was bloody well killed! Are you an idiot? Christ!'

Declan let Shaun rant. This was a man who quite happily stabbed a man over a recognition a couple of days ago. He had to tread carefully.

'Why?' he asked in the calmest voice he could muster under the circumstances. Shaun leaned forwards, seemingly calm once more as he placed the half-drunk mug of tea back down.

'Michael was writing a book,' he said. 'He'd been talking to his solicitor and they reckoned that with the cancer, and the fifteen years done already he could be released. But he would be coming out to nothing; Susan had taken everything while he was inside, and even his nest egg had been spent by Francine without his knowledge during the trial.'

'Francine Pearce?'

'Yeah. She held it for when she wanted to create her own

company a few years after. Anyway, Michael? He was broke. And because of that, he was working on a tell-all. His side of the story. He'd been offered six figures for it, and in it he was going to talk about the donations he gave, the party politics ...'

'Yeah, I could see a lot of people being pissed at that.'

'But he was going further,' Shaun said. 'He was in for a penny, in for a pound, you know? He was opening the lid on Devington Industries, on the relationship Vicky had with her sister, what she did that night, everything.'

'How did you find out about this?' Declan reached into his jacket, pulling out his notebook. This was turning into an enlightening interview. 'I mean, I'm assuming you were a large part of the book.'

'Why? You think I'm part of—' Shaun took a deep breath, calming himself. 'Sorry. He called me from prison. Wanted to talk to me. And I agreed.'

'Why you?' Declan asked. 'No offence but you wouldn't have been my first point of contact.'

'I don't think I was,' Shaun leaned back into the sofa, pulling his glasses off and rubbing at his eyes, the headache getting worse. 'But who else was going to take his call? Susan was running the company. Francine hadn't spoken to him since the night of the murder. Andy MacIntyre was now Andy Mac, the YouTube Prophet. And Charles was pushing his way up the Tory backbenches.'

'And you had nothing to lose.'

'Only my marriage and my family, but I was losing those anyway,' Shaun snapped, the anger returning, his emotions yoyoing back and forth. 'The guilt of the murder had made me make some bad choices ...'

'Yes, the murder. Tell me about it,' Declan asked,

switching topic. He didn't want Shaun getting comfortable telling a story, and changing tact seemed to stop the anger.

'What do you want to know? I pushed her off the roof,' Shaun confessed. 'She fell.'

'And how did you do it?' Declan asked. 'How did you get to the roof?'

Shaun paused, as if reaching for an answer.

'I walked up the stairs.'

'Past the guard?'

'I suppose.'

'Describe the roof.'

'What?'

'Describe it. What did it look like? Smell like? How cold was it?'

'I don't remember,' Shaun shook his head.

'Of course, you do,' Declan placed the notebook to the side. 'The act of killing someone embeds itself inside you. You'll remember everything vividly. Dream of it constantly. Unless of course you didn't do it.'

'Are you saying I'm a liar?' Shaun swiped at the mug, sending it crashing across the room. Declan waited a couple of moments before speaking, forcing himself not to react, not to move. He'd faced many people like this in his time in the Military Police. The one thing you didn't want to do was give them a reason to attack.

'I'm saying that you believe it for some reason.' Declan said carefully, walking on eggshells. 'But I don't think you remember killing Victoria Davies. I think you don't remember anything from that night.'

There was a silence between them.

Eventually Shaun broke it, his voice no more than a croak.

'How would you know that?' he asked.

'Because in the last two days I've spoken to you, Andy and Charles about that night. And the one thing that links the other two was that they both admitted that they were blackout drunk at the time of Victoria's murder. It makes sense that you were too.'

'Why?'

'Because I think you were all deliberately made that way,' Declan said, rising up and pacing around the room as he spoke. 'I think someone wanted all three of you to have no memories of that night. If you can't remember it, how do you know you were the killer?' he asked.

Shaun's body language changed as he slumped down in the sofa. The angry man was gone for the moment.

'Because they showed me the necklace,' he said.

'Who did?'

Shaun went to speak, but then stopped.

'I can't say,' he said. 'They might hurt my family. My daughter, she's been helping me—'

'I'm sorry Shaun, but she hasn't.' Declan sat back down, facing Shaun again. 'Your daughter Sally hasn't been paying in the money. Someone else has. Your family's moved on.'

Shaun took a deep, shaky breath and nodded to himself.

'I wondered that,' he said. Then he straightened, as if making a decision. 'It was after the election, right after Michael was convicted,' he said. 'Francine Pearce met with me.'

'Michael's PA?'

'Yes, but not by then. Francine worked for Devington in their law department before she started sleeping with Michael, and when he was removed, she found a new way to move up in the company.'

'Susan?' Declan asked. Shaun didn't answer, continuing on.

'Anyway, she meets with me. It's September, just after the 9/11 stuff happened. She said that Devington were going to push for some kind of arms infrastructure deal with the government. It was the first big deal that Susan had helmed since taking over, and Frankie needed me to help push it through Parliament.'

'And you said yes?'

'Christ no!' Shaun rose now, the furious anger returning to his voice. 'I was completely against that. And then she showed me the envelope with the necklace in it!'

Declan rose to face Shaun, his hands out and in front of him, palms facing Shaun.

'Easy Shaun, I'm just asking questions. No need to feel threatened. You mean Victoria's necklace?'

Shaun nodded. 'She explained that she'd found it on me that night. I'd cut my hand, and the blood was all over it. She'd hidden it from the police.'

'She'd saved you from being accused as the murderer.'

'Yeah,' Shaun spat the word. 'But because of that she owned me. And of course, I did what she asked. To say no would kill my political career and have me locked up.'

'So rather Michael did the time?'

'He was no angel, believe me, but you're right.' Shaun looked to the floor, and Declan could see the shame in his expression. 'Over the years she'd come to me, usually on Susan's request. She'd ask me to vote on things. And I did so. Until I lost my seat.'

Declan sat back down and wrote this down in his notebook, using the time to think. Andy Mac had mentioned the same thing.

Had all three MPs been given the same story? Had they all voted for Susan, believing that they were the murderer, with their blood on a necklace?

'Tell me about Sarah Hinksman,' he continued. Shaun looked surprised at this.

'Sarah?' he asked. What about her?'

'The night of her death,' Declan continued. 'She turned up looking for you at the conference, and you asked Andy Mac to keep her busy.' He stopped as Shaun sat back down and started to cough. Or cry. Long wheezing *huffs* that Declan slowly realised was actually Shaun laughing.

'You think she came to see *me?*' he said. 'God no! She called me at the hotel the night before, told me to take my wife and ensure I wasn't around because she was turning up to settle a score!'

'She wasn't coming to out you as the father of her baby?'

Shaun shrugged. 'I don't know what she was doing, as she never got to say what she wanted to. And then she had the accident.' He stopped, his face sobering up.

'You don't think it was an accident.'

'Who was she coming to see, Shaun?' Declan asked. 'That night. Who was it she wanted to out?'

'I don't know.'

'Were you the father?'

'I don't know. And God help me, I never wanted to know.'

Declan picked up his phone, opening an email that Billy had sent fifteen minutes earlier. The photo attached showed an image of Charles and Sarah laughing in 1997. He turned the phone around and showed it to Shaun.

'Was it Charles, Shaun?' he asked. 'Was she about to destroy Charles Baker's career and not yours?'

Shaun examined the photo. 'You should take a look at the

original,' he said. 'There's more to see—'

Shaun stopped as there was a banging on the front door.

'They've found me!' he hissed, jumping to his feet, the screwdriver out again. 'You set me up you son of a bitch! I'll kill you for this!'

Ignoring the insult while keeping an eye on Shaun, Declan rose up, walking over to the door.

'Calm down, it's my boss,' he said. 'I'm sorry, Shaun, but when you passed out I called him and told him what happened. He said he'd bring a couple of uniforms up.'

'You traitor!' Shaun's hands were clenching and unclenching as he stood, gripping his makeshift weapon, standing like a feral creature in a cage.

'You confessed on my doorstep!' Declan replied as the door banged again. 'Of course, I was going to call Monroe.'

'Detective Sergeant Alex Monroe?'

'DCI now, but yeah,' Declan paused. 'Why?'

The door banged harder, the wood visibly shaking. Declan walked to it, opening it—

To find a trio of red laser points on his chest.

There was a man in a suit standing on the step; overweight, but with overpowering odour of "don't mess with me". In the background, at the gate to the house were three more suited men, and a familiar van at the driveway.

An *SCO19* armed police unit.

'Declan Walsh?' the man said, showing his warrant card. 'I'm DCI Sutcliffe and you have my suspect inside your house. I'd like him back. Now.'

'Or what?' Declan asked.

'Or else I'll have you shot and take him out myself.'

22

STAND OFF

DECLAN LOOKED DOWN AT THE LASERS AIMED AT HIS CHEST.

'I don't know what you're talking about,' he said. 'I don't have anyone in my house. I'm just clearing out my father's old things.'

'Then you won't mind me coming in and having a look?' Sutcliffe said, trying to peer past Declan and into the house.

'Of course not,' Declan smiled. 'We're all police here. Just show me the warrant.'

Sutcliffe hissed in frustration at this. Declan stood his ground. Looking at the men at the gate, he paused on one of them.

'Tell you what, DCI Sutcliffe, why don't you get your man over there to come ask me?' he said. 'The one with the rimless glasses? I'm sure we have a lot to chat about.'

Sutcliffe sighed. 'Don't make this harder than it is,' he said.

'It's not hard at all,' Declan replied. 'It's incredibly simple, actually. You go tell whoever sent you that I don't respond well to bullying. No warrant? No entry. And you can tell the SCO19 guys that I'm not intimidated by the lasers. This isn't the first time I've faced off a possibly corrupt DCI with guns aimed at me. Christ, it isn't even the first time this month.'

And with that Declan slammed the door in Sutcliffe's face, locking it quickly.

'What are you doing?' Shaun asked, standing at the window, looking out at the policemen. Once again, he seemed calm. This surprised Declan, because currently Declan's body was filled with adrenaline. Declan quickly pulled him to the side, against the wall.

'Buying us time,' he said. 'There's something really wrong with those coppers. For a start, the prick that attacked me last night's hanging out with them.'

He walked across the room, away from Shaun.

'Keep out of the line of sight for the moment,' he suggested. 'Sit back down. They won't storm in until they can find a way of proving it was required. All we have to do is wait for backup and hope it comes first.'

Shaun sat down reluctantly.

'You said "they've found me" when they banged on the door,' Declan said. 'Who's they?'

'Francine,' Shaun said. 'She found me earlier today. I know they don't want me to speak to anyone, and they didn't want you distracted from the direction they wanted you going.'

That was interesting. Someone was guiding the investigation. But who?

'Let's carry on speaking then,' Declan pulled out the note-book. 'Unless you have something better to do?'

Shaun shrugged, staring at the door. 'I could really do with a drink.'

'Drink later. Talk first. Now, why did you come and see my dad five years back?'

'Because of the book,' Shaun said. 'Michael's one. Your father would have been in it. Michael reckoned he had proof that the detectives on the case had been bought off.'

'My dad wasn't corrupt,' Declan snapped, but at the same time there was a small doubt niggling in the back of his mind. A couple of weeks earlier he'd had a run in with Johnny Lucas, one of the criminal "twins" of East London while working the Mile End case, and it had come out that he was chummy with Patrick Walsh in the nineties.

Hell, the twins had their own chapter in Patrick's memoirs.

'I didn't say your father,' Shaun said, bringing Declan back to the present. 'I said detectives. Plural.'

'We'll come back to that,' Declan said, also watching the door now. It'd gone silent outside. That was never a good sign. 'Let's go back to Francine Pearce and the Bill you were asked to put through, back when you were shown the necklace. Did it pass?'

'Yes, by two votes.'

'All three of you voted for it.'

'How did you know?'

Declan steepled his fingers as he considered this. 'All of you lost your memories that night. Michael Lucas is accused of murder and convicted. A few months later Susan is made CEO, and Francine Pearce effectively blackmails you into doing what she said, in fear you'll be exposed as the murderer.' He smiled. 'And I bet you weren't the only one she spoke to. Andy Mac mentioned similar, but I didn't realise it at the time.'

'What are you suggesting?' Shaun flinched as the sounds

of shouting rose outside, his agitation starting to return, the screwdriver still in his hand. Declan walked over to the window, looking out.

'I think that all three of you were told by Francine, individually, that you were the killer. She stopped you telling each other and kept you working for her.' He thought for a moment, watching through the glass.

'You were telling me about Michael,' he said. 'Why he called you to visit him.'

'This is stupid. We should be getting out of here.' The irritation was rising dangerously high in Shaun's voice.

'We'll get out of here, but not the way you're thinking. Talk.'

'Fine. He told me that before the murder, he'd been stockpiling data, files on everything and everyone. I think it was so he had leverage if Vicky divorced him. He said he had proof she'd done something bad at a Labour Conference. I think it was to do with drugs.'

'Did she take drugs?'

'It was the late nineties. Everyone took drugs. Vicky was a multi-tasker. She'd take something to get high and bring herself down with a downer.'

'Something like ketamine?'

Shaun thought for a moment. 'Possibly,' he said. 'I never saw her do it, but I know people who had. When she hung around with Andy, before I was around, I know he did K back then. And Michael had it all written down. He'd expected a monster pay-out if they divorced.'

'That makes sense. Victoria was the one with money in that relationship. What did he do with the files?'

'Nobody knows. He said he had them in a security box. Paid for lifetime service and would remove them when he got out. He was expecting a resolution in the next couple of weeks.'

'Because of his cancer?'

'Yeah. It might not have been terminal, but it was still there. He expected to be out within days. And then a week later he died.'

Declan nodded as he considered this.

'You spent time with Victoria at Devington House?' he asked.

Shaun's face darkened. 'My private life is nothing—'

'For Christ's sake, Shaun!' Declan snapped, his patience finally running thin. 'I'm trying to save your life here and find a killer! I couldn't give a damn about your sordid little past!'

Shaun stared in shock at Declan, the anger seemingly surprised out of him.

'I spent time there,' he admitted.

'How did you keep it from Michael?'

'We'd use secret passages.'

'Priest holes.'

'That's what Vicky called them.'

There were the sounds of approaching sirens as Declan carried on staring out of the window as he spoke. 'The passages take you outside?'

'One did. What relevance does this have to the murder?'

'Working on that part. Did you know Sebastian Payne?'

'Who?' Shaun's response was honest. Declan decided to skip past that. Time was running out.

'Why did you stab the homeless man?'

'He threatened to out me. I couldn't risk it.' Again, Shaun's anger turned to guilt, as if two distinct souls were fighting in one body. 'I didn't mean to stab him so hard.' He walked to the shelf, picking a photo of Declan up, in the red cap of the Military Police.

'You were a soldier?'

'Military Police.'

'No wonder you weren't scared of SCO19.'

'Not the first time I've had guns aimed at me,' Declan replied.

'I was in the Territorials,' Shaun said. 'Briefly, anyway. We never fired weapons; we had these things called blank fire adaptors attached.'

'A man with a BFA weapon is still scary if you don't know it's attached,' Declan said. 'To the average person, a gun is a gun.'

'I suppose so.' Shaun put the photo back on the shelf as Declan nodded, walking to the door. The sirens had stopped now and raised voices could be heard outside.

'What are you doing?' Shaun rose, terrified.

'Did you trust my dad?' Declan asked as the door was hammered on once more.

'Yes.'

'Then trust me.' Declan opened the door to reveal Monroe standing there.

'Cavalry's arrived, son,' the older man said, looking into the house. 'Hey, it's Shaun Donnal. Long-time no see. Put the screwdriver down, laddie. We're here to help.'

Declan looked past Monroe to see a standoff on his front garden. Billy, Anjli and half a dozen uniformed officers barred the way for DCI Sutcliffe. Declan also noted that the man with the rimless glasses had disappeared.

'He has a suspect of mine in there!' Sutcliffe shouted. 'I demand you hand him over!'

Monroe looked back to Sutcliffe.

'Name?'

'DCI Sutcliffe!'

'Well, I'm DCI Monroe, and by the looks of you I'd say I'm probably the one with seniority in years here,' Monroe smiled. 'And therefore, I don't see your suspect in there, I see my suspect. Shaun Donnal, grievous bodily assault in Soho. You can have him, but only when I'm done with him. Until then, take your overcompensation and your guns and sod off out of this sleepy little village.'

Sutcliffe looked around, and Declan could almost see the thought processes running through his head.

'I want him after you're done with him,' he hissed, nodding to his men. As one they left, leaving only Monroe's team on the grass.

'There was another here,' Declan said. 'The one that jumped me last night.'

'I don't doubt it,' Monroe replied. 'Just as much as when I search for our DCI Sutcliffe later, we'll likely find that he doesn't exist.' Standing in the doorway he looked to Shaun, then back to Declan.

'We'll talk about this later,' he said softly. 'But before that I think we should get Mister Donnal here somewhere safe and in a secure location under a fake name. He seems to be rather popular tonight.'

'I'll come with you,' Declan said. 'I've got what I came here for. Donnal was an extra bonus.'

'More of your father's ties?' Monroe smiled. Declan pointed back to the coffee table.

'His files from the Davies case,' he said. 'Thought they might help.'

'Don't know what difference they'll be to the ones we have, but anything will help,' Monroe replied. 'Let's get back and reconvene tomorrow. I don't think any of this is going to change by then. And by then Doctor Marcos should have some news for us.'

As the police came in and handcuffed Shaun, taking his screwdriver as evidence in the process, Declan nodded to him. He'd ensure that Shaun was placed somewhere safe, and that his anger management problems didn't cause any more issues.

'Walsh, can I say something?' Shaun seemed furtive. Waving the police away, Declan leaned in.

'They weren't real police,' Shaun said. 'Or at least some of them weren't.'

'How do you know that?' Declan asked.

'There were three men by the gate when I looked out of the window. All three of them were chasing me earlier. The one with the glasses had this baton thing he hit me with.'

A cold chill went down Declan's spine.

'Rimless glasses?'

'You saw him?'

'We've met,' Declan nodded. 'Who do they work for?'

'Pearce Associates,' Shaun replied as the police, watching for Declan's nod returned and started to escort Shaun to a waiting vehicle. 'Look at the photo! Look for her!'

Declan stared after him, deep in thought. It was Anjli who brought him back.

'Nice place,' she said. 'Hope you're not thinking of selling it, as it's gonna be a bastard to get a good listing now we've made such a racket here.'

Declan laughed. 'I'm starting to think we've been looking at the wrong suspects,' he said. 'I think we need to get Francine Pearce in as soon as possible.'

'We've tried,' Billy said as he stood by the coffee table,

already rifling through Patrick's notes. 'Her solicitor already called, saying that she'd heard we were reopening the case, and that based on our investigation so far she's already said everything she needs to.'

'And how does she know how our investigation's going?' Declan asked, taking the file from Billy. 'You can play with this after dinner. First I need you to find out something for me.'

'What?'

On his phone, Declan showed Billy the image of Charles and Sarah; the one that Billy had sent almost an hour earlier. 'I need you to take a real good look at the original of this,' he said. 'Shaun seemed convinced that there was something more to it. And then I need you to get Doctor Marcos to compare Sebastian Payne's DNA with the trace she gathered from that coffee cup.'

'The cup?'

'Yes,' Declan nodded. 'You see, I'm starting to think that Charles Baker was Sebastian's real father.'

23

FAKE NEWS

I⟶ took a couple of hours for Shaun to be signed in at an undisclosed location in North London, Declan himself signing the paperwork to ensure as minimal exposure between the police and Shaun as he could. As far as anyone was concerned, Shaun was some drunken homeless bum named Dave that needed to sleep off the night, and Declan would be back in the morning to pick him up.

That done, Declan returned to his house to finish reading through the notes he'd found earlier. He'd stopped off at his apartment and brought a holdall with a change of clothes and a toothbrush this time, purely to ensure that he wouldn't be caught out again and, following the visit by Shaun, he decided to swear off the alcohol as well. Which was probably for the best, as the notes that he read through were dull and uninspiring.

He couldn't place what was wrong with them; they just didn't feel like an investigation, it was if they were just going through the motions. It felt like his father had already made his decision on who was guilty and was simply ticking the boxes to look good.

There was one thing that stood out though: a piece of transcript dialogue, an interview between then-DS Monroe and Susan Devington, about three weeks after the murder.

DS M: And how long were you held in the station?

SD: They let me out the following day.

DS M: And why were you arrested?

SD: I maced a policewoman. By accident of course.

Declan pulled his notebook out, flicking back through it to his own interview with Susan. It felt so long ago now, but it was only yesterday when he'd spoken to her.

Kept in 48 hours. Kicking a policeman and stealing his helmet.

It might have been two decades worth of fake memories, but Susan Devington didn't seem the type of person to get such a simple fact wrong. Both the reason why she was arrested and the length of her incarceration had been changed.

Within his father's notes was the address and telephone number of the station that she'd been held at back then. Dialling it, Declan waited until he was connected, and then bounced from department to department for a few minutes, trying to get through to the desk sergeant. Eventually he was placed through and he began explaining why he was calling. The desk sergeant didn't recall the case; it was from two decades earlier and wasn't that exciting, so Declan would have been stunned if the sergeant had remembered it, but the sergeant did explain that all cases since 1996 were now digitised so it shouldn't be an issue to find. Declan gave his email address and was about to disconnect the call before something else came to mind.

'Before I go,' he said. 'Just wanted to check up on something. We had a letter sent to us that you guys found recently from twenty years ago.'

'Ah yes, the Davies murder,' the sergeant remembered. 'Is this connected to the road protest?'

'Maybe,' Declan admitted. 'But that's not what I wanted to ask about. How exactly did you find the letter?'

'I'm not rightly sure,' the sergeant said. 'I'll find out and put it in the email.'

Declan thanked the desk sergeant and disconnected the call, leaning back as he considered the erroneous responses that Susan had given. There was something off there. He just needed to work out what it was.

Deciding to put this aside for the moment, Declan now flicked through the remainder of the folder's backmatter, pausing when he found notes taken during an interview between his father and Francine Pearce. Reading through them, he saw a woman scorned, angry even at the betrayal of the man she loved. He felt sorry for her; Francine was a wronged woman who'd made a mistake, but here again was something that he couldn't believe that his father hadn't picked up on.

Declan re-read the notes. For a woman who claimed to have loved Michael so much, Francine seemed very happy to throw him under the bus. Her statement was filled with countless observations on how he was angry about Victoria's infidelity, how he'd found out about the affair while ignoring his own hypocrisy, how he had explained to Francine one night that he couldn't have been the father as he'd had a vasectomy. Declan assumed that someone so much in love would have at least given their lover the benefit of the doubt, but reading it a third time, Declan started to see the words of a woman who seemed to be deliberately damning the suspect. And with Shaun's line on how she was emptying his bank accounts while he was going through this, Declan couldn't help but wonder if this was deliberate.

The vasectomy line caught his eye again. Michael was the cuckolded husband, obviously unable to father the bastard in his wife's belly; of course, he would murder her for this unfaithfulness, this embarrassment. But something nagged at him. Things said about this over the last couple of days.

'Michael claimed he had the snip, but I know Charles claimed he'd put the kibosh on that too.'

'Susan Devington should mind her own bloody business.'

'Charles was already working out how to use this to his advantage, like he'd done the snip.'

Declan flicked through the pages at the back of the folder once more. He'd seen a number on a card as he'd looked earlier; finding it, he held it to the light so he could read it properly.

THE LONDON ANDROLOGY CENTRE
DR A. KHAI

There was a telephone number underneath it. Declan looked at the clock on the wall; it was almost ten in the evening now. There was every chance that the clinic would be closed now. Also, this was a business card from over two decades earlier. The clinic and the number might not even exist anymore.

Declan picked up his phone and dialled the number. At

least he could leave a message for them to call him in the morning. Surprisingly, it rang. After a couple of rings however, Declan realised that this was a pointless act. People wouldn't still be—

'Hello?' A man's voice, old and croaking answered the phone.

Declan sat up.

'Sorry to call so late,' he said. 'Is this the London Andrology Centre?'

'It used to be,' the man's voice replied. 'Now it's the Khai Andrology and Fertility Clinic.'

Declan grabbed his notebook, cradling the phone at his ear as he wrote the name down.

'Excellent. I'm looking for a Doctor Khai?' he said.

'Call back in office hours,' the voice replied, obviously tired.

'No, I understand that, but I was hoping to gain a contact number for him,' Declan continued. 'This is Detective Inspector Walsh of the City Police.'

There was a moment of silence as the voice on the end of the line mentally reassessed the call from enquiry to police.

'Is there a problem?' The voice seemed concerned.

'I can only really talk about it to Doctor Khai.'

'This is Aston Khai,' the voice confirmed. 'What's the problem?'

'I'm following up on a cold case you were involved in,' Declan said quickly. 'Michael Davies. Would have been over twenty years back.'

'I remember it,' Doctor Khai replied. 'Hard to forget when your work hits the evening news. I'd given him a vasectomy several months earlier.'

Declan decided to go with a hunch. Too many things

didn't add up here. And according to his father's notes, Doctor Khai was never around to be interviewed.

'But you didn't, did you,' a statement more than a question. Declan made his tone as menacing as he could as he continued. 'Tell me Doctor Khai, how much did Charles Baker pay you to fake the procedural?'

There was a long pause on the telephone. A too long pause.

'If you don't tell the truth now, Doctor Khai, I'll be forced to make a more public enquiry,' Declan added for good measure.

Another pause. Then ...

'I agreed to do it with Charles Baker, but it wasn't Baker who paid me.'

'Who was it that paid you?'

'A woman.'

This was a surprise, but Declan didn't comment on it. There were only two women he could think of that would gain from this.

'Was her surname Devington? Pearce?'

'Neither.' Another pause. 'I only spoke to her once, I think it was Wooton, or Wilson.'

'Frankie Wilson paid you?'

'Yes.'

'How much?'

'Fifty thousand pounds.'

Declan almost punched the air.

'So, Michael Davies wasn't given a vasectomy?'

'No.'

'But he believed he had?'

'Yes.' Doctor Khai's voice was soft, as if the man knew that by saying this, he was signing his career away. 'And I've regretted it for years.'

'I'm sure you have,' Declan said. 'One of my colleagues will be visiting you in the morning, so I'd suggest you spend the rest of the evening writing out a full and honest statement for them.'

With that he disconnected the call, leaning back in the sofa.

Michael Davies wasn't sterile. He could have fathered the child Victoria had. For some reason Charles Baker had teamed with Sarah Hinksman's old assistant and had deliberately set out to destabilise the marriage. No matter what happened, the moment Victoria became pregnant, even if she had remained faithful, Michael would believe it was someone else's child. Granted, he probably didn't expect a murder to be the outcome, but it was a pretty Machiavellian thing to do, especially to one of their biggest donors. And Frankie Wilson had disappeared when Sarah died. Why did she return a few months later to do this?

His phone beeped. Declan looked down to see that the Derbyshire police had sent Susan's arrest report over as an email attachment. Opening it up on the phone, he scrolled through the PDF file. There wasn't much to it: Susan Galloway *née* Devington had been arrested in a road protest scuffle on New Year's Eve, 2000. From the report given of the affray it looked like Susan had actively started the scuffle, pepper spraying a policewoman in the face while spitting and swearing at others. Easily enough to be arrested on, with both sides spoiling for a fight. She'd been taken to a local Derbyshire police station where she'd been held, screaming and swearing bloody murder until January 2nd, when she was released.

Everything here fitted her story, but there was one thing that didn't.

Declan zoomed in on the photo of Susan, taken the night she was processed. Picking up the folder from the table once more, Declan flipped through the notes, finding a photo in it, taken in 2000 at some gala. Michael and Victoria were obviously the focus of this paparazzi photo but to the side, almost off camera was a mid-twenties Susan Devington. There were only a few months difference between the photos, but whereas Susan was easily recognisable in the one from the party, the Susan that was on the crime report wasn't.

She was close, she was similar in looks, but it wasn't close enough to someone who knew Susan, who had seen Susan up close and personal.

Because it wasn't Susan Devington.

That's why she'd got the facts of the arrest wrong. Someone else had been arrested in her name. Which meant that Susan Devington's alibi, that of being in a police cell at the time of the murder was a complete and utter lie.

Which now gave Declan a new line of enquiry. *Did Susan Devington kill her sister?*

He went to send a reply back, to thank the desk sergeant, but saw that there was more to the email. The sergeant had been quite detailed in explaining how the letter had come to be in their possession once more.

Declan read the note twice, before leaning back. He now knew for certain that there was a traitor in the Last Chance Saloon.

And, because of the email, he knew who it was.

24

A QUIET EVENING

Billy Fitzwarren didn't often eat in expensive restaurants anymore. He'd spent his life eating out; as a child he was allowed by his parents to eat wherever he wanted, as long as it wasn't junk food. This meant that Billy became very creative with his list of locations, and the specialist orders that he would place while there. In fact, he'd spent his entire teenage years never stepping foot in a McDonalds, while having the greatest chefs in the world whip him up a Big Mac at five times the cost.

You could do that when you were wealthy.

Now, of course, Billy didn't have those luxuries. Ever since he'd chosen the police over a life on the family's Board of Directors, his family had started to distance themselves from him. And when his uncle, Bryan Fitzwarren had started a Ponzi scheme using cryptocurrency as its base, it was simply bad bloody *luck* that Billy was the one to not only solve the case but also arrest his uncle.

Yeah, that hadn't gone down well.

But tonight was different. Tonight, was date night. He'd

worried that it would be postponed after he had to drive into Berkshire, but he'd managed to reschedule for eight thirty. And so here he was, dressed in the coolest clothes he could find, sitting in Cecconi's in The Ned, waiting for his date to show up.

He knew people were watching him as he sat in the booth. He always knew that people were watching him. The man who obviously hated money; the man who sold out his family. He was used to this. He ignored them.

Looking up, he saw a young, blond man enter the restaurant. He wore a simple Tom Ford blazer over a Luis Vuitton jumper, his black jeans seemingly label-less, but festooned with jewelled designs down either side. Billy grinned. They were most likely Roberto Cavalli's, and cost more than the rest of his wardrobe put together.

The young man looked around the restaurant, and Billy waved his hand to catch his attention. The young man looked to Billy and then his face fell.

Well, that wasn't the reaction Billy had wanted.

The man walked over to the booth, but instead of sliding in to face his date for the evening, the man stood, awkwardly, just out of reach.

'Something the matter, Simon?' Billy asked. 'You look like someone died.'

Simon looked around, as if expecting to see someone. He looked back to Billy, a tear forming in his right eye.

'Sorry, Will, I have to go,' he said. 'I can't do this anymore.'

'Do what?' Billy rose from the chair, trying his best not to draw any attention. 'It's just dinner.'

'I can't.'

'We can go somewhere else,' Billy pleaded. 'What about Chinatown?'

'My family have said we can't see each other anymore.' Simon looked away, as if ashamed to look at Billy.

'Oh, it's your family, is it?' Billy's tone grew angry. 'And we wouldn't want to upset family now, would we?'

He sat back down. 'Go on then, piss off,' he said through clenched lips. Simon wavered for a moment, as if changing his mind, and then left the restaurant quickly. Billy bit back the urge to leave the restaurant and run after Simon, tell him that he'd do whatever was needed to make things work. Instead, he waved to a waiter and asked for the wine list. If he was going to eat alone in a fancy restaurant, he'd eat well.

Writing and sending a quick text on his phone, he sat back, ignoring the hushed words and stolen glances his way.

The waiter came by with a wine list and, after a few minutes of deciding which one to take, Billy eventually picked an expensive Shiraz and sent her on her way. She was replaced by a smiling businessman.

He was older than Billy, but not by much. He wore a dark-blue Hugo Boss number over a black shirt, and his tan brogues were expensive, but completely wrong. *You never wore brown in town.* He wore his brown hair shaved at the sides and slicked back, the amount of gel in it making it look like a Lego hair piece and he had a large, recognisable cygnet ring on.

'William Fitzwarren!' the man breathed. 'Fancy seeing you here!'

'I'm sorry, I don't think we've met before,' Billy couldn't place the man from anywhere in his past. But the man obviously knew Billy.

The man slid into the chair, smiling as he did so. 'Course you do! Rufus Harrington! We went to Harrow together!'

Billy leaned back in the booth. 'No offence, Rufus, but if

we did, you had to be a few years above me. And if so, we didn't go to Harrow together, we attended the same school, and visited the same building at the same time. Not quite the same as going together.'

The smile wavered. 'No love for the old school tie, then?'

Billy shrugged. 'I think they took a pair of scissors to it the moment I joined the police.'

He indicated the ring.

'You'd have more chance using your lodge membership.'

The ring that Rufus wore bore the square and compasses emblem of the Freemasons on it, but he wasn't from the same lodge as Billy was. Rufus hid the ring from view, as if having it announced would suddenly out him or something.

'Look, I'm waiting for my date,' Billy said. 'So, whatever you want, just say it. But if it's asking for a referral to my father, you've really backed the wrong horse.'

'I thought your date walked out on you,' Rufus replied, the smile now gone. 'I thought a lot of people had walked out on you since you walked out on them.'

Here we go, Billy thought.

'Little birdy says that you're digging into Devington Industries,' Rufus said, lowering his voice.

'And what's that to you?' Billy smiled at the waiter as she returned with the Shiraz, offering his glass to be poured. He tasted, nodded and then allowed a small measure to be poured. He looked to Rufus. 'I'd offer you some, but you're not staying,' he said. 'My date will be here soon.'

Leaving the bottle on the table, the waiter walked away. Rufus leaned closer.

'Don't screw around with Devington,' he said. 'This is a friendly reminder that no matter what uniform you're cosplaying in today, you're not one of them. You're one of us. And we look out for our own.'

'One question,' Billy replied, sipping at the wine. 'Has this come from Devington, or have they got my family to ask you to do this?'

'Blood calls to blood.' Rufus leaned back in the seat, watching Billy. 'One day you'll get bored of playing police-man, or they'll get bored of being a rich boy's toy. You don't want to be without friends then.'

'I have friends,' Billy said. 'In fact, I'm waiting—'

'I know, I know,' Rufus picked up a bread roll from the table, tearing it in half, tossing one half back in the bowl while gnawing on the other. 'You've got a date. But even your date knew that you're toxic to be around right now, didn't he?'

Billy grinned.

'That wasn't the date I talked about,' he said as beside Rufus Anjli Kapoor appeared.

'Excuse me, mate, I think you're in my seat,' she said, the tone in her voice menacing while her face was open and smiling. Rufus looked at her, noting her off-the-peg clothing and easy style before rising from the seat, allowing Anjli to sit.

'Great catching up, buddy,' he said to Billy. 'Think about what I said.'

And with that Rufus Harrington left.

'Did I interrupt something?' Anjli said, picking up the bottle and looking at it. 'This looks expensive. You sure about this?'

'Firstly, no you didn't. Secondly, I didn't want to eat alone and it's far nicer to do it with friends. And thirdly, yes, it is very expensive.'

Anjli grinned as she poured out a generous glass. 'What did he want?'

'He was warning me from digging around Devington Industries,' Billy said. 'Which was bloody stupid as that's just catnip to a copper.'

'And your date?'

Billy's face fell. 'I think they got to him. He bailed on me a few minutes before Rufus turned up.'

'Sorry, dude,' Anjli said. 'Still, this is nice. I was about to go get some dinner near Temple Inn anyway. What's good here?'

'Whatever you want,' Billy grinned as a waiter walked over. 'Hi, just checking, does your chef know how to make a Big Mac?'

He looked back to Anjli. It might not be the night he was hoping for, but he'd rather spend it with friends than any of the old school brigade.

ALEXANDER MONROE PARKED THE CAR DOWN A SIDE AVENUE, just off the Mile End Road. He didn't want to take it into the estate; the chances were that he'd return to find it gone or stacked up on bricks while the alloy wheels were removed. Locking it he started north, walking under the railway arches that divided Mile End with Bethnal Green, entering Globe Town.

He hadn't been here for a while, but he still knew the route to the boxing club on Bullard's Place, walking past tower-block estates, feeling the eyes on him as he walked. He was something new. They would be watching before confronting. Also, they would see that he walked with purpose. The watching eyes would wonder why he was so confident.

Monroe wasn't confident; he put on a good show. There was every chance that he might not come out of this confrontation, depending on who he met.

Everyone in the East End, even London itself, knew of the *Kray Twins* who, with their *Firm* ran the criminal side of East End London during the fifties and sixties. London had a long list of criminal organisations: *the Clerkenwell Crime Syndicate, the Richardson Brothers, Billy Hill and Jack Spot, the Sabinis,* the list went on. And there, from the nineties, working from a boxing club in the heart of Globe Town, East London were *The Twins*: Jackie and Johnny Lucas.

Made out in the press to be a modern-day version of the Krays, Johnny and Jackie were different. They famously never appeared together, an agreement allegedly planned so that if one was killed, the other could gain revenge for them. When people turned up to speak with them, they never knew which of the twins they'd meet with, as Johnny and Jackie changed around their schedules constantly. They looked identical. They wore almost identical clothing. Their haircuts were the same.

The problem was that even though this was all well known, it was also well known that Johnny and Jackie weren't twins. They weren't even two people. Johnny and Jackie were just one person: a person with a very particular multiple personality disorder. There was "Johnny", the rational, business-like one and then there was "Jackie", the out and out psychopath. And over the years people had learned not to peek behind the curtain. *The Twins* were twins and that was that.

Monroe knew this. He also knew there was a very strong

chance, even more than a coin flip, that he could be walking into Jackie Lucas's fun house right now, rather than the safer option of Johnny Lucas's club.

Walking into the boxing club, Monroe took a deep breath, taking in the mixture of sweat and leather. The club had been here for decades; the paint on the walls was cracking, covered over with aged boxing event posters, the boxing ring in the middle had seen better days and the equipment surrounding it was a mixture of leather and duct tape. Glancing about, Monroe saw that only a couple of boxers were training right now, working on the heavy bags to the right. As he walked through the club, one of the trainers – a meaty looking man in his forties tracksuit over a tank top and his hair gelled back – walked out.

'Whatever ya selling, we ain't interested,' he said. Monroe smiled.

'Hello Petey. Haven't seen you since you were what, fifteen?'

The trainer stared at Monroe for a second and then swore softly.

'Boss,' he said. 'We got another copper in.'

There was movement from the back room. A man, well-built and in his early sixties entered the boxing club through a door that probably led to an office. He wore a black suit and shirt, but no tie, his salt and peppered hair blow-dried back, giving him a little quiff at the front.

'Bloody hell,' he said. 'Back from the dead. Hello, Alex.'

'Mister Lucas,' Monroe replied. 'Jackie or Johnny?'

'Johnny,' Johnny Lucas smiled, walking to a water bottle and pouring himself a cup of water. 'Jackie's up north today.'

'Course he is.' Monroe's smile never fell.

'What do you want, DCI Monroe?' Johnny asked.

'You hear about Patrick Walsh?' Monroe asked.

Johnny shrugged. 'Had his son in here a couple of weeks back if that's what you mean. Cocky little bastard. Blamed me for a murder in Mile End,' Johnny smiled. 'That said, he made sure that I wasn't out of pocket, so I owe him that.'

Monroe shook his head. 'I'm not on about the Mile End issues,' he said. 'I'm here because Patrick Walsh died a couple of weeks back.'

Johnny's face didn't change. If any emotion was behind it, he hid it well.

'I didn't do it,' he stated.

'I didn't say you did,' Monroe replied. 'I know you're not that stupid.'

'Jackie is,' Johnny mused. 'But we liked Patrick. So why tell us if we're not involved?'

'Because Declan's got it in his head that his dad was murdered,' Monroe explained. 'And he's hunting for the killer.'

'Do you think he was murdered?' Johnny asked.

Monroe shrugged. 'It was an accident,' he said. 'Most likely a heart attack, country lane, late at night.'

'You didn't answer me,' Johnny tutted, waggling his finger. 'You did what you always do and changed the subject.'

'What I think doesn't matter,' Monroe snapped angrily. 'What I know is that Declan Walsh will stop at nothing to find the man that killed his dad. And you're on that list.'

'And why are we on this list exactly?'

'Patrick was writing a book,' Monroe said. 'And you were in it.'

There was a silence over the boxing club as Johnny considered this. 'He's got nothing on anything I did back then. Nobody has.'

'I didn't say he has,' Monroe looked around the boxing club, keeping an eye on the other inhabitants in there. This was the make-or-break moment. 'But I came to give you a warning.'

Johnny Lucas raised his eyebrows at this. 'You're warning me? That's a bold statement.'

'I'm serious,' Monroe snapped back. 'You tell him anything about his father; you tell him the truth? I will use every resource at my disposal to destroy you.'

The men around him grumbled at this, but Monroe carried on.

'I know Declan removed your pet copper, so you're probably not getting the news on the hour like you used to. So, here's the news,' Monroe's voice started to gain a Glaswegian twang as his temper flared. 'I will tear down this poxy little boxing club and stick you behind bars so fast you won't even have time to change shirts.'

Johnny stared at Monroe. The whole room stayed silent.

'All you had to say was please,' Johnny said. 'I'm a reasonable man. And I don't want a grieving son to learn such things about a parental figure.' He turned and walked back into the office, but stopped at the door to it, still looking away.

'But you come back in here again with this attitude, and I will gut you like a pig and lace you into one of my heavy bags. By the time anyone finds you, they won't recognise your face. Understand?'

But Monroe didn't hear Johnny's threats, for he had already left the boxing club.

25

LAST RITES

ANDY MAC COULDN'T WATCH THE NEWS. TODAY IT HAD BEEN mainly continuing reports of the upcoming Conservative leadership battle, but with nobody actively entering it yet, all that could be discussed by the newsreader and some "expert" that Andy had never heard of before was hearsay and rumours, talks about how the party needed a fresh face while shilling old faces for opinions. And of course, as most of the hearsay and rumours were about Charles Baker, as while Andy watched, Baker was being mentioned constantly. The other candidates in the rumour mill, Kent MP Nigel Dickinson, who was a teeny bit to the left of UKIP, and Tamara Banks, who seemed to be the living reincarnation of Margaret Thatcher wearing Prada, were mentioned almost as a courtesy, but it was Charles Baker everyone spoke of.

Charles sodding Baker.

And then the news had moved to a murder enquiry; a body found in a wood not more than ten miles from here. The identity was unannounced as yet, but Andy knew that it was only a matter of time before the world knew that Sebastian Payne was dead and that Andy Mac was the murderer. Even if it couldn't be proven, even if the police were swinging in the dark like that damned DI Walsh was, the public would form their own opinions. The news would leap onto it like buzzards on a corpse. Just like Charles Baker was the "news-worthy" candidate for the election, Andy Mac was a target that many people would delight in tearing down. In the face of public opinion, YouTube would most likely turn from him, his videos would be de-monetised and God's Will TV would die.

His wife had known that something was the matter with him when he'd arrived home the previous night; there was no way that he could have disguised it as he was wet, stressed and sooty, having dumped the Land Rover down a back road on private land three miles west and walked home across the fields so as not to be seen by any late-night drivers. He'd only intended to dump the box in there; the land was wild and untamed, out of sight within the woods, and the land was long disused, becoming a bit of a fly-tipping ground over the last few months. He thought he could hide the box until he could find a better place to sink it. But when he arrived at the entrance to the land, from just looking at his vehicle he realised that the Land Rover was more of a hindrance than he'd hoped for.

It was covered in mud and scratches and the back bumper was way more scuffed and damaged than he had hoped for. If the police found it, they could easily match the paint marks and residue with a flight case. The inside of the Land Rover was also damaged from where he'd used the ratchets to pull it up. In the middle of the night and pumping with fear and adrenaline, Andy had decided that if Walsh returned – if any police returned in fact – there was no way that he'd be able to bluff his way out of the truth. And so, he had set fire to it, just like he had done the box earlier that evening. And leaving the Land Rover burning, he'd walked home through the fields.

He'd told his wife that there were some problems with the channel, that he was being targeted online and needed to change the narrative of his life. It wasn't the first time that hate groups had targeted him, and he knew that having seen this in the past, his wife would most likely believe him this time also. Explaining that he'd struck someone on the main road – not killed them, but enough to force him to drive from the scene – he said that if the press found out they'd use it to attack him, to take away everything he had. That *they* had. His wife liked the things that they had and she really didn't want to go back to any kind of prior, less affluent life, and so she agreed to state that he had driven the Tesla back that night, giving him an alibi for the fictional motoring incident, unaware that she was giving him an out for a far worse crime. And he'd contacted his team at God's Will TV, asking them to pick up something from the Land Rover, giving them the opportunity to learn for themselves that it was missing and call the police. This way he had at least one degree of separation.

But then Walsh had returned, and the detective knew, he damn well knew that Andy had killed Sebastian. He'd even told Andy how he believed it had happened and had been exact on every step of the crime. Andy knew that it was a matter of time before Walsh and others came for him. Maybe even that night.

He had to get away now.

There was a number that he had in the back of a book in his study; a number that he hadn't called, hadn't needed to call in years. It was her number. *The bitch*. He didn't want to dial it, but there was nothing more that he could do. He was one step away from a life in jail. Of losing everything.

He choked back a sob as he dialled it. It was answered on the third ring.

'Well, you've been a little ray of light recently,' she said as she answered. 'I've been monitoring everything that the police have learned about Sebastian's murder. What the hell were you thinking?'

'It was an accident,' Andy whispered, ensuring that nobody else in the house could hear him speak. 'I gave in to my needs. It won't happen again.'

'You're damn right it won't happen again,' the woman continued. 'After all I did to get you going, the money I funded you with ...'

'I paid you back!' Andy snapped. 'Don't you dare throw that on me!'

'How about I throw another death on you then?' The voice was calm. Andy slumped; he knew she was right. She was right ever since she showed him the necklace in the envelope and explained what he had done that night.

'I need you to get me out of here,' he whispered. 'Please, I have money.'

'And where would you go? The police will be coming for you anytime now.'

Andy glanced around his study, looking for inspiration. 'I could go and be a missionary,' he said. 'I could go somewhere remote, Francine.'

'And somewhere extradition free, I'm assuming?' Francine Pearce chuckled. 'Face it, Andy. You've screwed up. Your base needs have ruined everything. Your wife, your children? They'll be pulled through the court case. They'll be hounded for the rest of their lives. How could they not have known? How could they have stayed beside him?'

Andy started to cry softly. 'Help them,' he said.

There was a long pause down the line, as if Francie Pearce was coming to a decision.

'I can help them,' she said. 'But I can't help you, Andy. You have to make this right, somehow.'

'And how do I do that?' Andy snapped, looking around nervously in case he had woken his wife. His eyes widened as he realised what was being insinuated. 'I can't commit suicide! That's a mortal sin!'

'Oh, Andy. As if you haven't sinned enough,' Francine replied. 'You think you're still going to Heaven after what you've done? To Vicky, to Sebastian, to Sarah? How many commandments do you need to break before you realise you're going straight to Hell?'

Her tone softened. 'Think of it like this,' she said. 'It'll be quick. Easy. All your fears, all your concerns will melt away. No more secrets. No more being chased. And I'll personally ensure your family won't be touched by this. They'll live the rest of their lives in the manner they're accustomed to. They'll be okay, Andrew.'

Andy Mac wiped the tears from his eyes. 'What do I need to do?' he said, his voice shaking, but resolute.

Francine Pearce told him.

WHEN THEY'D MOVED INTO THE HOUSE, ANDY HAD DEMANDED that the basement be converted into a home gym. Being on TV meant that he was constantly being scrutinised, examined by the masses and he needed to ensure that he looked healthy; that he looked radiant at all times. He would attend virtual spin bike classes and had three different personal trainers on speed dial in London. And when he was home, he needed to ensure that he carried on with this regime, even if it was in a modified basement.

The basement itself was painted in an off-white colour called *Polished Pebble*. The floor was covered in those black, rubber mats that came in squares and jigsawed together to make a complete flooring. One of the walls was a full-length mirror, while the facing wall had two flat-screen televisions screwed onto it: one in front of the treadmill, and the other in front of another spin bike. Both were constantly linked to one of the religious cable channels with the sound off. Andy didn't watch them for fun when running or cycling; this was more reconnaissance on the enemy.

There was a weight rack and a pull-up tower beside the televisions and resistance bands and water bottles were against the far wall, a rowing machine and an elliptical trainer beside them. Andy was proud of this gym. It was more stocked out than half of the ones he attended while in London.

Grabbing a resistance band, he reached up, looping it around the very top of the pull-up bar, keeping it nice and tight as he tied it down. It was so high that he had to half-step onto a Pilates ball to ensure he could reach it. Using his hand to steady himself, he felt, one last time, the letter in his pocket.

They would be safe.

He looped the other end of the resistance band, ensuring it was tight, opening it as wide as he could. It was the hardest one to work with in his gym as there was barely any give in it. Even his full weight wouldn't stretch it.

They would be safe with him gone.

Pulling at the loop he dragged it over his head, already feeling the tightness at his throat as it retracted, the rubber biting into his neck. He wobbled a moment on the Pilates ball, holding the bar to steady himself.

He wasn't ready to go yet.

'Lord,' he said, looking up to the ceiling. 'I'm sorry for what I did. I truly am. And I hope that you'll see the good things in my life before you—'

He didn't finish.

The ball slipped out from under his feet and Andy Mac fell, the noose around his neck snapping tight as he jerked to a stop, his feet no more than an inch from the tower's floor. He grabbed at the band, his eyes bulging, suddenly scared, worried that God himself had moved the ball, that he was going to Hell ... But it was too late. The band was too tight. He couldn't get purchase. He couldn't stop this now.

His dead eyes were now wide and staring, his face contorted in a last expression of pain and terror, seemingly watching himself in the mirror as he rotated slowly, hanged by the neck. And this is how he was found, an hour later when his wife led the police, finally here to arrest him, down to the basement.

Andy Mac would never preach again.

SHAUN DONNAL ROCKED BACK AND FORTH ON THE BENCH IN HIS cell, pulling the blanket that he'd been given tightly around him. This was a bad idea. He shouldn't be here. He should be back on the streets, hiding, ensuring that he wasn't found. Sally would—

No. Sally wouldn't send him any money. Apparently Sally had never sent him any money. His family didn't even know if he was alive or not. Shaun had assumed that by seeing the money going out of the account, they'd at least know he was safe; now however he didn't know what to do. Should he contact them? Let them know that he was alive?

No. Because then Francine would move on them. Shaun's family would be hurt. And he'd hurt them enough over the years.

Shaun thought back to what DI Walsh had said. Could it be true? Had he believed a lie for twenty years, and taken the blame for someone else's murder?

If he had, then someone was going to pay for the last five years of hell. And he knew exactly who that someone was.

The night hadn't been that bad, actually. They'd fed him, even allowed him to use a shower, providing him with a little travel-sized shampoo to wash what was left of his hair and beard. It wasn't combed, just finger-straightened, but he felt cleaner than he had in ages.

He didn't have a watch on, but Shaun had always had a pretty accurate internal clock, and this clock told him that currently it was about 5am. It was the midst of the graveyard shift. The pubs were closed, the nightclubs emptied. Anyone who was being brought in from either of these would already be here. This was the time for it to be as silent as the grave until the dawn in an hour or two started the Saturday rush.

But it wasn't silent as the grave.

He could hear locks being turned, of heavy doors being opened. He could hear whispered words being spoken and footsteps walking down the corridor. Footsteps stopping at his door.

He pushed himself back against the wall as the door to his cell opened. A policeman leaned in. 'Sorry to wake you,' he said, the tone of his voice insinuating that he wasn't sorry at all. 'But your ride is here.'

'DI Walsh wasn't supposed to arrive until morning,' Shaun said nervously.

'Mate, it is morning,' the policeman said, still standing by the door. 'He probably wants to get you out of here before the Saturday shops open. Chop chop.'

Shaun reluctantly rose from his bench, placing the blanket down. The policeman didn't know who he was. Nobody knew who he was. Only DI Walsh and his department knew his true identity. If they were here to take him this early in the morning then something bad must have happened.

'Is everything okay?' he asked as they walked down the corridor.

The policeman shrugged. 'I thought I'd be doing day shifts by now, but apart from that I assume so.'

They didn't walk through the station, instead, they walked through the loading bay, out to where the police cars were parked at the back. Shaun could see that the dawn was approaching, the sky lightening into a hazy turquoise before the morning sun.

There were two detectives standing by a grey car, waiting for him. One was an Indian woman, the other a young man.

'DC Fitzwarren and DS Kapoor,' the young man said. 'We work with DI Walsh.'

Shaun nodded, looking around. 'Is he here?' he asked. Kapoor shook her head.

'What about Monroe?' Shaun asked again. He trusted Walsh, but Monroe was still an unknown entity here. *Christ, he needed a drink.*

'No Monroe either,' Kapoor replied as they signed the

paperwork. Shaun looked to the car; in the back seat, just out of sight of the policemen, he could see that someone was sitting there.

'So, it's just the two of you?' he asked. Fitzwarren looked back to him.

'What is this, bloody twenty questions?' he snapped. 'No, there's nobody else here. Shut up and wait for a moment.'

Shaun felt a sinking sensation in his stomach. Yet again he'd been lied to. This wasn't the reception he'd been promised. These weren't the police he'd been promised.

'It's just that Monroe said that she'd be here personally,' he said, watching Fitzwarren.

'Well, she's busy—' Fitzwarren paused.

'Oh, you little bastard,' he said.

The policeman that had brought Shaun down to the car looked up from the paperwork.

'There's no need for that kind of language,' he said, but Fitzwarren wasn't listening. Instead, he'd pulled an extending baton out of his pocket and had turned to Shaun. Kapoor too had a weapon out, but now Shaun was ready. This was a set up. He wasn't going anywhere. The back door of the vehicle opened, and the man with the rimless glasses emerged.

'Get in the car, Donnal,' he said. 'Don't make this more painful than it needs to be.'

Shaun looked to the policeman, now staring confused at this third arrival.

'They're not police!' Shaun cried. 'They're going to kill me!'

The policeman didn't get a chance to reply as Fitzwarren swung his baton up hard, catching the policeman in the throat. But, as the policeman fell to the floor clutching at it, sirens started to blare out.

'Goddammit!' the man shouted. 'Just kill him now and be done with it!'

But it was too late. The doors were opening and more police stormed out, several pulling out yellow X26 tasers as they did so. The man with the rimless glasses swore, looking around for Shaun, but the target had gone.

'We're done!' he cried. 'Go!'

The two fake officers leapt into the car and, with a squeal of rubber, it reversed at speed out of the car park, sliding into the early morning traffic, leaving behind a small gathering of incredibly confused policemen who were now wondering who the hell their late-night guest really was.

And two streets away, hiding in a doorway and holding his breath, almost as if the simple act of breathing would give his position away, Shaun Donnal waited for his heartbeat to calm down as one line repeated itself over and over again.

'Just kill him now and be done with it!'

They were really going to kill him. They'd given up on just scaring him. Shaun shook himself from the memory and was about to carry on walking, when one of the televisions in the window of the shop he was currently using as cover caught his eye. It was a news channel. The sound was off, and it was showing something to do with American politics on the screen, but the news ticker along the bottom of the screen tightened his chest.

YOUTUBE PREACHER 'ANDY MAC' FOUND DEAD IN
AVEBURY HOME – BELIEVED TO BE SUICIDE

Andy was dead.

Shaun would have been next.

There was only one person who could have done this.

And they would have had help. It was time to take the whole bloody lot of them down in one go. To cut the head off the snake, in fact.

Shaun looked around. From the road signs he could see, he was in a suburb of North London; it would take a couple of hours to get back to King's Cross, where his rucksack, gathered back up after his beating yesterday had been hidden somewhere safe before he'd made his way to Hurley and DI Walsh.

And in that rucksack was the gun he had stolen from Francine Pearce's car.

The police weren't going to be able to help him; they hadn't even been able to keep him safe for twelve hours. No, it was time to end this, before Pearce and the man with the rimless glasses found a way to end him and ensure that he was also nothing more than a line on a news tickertape, just like poor Andrew.

Gathering his courage, Shaun stepped out onto the street and headed south.

26

POST MORTEM

DECLAN HAD WOKEN UP AT 7.30AM WHEN THE CALL CAME through from the North London police station that he had visited the previous night. It was muddled but seemed to be that Shaun Donnal had manufactured some kind of escape, using fake police to distract the officers on watch.

To be honest, there was no way that Shaun Donnal would have been able to manufacture anything in his current state of mind, not to mention the fact that only Declan and Monroe had known where he was. But with Shaun now gone and nothing to be done about it until he either resurfaced or contacted the number Declan had left with him, Declan decided instead to shower, dress and, skipping breakfast, grabbed his father's file and drove into London before the Saturday morning traffic kicked in.

He'd just passed Heston Services on the M4 when Monroe called to give him the news about Andy Mac. And because of this, it was a sombre and thoughtful Declan Walsh who arrived at Temple Inn at 9am to find that even though it was a weekend, he was still the last officer in. Downstairs

Doctor Marcos and her assistant, DC Davey – a tall, slim bespectacled woman with frizzy ginger hair – were knee deep in microscopes, while on the first floor Anjli was poring through old files as Billy and Monroe were watching security footage on Billy's monitor. Even Trix was in, strangely silent, working on some file entry in the corner of the room.

Looking at the people in the office, Declan forced himself to smile, to look as if nothing was wrong.

But everything was. Because there was a traitor right in front of him.

Monroe, seeing him waved him over. 'Come look at this.'

The CCTV was from the police station car park. It was blurry, mainly because it was early in the morning and the lights around the station were turning off, but Declan could see two people – a man and a woman talking to a policeman –while Shaun Donnal stood to the side.

'He doesn't even look like me,' Billy snapped. 'Christ, his suit looks like it's polyester.'

Declan looked to Monroe.

'Shaun Donnal didn't break out, no matter what they say,' Monroe explained. 'Firstly, Donnal didn't know where he was and secondly, he hadn't made any calls. But at around five in the morning these two officers arrived to take him.'

He pointed to the screen.

'Meet DC Fitzwarren and DS Kapoor, as they identified themselves to the police on site.'

'They used our names?' Declan whistled. No wonder Billy was annoyed. 'That's ballsy, to walk right in.'

'They had the paperwork and everything,' Billy muttered. 'Whoever did this was very well organised. Like James Bond organised.'

'Except Shaun didn't seem to believe it,' Monroe

pointed to the screen where, moving back from the car, Shaun was obviously distressed. There was no sound with the footage, but Declan could see a third man emerge from the car.

It was blurry, but he'd recognise the man with the rimless glasses anywhere.

'That's the bastard that sucker-punched me, and who was at my dad's house last night,' he said. 'Shaun mentioned he'd had a run in with him before as well.'

'Well, he definitely recognises him,' Billy indicated the screen where Shaun stared at the new arrival. But it didn't last long; the fake Billy struck the policeman as other officers ran out of the building with what looked like standard police issue tasers in their hands. Shaun took this opportunity to run, while the three imposters leaped into the car and drove off at speed.

'Shaun said that bastard works for Francine Pearce,' Declan said.

Monroe nodded. 'Well, we can have a chat with her when she eventually agrees to come in,' he replied, noting Doctor Marcos and DC Davey emerging from the stairs. 'Until then, let's have a chat in the briefing room.'

Nodding to Anjli to join them, Declan and Billy followed Monroe, Doctor Marcos and her assistant into the briefing room. Shutting the door behind them, Anjli sat down at the desk beside Declan, resting her head in her hands for a moment. He glanced to her.

'Are you hungover?' he asked. She threw back a weak grin.

'Billy likes very expensive and very drinkable wines,' she simply whispered.

'So, we have some new developments,' Monroe said.

'Andy Mac has committed suicide, which obviously puts a massive crimp into our case.'

'How so?' Declan asked. 'I mean, obviously, but surely we have more from Baker and Donnal's testimonies?'

'Because he apparently had a full confession on his person when he hanged himself in his gym,' Monroe replied. 'Stating that not only did he kill Sebastian and hide the body, but also giving the location of where he hid the Land Rover. And while he was at it, he also admitted to the murder of Victoria Davies, and even threw in the murder of Sarah Hinksman as well, claiming that this was why Sebastian had attacked him.'

Declan scratched at his chin. 'He wasn't suicidal when I left him,' he said. 'If anything, he was looking like he wanted a fight. He genuinely thought he could beat this, or at least keep it going long enough to find some other escape route. Not this.'

'Well, we'll need to work out what was going on in his mind pretty damned quick,' Monroe said. 'The case is being mothballed again.'

'What?' Now it was Billy's turn to reply. 'You can't be serious!'

'I am, laddie. Sebastian Payne's murder was never ours. It was Newbury plod's. We were following the murder of Victoria Davies, and one of our main suspects killed himself after confessing to it. Powers that be are happy to let this pass.'

'That's rubbish,' muttered Billy as he slumped back into his chair.

'Oh, I agree,' Monroe said. 'And that's why I said it'd take us twenty-four hours to tie everything up.'

'Does that really work?' Declan looked around. 'I mean, that just sounds like a movie plot.'

'Of course, it never works,' Monroe replied harshly. 'They gave us six hours. Which means that we have until football kicks off this afternoon to work out who killed Victoria Davies, who killed Sarah Hinksman, who tried to abduct Shaun Donnal this morning and now who killed Andy Mac, because that's the dodgiest suicide I've seen in thirty years.'

'It could have been Charles Baker,' Doctor Marcos suggested. 'DI Walsh's suggestion to check the DNA was right. Baker was Payne's father.'

'Too flimsy. We need more,' Monroe was pacing now. Declan raised a hand. 'You don't need to ask permission here, laddie.'

Declan rose, walking to the front and turned to look at the others. Through the glass he could see Trix, still on her phone, music in her earbuds as she rocked along.

'I think I've worked it out,' he said. 'But I need to check something. And I wanted to do it when everyone was here.'

'Christ, it's bloody Hercule Poirot,' Monroe muttered. Declan looked to him.

'Could you phone Anthony Farringdon, please?' he asked. 'And could you put it on speakerphone?'

'Well, this is a bit odd, but okay.' Monroe pulled out his phone, dialling.

He waited.

'Anthony,' he eventually said into it. 'I was; you were? Oh.' He turned the speaker on.

'I emailed the photo that Billy sent to me over to Mister Farringdon this morning,' Declan explained, nodding to Billy. 'Could you put it on the screen?'

Billy nodded, tapping on the computer tablet beside him.

The photo of the 1997 Election's new members of Parliament and their aides appeared on the screen.

'Billy sent this to me as it showed Baker and Hinksman getting chummy,' Declan said, tapping on the area where Sarah and Charles were seen laughing. 'But we were so busy looking at them, we didn't look at the others. Mister Farringdon, the woman on the far left, with the black hair and the cap on. Do you remember who she was?'

There was a pause down the line as Farringdon examined the image.

'Frankie Wilson,' he eventually said. 'Hinksman's assistant.'

'Thanks, Anthony, you've been a massive help,' Declan said, indicating for Monroe to disconnect. Walking to the wall, he used the touch screen of the plasma to enlarge the image of Wilson.

'This is Frankie Wilson, the assistant to Sarah Hinksman,' he looked to the officers in the room. 'She booked the rooms for Hinksman and Donnal, she arranged the adoption of Sebastian. We've seen her before in other photos of Sarah, but we've never had a clear view of her face.'

Tap. He brought up another image. A stern, older woman with black hair.

'This is Francine Pearce, taken from the Pearce Associates website.'

Monroe looked at the images. 'Jesus, it's the same woman.'

Declan nodded. 'We've been looking at the wrong women,' he said, tapping the screen again and opening a file image. The photo that Derby police station sent the previous night appeared. 'This is the mugshot of Susan Devington that was taken the night that Victoria was murdered. As you can see, it's close, but it's not her.'

'She used a double to give her an alibi?' Anjli was surprised at this. 'You think Susan was the killer? Why would she want her own sister dead?'

'Well, I wondered that too,' Declan replied. 'Until I realised after reading the arrest file that it was Francine Pearce that bailed her out the next day. We all missed it because she used her other name back then. Frankie Wilson, as Frankie is a common nickname for Francine.'

'She changed her surname?' Billy was already looking through the files. 'We have no knowledge of that.'

'That's because our reports and files were tampered with before we received them,' Declan said. 'My father's ones, however, were still intact. Francine Pearce had recently divorced before starting with Devington Industries, where she began her affair with Michael Davies. Her married name was Wilson.'

'Frankie Wilson, Sarah Hinksman's loyal assistant,' Monroe said. 'Wait, what do you mean, our files were tampered with?'

'Oh, that's simple,' Declan said. 'We have a mole in the department. Someone who's been working for Pearce from the start, who ensured that we'd get the letter, and who led us by the nose to where Pearce wanted us.'

Everyone in the room now started to look around, their faces filled with suspicion.

'Don't worry,' Declan smiled. 'It's nobody in here. It's Trix.'

As he watched her through the glass, he saw Trix jerk in her chair, glancing nervously at the briefing room.

'I know you have a bug in here, and I know you can hear

everything we're saying,' Declan waved to her. 'It's why you have those bloody ear buds in all the time. So, I suggest you get your arse in here and explain everything before I call the two Middle Temple guards I borrowed when I came in this morning, who are waiting just outside, and have you brought in by force.'

Slowly and shakily Trix got to her feet, looking to the main entrance.

'You won't manage it,' Declan shook his head. 'Feel free to have a go, though.'

Anjli opened the door as Trix walked into the room.

'I think you need to sit down, lassie,' Monroe grumbled as he looked to Declan. 'Are you sure about this?'

'I wasn't until just now,' Declan admitted. 'I actually thought it could have been you.' Monroe's eyebrow raised, so Declan continued. 'I only told you I was going to my Tottenham apartment, and the man was waiting for me. Only you and I knew where Shaun was, yet somehow someone was able to move things around. It was a small list.' He looked back to Trix.

'Until I spoke to Derby, and they explained how their work experience girl found the letter while filing,' he said. 'They couldn't remember the name of the girl but remembered that all she did was sit on social media all day. And, after they sent the letter on, she stopped arriving.'

'Doesn't mean that's me.' Trix's expression was belligerent.

Declan nodded. 'True, so let's go through everything. Our records have been tampered with; and you've been working on the record entry system all week. We're an antiquated system here, and it's easy to delete what's not required. And let's face it, by making a point of not knowing what

HOLMES2 was, you ensured that we'd all dismiss any computer skills that you had. Then, you conveniently took the phone call that brought the first footage of Shaun Donnal to us. When I called to let the Guv know I was going back to my apartment, you took the call. And when I arrived, there was a man waiting for me.'

'Oh, come on,' Trix complained. 'Answering the phone isn't a crime.'

'True, but you made a point of checking which house I was going to,' Declan said. 'The next day, when you saw my face, you seemed concerned. You even said, *"they shouldn't have done that to you,"* as if you knew who "they" were. I thought it was compassion, but now I realise it was guilt.'

'Susan Devington knew to come here,' Monroe thought aloud. 'And Charles Baker knew that we were visiting him even before we did. Have you bugged all of the rooms?'

'They haven't bugged downstairs,' Doctor Marcos stated. 'We do a bug sweep every morning.'

Declan almost wanted to ask Doctor Marcos why she did this but decided to shelve that thought for the moment. Trix glanced around the room as if looking for allies, and then like a deflated balloon all the fight left her body as she slumped back into the chair.

'He was supposed to warn you, not attack you,' she said softly. 'He was supposed to make you think he was Government; make you look at Charles Baker more.'

'Why were we being aimed at Charles Baker?' Billy asked.

'Because that was the plan all along,' Declan said. 'Revenge.'

Trix nodded. 'Ms Pearce wanted to get revenge on them all for what they did to Sarah Hinksman. I never knew why, just that I was to ensure you followed the breadcrumbs.'

'What was the endgame?' Doctor Marcos asked. 'Destroy the reps of Andy Mac and Baker?'

'Probably,' Declan replied. 'However, Pearce had all three of them under her thumb, so something had to have set this off.'

Trix nodded again. 'Michael Davies had information, all locked up in a vault. She always had a fear that if one of them worked out where it was, if they got in there, they could destroy everything she'd built up.'

'So, this was a scorched-earth ploy,' Monroe mused. 'Remove all targets, make them so distrusted that no matter what they said later, it'd never work.'

'I think so.'

'But why?' Anjli looked around. 'I mean I understand revenge for what happened to Michael, but the whole Hinksman thing—'

'I think I've worked that bit out.' Billy looked up from his laptop at Trix. 'You might have deleted files to stop us learning that Francine Pearce was Frankie Wilson, but there are other ways to search. I'm in the Law Society database.' He shared his laptop's display onto the plasma screen. It was a list of names and years.

'When people get their law degrees, they then have to do two years on a Legal Practice Course,' he read from a page on his phone. 'After that, and after they complete a period of recognised training they collect their certificate and are admitted to the roll of solicitors. And right here in 1993, we have written down on the roll Francine Wilson, *née* Pearce.' He highlighted a list of names. 'You'll also see here that in the same year her sister, Sarah Pearce was admitted to the roll of solicitors as well.'

'So, Francine became a solicitor while she was married.'

Monroe nodded. 'That's why we didn't link the PA Pearce with the solicitor Wilson.'

'And Sarah Pearce became a solicitor before she married,' Declan said in realisation. 'She married Liam Hinksman at the start of 1994.'

'God,' Anjli looked to Trix. 'Sarah Hinksman and Francine Pearce were *sisters*?'

'Makes sense,' Declan replied as he picked up his notebook, opening it. 'Sarah becomes an MP, and Frankie joins her in an advisory position.'

'Still doesn't explain why she ended up working for the Devingtons.' Monroe looked to Trix, who refused to catch his eye.

'I think I might have that as well,' Declan said. 'Something that Andy Mac had said yesterday about speaking ill of the dead. I think Victoria Davies was the one who spiked Sarah's drink with ketamine.'

There was a silence in the room as the others took this in.

'Andy Mac said that Victoria was well versed in such drugs. And she and Michael were grooming Shaun to be their big socialist replacement for Blair. I think that Hinksman turned up to reveal Baker as the father of her child and Victoria, thinking it was Shaun about to be revealed, tried to find a way to stop her. I don't think she expected Sarah to drive. But either way, Sarah dies. This is why Victoria becomes the shoulder for Shaun to cry on; guilt for the manslaughter.'

'Somehow, Frankie finds this out,' Monroe was speaking now. 'She's not known by Michael and Victoria and so she joins Devington under her maiden name and over the next year gets close to Michael, looking for a way to destroy them both.'

'She reconnects with Baker around now,' Billy added, flipping another document, a typed statement, to the screen. 'Doctor Khai sent his statement in last night and says that Baker and a solicitor named Wilson were the ones who bought him off. Therefore, Michael thinks he's sterile when in fact he's as virile as ever.'

'Baker sees this as a way of removing Victoria and Shaun,' Anjli was writing in her notebook now as she spoke. 'If Victoria becomes pregnant then Michael will believe it's an affair, even if it's actually his child.'

'Francine carries on with her mission of revenge, and turns on Victoria,' Declan continued. 'She makes alliances with Susan, most likely showing her how much of a nightmare daddy's company is becoming with those two in charge. Susan agrees to help. Francine ensures that all three MPs are given something to cause them to black-out, and after Victoria dies, Francine uses a necklace to convince each of them that they were the murderer. And for fifteen years, they each do whatever she and Susan desire, because if they don't they each believe that their careers will be ruined.'

'But if Baker became PM, he would have more powers,' Monroe mused. 'He would be able to find the necklace and remove it. Also, with the information Michael found. He'd be able to open the security box.'

'Maybe Francine didn't want Baker to go that high?' Anjli added. 'Maybe he was more use to her in the Cabinet?'

'Either way, we know that things have gone horribly wrong,' Declan finished. 'Andy Mac wasn't supposed to kill Sebastian. I don't think Francine planned for Sebastian to return after he was adopted. I think he was working with someone else.'

'So, what now?' Monroe turned to Trix. 'What were you supposed to do next?'

Trix didn't reply, as if unsure what the answer actually was, but she was saved by Declan's phone as it rang.

'DI Walsh,' he answered. After a moment, he clicked the phone to speaker.

'Sorry Shaun, could you say that again?' he asked.

The voice of Shaun Donnal, half crazed and furious spoke down the line.

'I'm ending this, Walsh,' he said. 'I'm taking all the traitors to the tower and I'm cutting their heads off!' There was a background noise, as if Shaun was driving.

'Shaun, don't do anything stupid,' Declan said.

'They killed Andy!' Shaun hissed. 'I've got one of their guns. The man with the glasses and his buddy. And they won't kill me before I BFA their asses. You hear me? It ends now, right where it started!'

And with that the phone was disconnected. Declan looked to Billy, who glanced up from his laptop in horror. 'That was Charles Baker's personal mobile,' he said.

'Jesus Christ on a cross!' Monroe exclaimed. 'And now we're gonna have more bloody deaths!'

'I don't think so,' Declan smiled. 'Do you trust me?'

'Do we have a bloody choice?'

Declan looked to Billy again. 'He's left the phone on, right?'

'I'm tracking it now. He's heading south, down the ...' he trailed off. 'He's heading to Devington House.'

Declan nodded. 'I thought as much,' he said, looking to Trix. 'You've got one chance to get out of this mess. You text your boss and you tell her that I'm on my way right now, alone, to arrest Susan Devington for Victoria's murder. You tell her to get there before me.'

Trix nodded, typing in a text, pressing send. Declan took the phone from her, passing it to Billy.

'Check where that's gone to, and who else has contacted it recently,' he ordered as he looked back to Monroe. 'Very soon the Parliamentary Protection plod will realise that their next Prime Minister is missing, and they'll race after him. I need you to delay them somehow, Guv. Call in favours, whatever.'

'So, you want Baker, Donnal, Pearce and Devington at the house?' Monroe frowned. 'Why?'

'Because Shaun's going to take them all up to the roof,' Declan said with a smile. 'And then just like *Poirot,* I'm going to arrive and let them tell me what really happened.'

27

AGAINST THE CLOCK

CHARLES BAKER WAS A MAN OF VERY FEW HABITS, BUT THE ones he had were ingrained over the years. Every Saturday he would get up at 7am, drive to a small, unobtrusive gym about two miles away and spend a couple of hours running on the treadmill. He hated running on the street as he was always harassed by paparazzi, protestors and ungrateful constituents. He lived on the third floor of a rather exclusive apartment block and they had banned treadmills above the ground floor and to be brutally honest he was simply too busy to go down to the Parliamentary gym, as he could guarantee that for every ten minutes he spent in there, five of them would be spent telling backbenchers to sod off and leave him be.

So instead, he found other ways to keep fit during the week, and every Saturday he would run a half marathon on a treadmill, staring out at the front at the small non-league football club that was situated beside the gym. Sometimes footballers from the club would join him, preparing for match fitness, but they didn't talk to him. Nobody there knew who he was, and that was exactly how he liked it.

Part of the plan to keep this as off the books as possible was that he did this journey alone. As a high-ranking member of the cabinet, he was supposed to have Specialist Protection bodyguards at all times; that stopped about three weeks after he took the position when he realised that running on a treadmill while non-uniformed muscle glared menacingly at anyone who approached didn't really help with the anonymity. And so, he'd joined a new club under a fake name while paying for a year in advance and informed his protection unit that Saturdays effectively didn't start for them until 10am. It was a plan that had worked well for close to a year.

But Charles Baker was regretting it right now.

He'd arrived at the gym as usual and was happy to put out a personal best on the treadmill. He'd taken a shower, walked back to the car in the gym's underground car park and had prepared to drive back to his London residence. He had a fete he was supposed to be attending that afternoon that he didn't really want to go to, but he knew that hearts and minds of voters were important, especially while trying to grab the prize within his grasp. He'd also been told that Nigel and Tamara were also attending fetes and fairs that day, so he knew that if he didn't, he might as well kiss goodbye to holding the news cycle. In fact, he was so absorbed in the ways that he could use the fete publicity to his advantage, he completely missed Shaun Donnal walking up behind him as he opened the door to his car.

He did however acknowledge the gun rammed into his back.

'Hello, Charlie,' Shaun hissed into his ear. 'Time for a drive.'

Charles hadn't argued. What was the point when a paranoid drunk had a gun aimed at you? He simply climbed into the driver's seat as Shaun clambered into the back. Shaun had demanded his phone and then, once Charles was about to start the car he felt Shaun move about in the back and then a noose of some kind of leather was looped around his neck, pulling his head against the headrest of the car. He wanted to pull at it, suddenly scared that Shaun had finally lost it and was going to strangle him in the vehicle but, before he could, it loosened.

'Don't worry, I'm just keeping you in the seat,' Shaun hissed, again into his ear. 'It's just my belt. If you pull forward? I pull back. So just sit calmly and keep your hands on the wheel at ten to two.'

'What do you want, Shaun?' Charles asked. 'Money?'

'Did you hear about Andrew?' Shaun leaned in again. 'Stupid bastard only went and hanged himself last night.' He pulled on the belt, momentarily doing the same to Charles. The noose loosened again, and Charles gasped in a lung-full of air as the *click* of a gun cocking was audible behind him.

'Maybe I'll just shoot you here,' Shaun said, almost as if talking to someone else. 'Nah. Not yet. We're going to see some old friends first.'

'Where are you taking me?' Charles asked.

'Start the car, Charlie,' Shaun said, almost laughing. 'We're going to see your ex-girlfriend.'

They'd been driving for about ten minutes, Shaun barking directions like some kind of manic sat nav before Charles realised that they were heading for Devington

House. Shaun had used Charles's phone then, calling some number that he'd read off a card in his hand.

'I'm ending this, Walsh,' he said into it. 'I'm taking all the traitors to the tower and I'm cutting their heads off!'

Charles assumed that Shaun was talking to DI Walsh, one of the two detectives that had spoken to him that week. This was good. The police knowing that Shaun was calling from Baker's phone would surely bring the cavalry once they tracked it. All he had to do now was keep calm, drive to wherever they were going, allow Shaun to act out whatever weird suicide fantasy this was and stand by as the mad bastard was shot by armed police snipers.

The image made him smile.

'They killed Andy!' Shaun hissed. 'I've got one of their guns. The man with the glasses and his buddy. And they won't kill me before I BFA their asses. You hear me? It ends now, right where it started!'

With that Shaun tossed the phone aside. Charles was happy to see that it was still turned on.

They could still track him.

He could still find a way out of this.

As if reading his mind, Shaun leaned forwards.

'Did they tell you that you killed Victoria?' he asked. 'Did they show you the necklace, like they did me and Andy?'

Charles choked on a response, partly due to shock and partly due to the belt around his neck. Shaun started to laugh.

'Oh, you poor bastard,' he said, leaning back into the back seat, hand still holding the end of the belt. 'You're one step from being Prime Minister and you're still too stupid to realise you've been played from the start.'

Charles carried on driving, his eyes on the road. Soon they'd be at Devington House.

And soon this would end.

FRANCINE PEARCE RAN TO HER OWN CAR; THE MAN WITH THE rimless glasses alongside her.

'We should wait until support arrives!' he exclaimed. 'This could be dangerous. You need a plan, not just running into a fire like some—'

'A plan?' Francine stopped, glaring at the man with the rimless glasses. 'Like the one you enacted this morning? Like the one where you allowed Shaun Donnal to escape?' She opened the back passenger door. 'We don't need support. He's just one man and you took him out last time with two blows to the head and a knee swipe. This time you can finish the job.'

The man sighed with annoyance, but still clambered into the car behind the driver's wheel.

'At least take some protection,' he said as he leaned to the side, reaching under the passenger's seat.

He stopped as he grasped at air.

'Oh, that little bastard,' he hissed as he sat back up.

'Another problem?' Francine asked.

'Nothing I can't handle,' the man said.

'Good,' Francine replied. 'Then drive the bloody car now!'

The man with the rimless glasses slammed the car into first gear and with a roar of the engine, the car drove off down the London street, on its way to Devington House.

DECLAN'S AUDI WAS ALSO SPEEDING THROUGH LONDON; BUT Declan had the advantage of a blue light and a siren to get the Saturday morning traffic out of his way. Beside him sat Anjli, while behind working on a laptop, was Billy.

'Got an interesting link for you,' Billy said as he looked up. 'The number Trix texted was a number that Andy Mac called last night around 1am.'

'You sure?' Declan swerved around a Sainsbury's truck, beeping his horn as he raced over a crossroads.

'Yup, definitely the same number. No ID on who owns it, probably an old burner number, but they chatted for about ten minutes last night. I reckon this would have been an hour or so before he hanged himself.'

'Francine Pearce speaking to Andy Mac before he hanged himself feels to me more like Francine Pearce telling Andy Mac to hang himself,' Anjli muttered. 'Probably promised to look after his family if he fell on his sword.'

'Would explain why he confessed to everything, when we know he didn't kill at least one of the three,' Billy said, wincing as a car sped backwards past them. 'We hit a motorway soon, right?'

'Did we ever work out who Sebastian was texting the day he was murdered?'

'Another burner phone. Probably a journalist of some kind.'

Declan almost slammed the brakes on in realisation.

You should leave Andy for the press. We're already gunning for him on some less than savoury things.

'Do me a favour,' he said, keeping his voice calm. 'Send me the number.'

'Nobody answers it,' Billy replied.

'Humour me,' Declan insisted as his phone beeped. Anjli glanced at it.

'It's a text,' she said. 'Want me to read it?'

'Please,' Declan was concentrating on the road.

'It's Baker's phone, so it must be Shaun,' Anjli said. 'It's just a set of directions. Three steps east, fifteen feet north ...'

'Shaun's just given us his secret way into Devington House,' Declan said as the phone beeped again. 'What's he said now?'

Anjli looked at the phone. 'It's not Shaun,' she said, placing the phone back down. 'It's your ex-wife. She seems angry. Something about a day with your daughter?'

Declan swore. 'Tell her I'll be free by this afternoon.'

'What am I, your secretary?'

Declan glanced at Anjli. 'Do you want to steer while I do it?' he asked.

Reluctantly Anjli started typing on the phone while Declan pressed his foot on the pedal. He needed to finish this quickly, if only to keep Lizzie from killing him.

28

REMATCH

THE MAN WITH THE RIMLESS GLASSES PULLED UP OUTSIDE Devington House; the gates were open, the driveway inviting.

'What are you waiting for?' Francine hissed from the back seat. 'An invitation?'

'The gates are open,' he replied. 'They're never open.'

'Maybe the police are already here,' she snapped back. 'Maybe you weren't fast enough.'

The man sighed inwardly, driving through the gates and up to the house. There was another car on the driveway, the driver's door still open. It looked familiar, and Francine pursed her lips together as she saw it, making a *tch*ing sound.

'Bloody Baker's here,' she said. 'Why is he here? The last thing we want is Walsh turning up and finding the whole gang around.'

She got out of the car before it pulled to a halt, already walking to the main entrance as the man with the rimless glasses followed her. She stopped as a mobile phone fell from the roof, smashing on the gravel beside her. Looking up, she saw Susan Devington move back from the edge.

'Oh, for Christ's sake,' she muttered. 'She's on the bloody roof again.'

Pushing at the door, she found it unlocked. Entering the ornate hallway, she was struck by how empty it seemed.

'Where's the old man?' she asked as they walked through the hallway, her companion closing and bolting the door behind him.

'Day off?' he suggested. 'It is a Saturday.'

'That man will die in here,' Francine replied. 'He won't take time off. Look for him.' She started up the stairs. 'And make sure every entrance is locked. I want Walsh to be stuck outside.'

'And if he gets inside?' The man was already moving to the large windows, ensuring that they were locked.

'Well then you'll just have to do a better job on him than you did last time,' Francine muttered as she continued towards the ballroom, and the stairs at the back that led to the upper levels and the roof.

MONROE GAVE HIS MOST WINNING SMILE AS HE PULLED UP TO the SCO19 barracks.

'Alright lads?' he asked as the blue-capped policemen bustled around him, gathering equipment and readying their weapons. 'Looks like you're off on a hunt.'

'What do you want, Guv?' a Specialist Firearms Officer asked as he walked over. Monroe smiled warmly.

'Andrews, good to see you're moving up in the world,' he said. 'You the SFO of these fine chaps?'

'And what if I am?' Andrews was wary as he spoke to Monroe. He'd worked under him before joining the firearm unit and although he respected the DCI, he also didn't trust him fully.

'Got a treat for you,' Monroe said, pulling out a sheet of paper. 'Training mission. ASAP.'

Andrews looked at the sheet of paper. 'This is a to-do list, Guv.'

'It is? Oh, silly me,' Monroe kept the smile. 'Must have left the letter in the office. Too late to get it back. You'll have to take my word for it.'

'No offence, DCI Monroe, but I'm not taking your word for anything.' Andrews returned the paper. Monroe held his gaze.

'No offence, SFO Andrews, but I have an officer in grave danger and I need armed backup,' Monroe whispered. 'And if you don't help me, I'll ensure that people know exactly why I transferred you out of my department and how much you can probably be bought for.'

Andrews looked at Monroe. He knew the man; he knew Monroe never made light threats.

'Officer in danger?'

'Grave.'

'Right then!' Andrews shouted to his men. 'Suit up! We have a training exercise to get to!'

Monroe sighed. If Declan was wrong, Monroe would most likely be fired for this.

But then if Declan was wrong, he would most likely die.

DECLAN PULLED INTO DEVINGTON HOUSE WITH A SCREECH OF tyres. As the man with the rimless glasses had seen, but a few minutes earlier, the gate was wide open and strangely fore-boding. However, unlike the man with the rimless glasses Declan didn't pause, speeding through the gates and up the driveway, pulling to an abrupt stop beside Charles Baker's car, the gravel spraying up and chipping the paintwork. On the other side of the drive was a black car, its windows blacked out, most likely Francine Pearce's.

'She's here already,' he said, already exiting the car and running to the main doors. They were locked. Stepping back, he looked at the house.

'There could be a back entrance,' he said to Billy and Anjli as they ran up to him. 'Check for any entrances into the building, and when Monroe gets here help him keep Special Branch at bay.'

'What about you?' Anjli asked.

Declan held up his phone. 'I'm going to see if I can find the secret entrance,' he said with a smile.

'But what if Shaun Donnal shoots you?' Anjli replied.

'He won't,' Declan replied with the assurance of someone who knew something that the others didn't. 'I think I know what he intends to do.' And with that he started off to the side of the house at a jog.

Billy looked to Anjli, a concerned expression on his face.

'Yeah, shoot everyone,' he said.

DECLAN COUNTED THE FLAGSTONES ON THE LEFT-HAND SIDE OF Devington House, checking his numbers against the text that Shaun Donnal had sent him. Once he'd reached the required number, he moved through the foliage at the base of the house, finding himself in a small alcove where one of the four turrets jutted out a little. At the base was a large flagstone, slightly discoloured against the wall.

Looking around, Declan saw an old crowbar in the foliage, probably what used to be utilised to prise the stone open when Shaun would visit. Sliding it into a visible and possibly man-made chink on the right of the flagstone, Declan levered it open, marvelling as the flagstone opened out to reveal ancient hinges on the other side. Behind it was a narrow passage, no bigger than a crawlspace that sloped upwards.

Getting on his knees and turning on his torch, Declan crawled into the space, moving upwards for about twenty feet until it hit a stone wall. Above him was a narrow passage with a wooden ladder embedded into the wall as blocks of wood. It didn't look that safe, but Declan didn't really have a choice at the moment. Slowly he climbed up the makeshift ladder, working out in his head the height that he was currently at. He realised that he must have been at the ballroom level when he found the ladder stop at a ledge, with a narrow passage running to his right now.

There were two options here: one was another ladder, twenty yards further to the right which went up to another floor – most likely the upper levels of the house, while in front of him was a wooden door of some kind. The passage to the right was most likely how Susan had got past the guard but Declan didn't have the time to play explorer so he pushed at the door in front of him, feeling it give as it opened up into the ballroom.

Crawling out, Declan examined the door as he closed it behind him. It was flush to the wood panelling along the side of the room, and if you didn't know it was there, you'd never know there was a secret door beside you as you danced.

Or fought.

Declan rose to see that he was in the dojo that he had sparred Susan Devington in earlier that week. Down the other end of the ballroom was a set of stairs that most likely led to the upper levels and the roof.

Standing there on the mat, waiting for him, was the man with the rimless glasses.

'You took your time,' he smiled.

Declan smiled in response. He'd hoped that this man would be here. He had a score to settle.

He rose to his feet, shaking off the dirt and cobwebs that had accumulated around him while in the priest hole. 'Never got your name,' he said.

'Never gave it,' the man with the rimless glasses replied. Declan shrugged.

'Fair point,' he said as he moved in. This time however he was prepared and, as he walked towards his opponent, he let his right hand loosen, letting an extendable baton slide into it. With a flick he opened it up.

'Let's get this over with,' he said as he attacked.

Francine Pearce had expected to find Susan Devington on the roof, and since arriving she now knew that Charles Baker would be up there with her. What she hadn't bargained for was Shaun Donnal, a gun in his hand and a wild expression in his eyes joining them. And, as she left Devington House and walked onto the roof, feeling the cold air hit her skin, it was Shaun who walked up behind her, pressing the gun into her back.

'Throw your phone over the edge,' he hissed, 'and then join the others.'

Francine calmly took her phone out and tossed it over the barricade that ran along the roof. 'You'll not shoot me,' she said. 'Your family—'

'Haven't spoken to me in years,' Shaun hissed. 'I know it's been you, Frankie. I've known it's been you for years, but I haven't had the guts to admit it.'

'And now?'

Shaun pushed Francine hard, sending her stumbling into Susan Devington's arms.

'Now we all discuss what really happened,' he said. 'To Sarah, to Victoria and to Andrew bloody MacIntyre.'

He cocked the gun in his hand.

'And then I'll dispense justice,' he finished.

———

THE FIRST TIME THAT DECLAN HAD FOUGHT THE MAN WITH THE rimless glasses, he'd been sucker punched and unready. He'd been distracted by Kendis's arrival and, even though he'd spotted the man approaching from across the street, he hadn't expected to be struck so quickly. This time however, he was ready, eager even for the rematch.

His opponent had pulled his own extendible baton out as Declan attacked, using it to deflect the constant blows that Declan was raining upon him, losing ground with every *clack* of the batons. Declan was also kicking out with his feet, trying to trip the man as he continued to keep him off balance. The sparring with Susan aside, this was the first proper fight that he'd been prepared for in weeks, and he had a lot of anger to work out.

Clack. The anger at being suspended for doing his job.

Clack. The anger at DCI Ford's betrayal in Mile End.

Whumf. A solid blow to the solar plexus, powered by anger at the death of his father.

And another blow. And another.

The man with the rimless glasses may have been military trained, but Declan had been trained to defeat the military as part of his job. Finally he was utilising these skills to their fullest extent, spin kicking around as he took out his opponent's leg, connecting a solid right against the face, the weight of the baton in his hand acting like a weighted glove as he sent the man sprawling to the dojo mat, clutching at his twisted knee. He tried to get up, but Declan was already in; a knee to the face broke a nose as the man flailed backwards, landing back on the mat with a thud, wheezing through his mouth as his bleeding nose filled it with blood.

Declan grabbed the man's right hand and, pulling out his handcuffs, he cuffed the broken opponent to the weight tower.

'We're done here,' he said, already walking to the stairs. 'I thought you'd be more of a challenge.'

His dazed opponent just stared at him in a concussed stupor.

———

DECLAN OPENED THE DOOR TO THE ROOF OF DEVINGTON House to see Charles Baker, Susan Devington and Francine Pearce on one side, while Shaun Donnal stood the other.

'You shouldn't have come here, Walsh!' Donnal cried. 'They need to pay!'

Declan walked closer. 'They need to face the law, Shaun,' he said. 'If you kill them, you'll be just as bad as them.'

'Listen to the detective, Shaun,' Charles suggested.

'Shut up!' Shaun screamed, his gun rising, his finger tightening on the trigger. Declan moved in front of the gun.

'Don't,' he said softly. 'Think of your family. Think of Sally. The real one. We don't know what they're thinking. But if you let me take these criminals in, if you step down, we can look to getting your life restarted. You don't have to hide anymore.'

'They killed Victoria,' Shaun said, his eyes tearing up.

'And they'll pay for that,' Declan said. 'But not with you being judge, jury and executioner.'

Shaun thought for a moment, the gun lowering. Declan stood to the side, giving the gunman space.

'You're right,' Shaun said, tossing the gun to the floor. 'They're not worth it.'

'Thank you,' Declan said, looking to Francine, but she had already reached down and picked up the gun, aiming it at Shaun.

'You poor, deluded idiot,' she said as she fired it at him. *Twice.*

Shaun spun, falling to the floor, unmoving as Francine turned the gun onto Declan.

'Are you mad?' Charles said. 'How the hell do we explain this?'

'Easy,' Francine replied, walking over to the door to the roof and using a metal pole to bar it shut. 'DI Walsh here came to our aid in freeing us from this madman. Unfortunately, he was shot and killed before you, brave Charles

Baker fought and wrestled the gun from the crazed Donnal, the gun going off in the process, killing him.'

She looked from the dead body of Shaun Donnal to Declan.

'Unfortunately, it does mean that you have to die too,' she said as she squeezed the trigger.

———

29

THE FINAL SOLUTION

'WAIT!' DECLAN CRIED OUT, HIS HANDS IN THE AIR. 'AT LEAST let me know if I got it right first!'

Francine paused, lowering the gun. 'Go on then,' she said. 'Let's see if you solved your final case.'

Declan took a deep breath, glancing down at Shaun's body. 'I'll have to start from the very beginning,' he said.

Francine nodded. 'Nobody's getting up here for a while,' she said. 'Go wild.'

'We don't have time for this!' Susan snapped. 'He will have told others! They're coming for me!'

Francine waved Susan back. 'Let's see if he has you dead to rights first, yes?' She nodded to Declan. 'Go on. Tell your story.'

Declan nodded in return. 'First we have to go back to the beginning,' he said. In the distance he could hear police sirens. That meant that things were going to be ending one way or the other very soon.

'It starts with two sisters,' he said. 'Sarah and Frankie Pearce. Both want to be solicitors. Both want to be powerful.

Both become solicitors but one, Frankie has married and is now Frankie Wilson. After a few years though, Sarah gets bored of being a solicitor. She moves into politics. Joins the Liberal Democrats. Maybe Frankie does too, I don't know.'

'I did,' Francine admitted.

'So, now Sarah is pushing to be an MP. This could be big for the sisters. Sarah marries Liam Hinksman, and even though he works for Labour, she fights for a seat in the 1997 election for the Lib Dems, with Frankie at her side, advising her.' Declan watched Francine for any reaction, Seeing none, he continued.

'So now we're in Westminster in 1997. It's all exciting. Sarah starts to visit her husband in the Labour offices and somehow meets Charles Baker from the room next door. They hit it off and have a brief affair.'

'That's a lie!' Charles exclaimed. Declan waved him down.

'You'd have more chance with that denial if we hadn't just proved by DNA that Sebastian Payne was your son.'

Charles looked to Francine. 'Did you know this?' he asked. Francine simply shrugged.

'Doesn't matter now,' she said. 'He's dead. Andrew killed him.'

Charles fell against the side of the roof, his legs seemingly giving way. Declan looked to him and saw at the entrance to Devington House the first of the approaching police vehicles. Unfortunately, it looked like Special Branch had got here first.

'Whatever happened, it didn't last long,' he said. 'Because soon, possibly even at the same time, Sarah met Shaun Donnal.'

Francine looked down at Shaun's body. 'She wouldn't listen to me,' she said. 'She was the MP, while I was just the advisor. I knew that it wouldn't last; I just had to bide my time.'

'And you did that well,' Declan replied. 'You booked their illicit trips to Queen Anne's Chamber and you ensured that Liam didn't find out. Possibly even to the detriment of your own marriage. It was around here that you split with your own husband, right?' With no response he continued.

'But now a new problem appeared. Jet-setting socialists Michael and Victoria Davies, spending Devington money like their own personal piggy bank.' He looked to Susan. 'That made you angry, right?'

'I wasn't around,' Susan said, looking away. 'I was already on the road protests by then.'

'Of course, you were,' Declan replied. 'Anyway, Michael and Victoria were now making a name for themselves in the party. Michael wanted to push against Labour and Blair; a bit of the old Socialist in him returning. Victoria meanwhile was finding that a house full of male MPs, far away from their families was an all-you-can-eat buffet. And that was fine, until she also met Shaun Donnal.'

'I didn't control who she met.' Francine folded her arms, the gun still in her hand. In the distance there was shouting as Special Branch gathered outside the house, while an Armed Police Unit van was also driving down the drive. In the distance, a police helicopter could be heard approaching.

'True,' Declan continued. 'And to be honest, you were probably happy for Victoria and Shaun to fall in love as it freed Sarah up to sort herself out and be an MP again. But she didn't. She kept the child, lost her marriage and the scandal forced her to resign from Parliament. You both left.'

'True.'

'But Shaun didn't follow. He was supposed to leave his

wife, but he didn't. He was happy with Victoria now.' Declan looked down at Shaun. 'At the Labour conference, Sarah turned up unannounced. People started to panic. Michael knew that Shaun was likely to be the father of this six-month-old baby. Having Sarah reveal it publicly was bad press.' He looked to Charles.

'The problem was, she wasn't going to out Shaun. She was going to out you as the father. She actually gave Shaun advance warning to get out before the bomb went off. That's why he didn't stop Andy Mac from getting her drunk; he didn't know he was doing that.'

'Andy Mac killed Sarah,' Susan said. Declan shook his head.

'That's not true and we all know it,' he replied. 'He was a coke head, true, but he wasn't the one taking ketamine right then. Victoria Davies was. And it was Victoria Davies, thinking that she was helping her true love, who spiked Sarah's drink.'

Tears started to form around Francine's eyes. 'Bitch didn't even know what she was doing,' she said. 'I was told that she was so out of it, she had no idea what was going on.'

'Michael told you this, didn't he?' Declan asked. 'When you went to work for him?'

'Yes,' Francine replied. 'I started at Devington shortly after Sarah died. Took my maiden name back. They'd all met me loads of times when I was with Sarah, but none of them recognised me. Nobody ever recognises the *help*.' She pointed the gun at Shaun Donnal's body. 'Even that rat there.' She looked to Charles Baker. 'Only he knew who I was. He was the only one that saw me.'

'So, you started at Devington Industries, and your plan at the time was to destroy Michael and Victoria's relationship,'

Declan continued. 'And at the time, Charles was looking for a way to remove Shaun as a rival for Labour Leader. You started an affair with Michael, convincing him to have a vasectomy. And then you schemed with Charles to pay Doctor Khai fifty grand to fake it. Now, Michael believed erroneously that he was sterile. You knew that if he got his wife pregnant, he'd instantly believe that she was unfaithful. They'd fall apart.' He looked to Susan. 'But then you got involved.'

Susan raised an eyebrow at this. 'Can we just shoot him now?' she asked.

'No,' Charles replied. 'I want to hear this.'

'You and Victoria never got on,' Declan said. 'And as a child she'd lock you in the priest holes for fun.'

'Bloody Ratcliffe.' Susan almost smiled. 'I knew it was a mistake leaving him with you. I was hoping you'd join me instead.'

'Yes, bloody Ratcliffe,' Declan replied. 'You were the studious one, the passionate one. The activist who did things while Victoria just played at it, using your family money. The company was collapsing, the board were on the point of selling out. In a year, Michael and Victoria had destroyed almost thirty years of Devington goodwill. You needed to stop them, but you knew you couldn't unless Victoria was gone.' He waved around the roof. 'Which brings us to New Year's Eve 2000.'

'I was in a cell on New Year's Eve,' Susan forced a smile, but it was strained. Declan shook his head.

'Whoever she was, she wasn't you,' he said. 'We've seen the mugshot. I think you paid someone to create an alibi for you. And at this time, you're already talking to Francine here. Maybe she's brought you in on her crusade to destroy

Michael and Victoria by this point. Either way, I think you left, doubled back and entered the house again through the same priest entrance that I used today. There you stayed until Victoria went to the roof, most likely guided up here by a text. All it took was for Francine to let you out at the right time.'

'You've made an error there,' Francine said. 'If you read the statements, you'll see that Michael told security to ban all guests.'

'Oh no, I saw that,' Declan smiled. 'He said all guests. You were staff. You came up, let Susan out and then returned to the party. Susan meanwhile waited until Michael came back from the roof and then slipped up after him.'

He looked over the edge, now filled with police cars, their lights flashing.

'All those years of anger, all that fury, you couldn't help yourself,' he said. 'You pushed your own sister over the wall, while keeping the necklace that she wore.' He looked to Francine. 'Meanwhile, you'd been busy spiking the drinks of Andy, Charles and Shaun. I'm not sure with what exactly, but it was enough to give them all complete amnesia for the night.'

'Conspiracies.' Francine raised the gun again.

'Not so,' Declan replied. 'You brought in each of them – Charles, Andy and Shaun – into your office and showed them the necklace. You explained that they'd had it on them after the murder. They couldn't remember anything; they were terrified that it was true. You promised to keep it quiet as long as they helped you out.' He looked back to Susan. 'You'd replaced the disgraced and convicted Michael as CEO by this point, but you needed a big win. There was an infrastructure deal following the 9/11 bombings. You used Francine's three pet MPs to pass the bill that allowed you to bid.'

'She did,' Charles said finally. 'She told me I'd killed Victoria and I believed her. I became paranoid that Shaun or Andy knew about this. It's why we fell out, why I changed parties.'

'Everything worked fine for fifteen years,' Declan said. 'You even funded Andy Mac in his new life as a preacher. But then Michael came back. He told Shaun that he had evidence, that he could prove some big things. Shaun, ever the loyal servant, told you. And you had Michael killed.'

'He was dying anyway,' Francine snapped. 'I just sped up the process.'

'And then Shaun, scared for his own life went AWOL, hiding on the streets,' Declan finished. 'You found a way to convince him to be quiet, with these "payments from his daughter". He was a good boy. But he was still a liability. And then Charles pushes for Prime Minister. If he gets it, then you might find this all coming out. They're a lot more fastidious in the vetting process, you see. And Prime Ministers can open security boxes of dead prisoners and find all your little secrets. You needed to bring him back down. Maybe the two of you had a falling out, I don't know. All I do know is that a couple of weeks back you sent one of your crew into a Derby police station and "found" this letter from twenty years ago. I think you hoped that it wouldn't go anywhere but would throw some shade on Charles to affect his leadership bid. The one thing I can't explain is how you found the letter.'

'She never sent it,' Susan spoke now. 'It was left in her drawer. I found it when I was cleaning the room out so I passed it to Francine just in case. You never know when such things can be useful.'

'True,' Declan said, looking to Francine. 'So how did I do?'

'Very well,' Francine nodded. 'You pretty much nailed everything. Such a shame you won't be able to tell anyone.'

And with that, Francine Pearce aimed the gun at Declan Walsh for a second time and pulled the trigger, shooting him at point-blank range.

———

30

THE DEAD SPEAK

THE PARLIAMENTARY AND DIPLOMATIC PROTECTION COMMAND were furious. They'd allowed Charles Baker this one request for several months now: a lone exercise time with nobody around, but now he'd taken it a step further, driving off on some joyride.

Then Pearce Associates had called, explaining that they had information that showed Baker to be a hostage, at the whim of a mad gunman that they'd been keeping tabs on. Immediately at alert, the PaDP had tracked Baker's phone to Devington House, speeding to the destination as fast as they could while sending out for helicopter and armed assistance. They had no idea what to expect when they arrived; all they knew was that Charles Baker was never going to be allowed out of their sight again.

What they didn't expect to see when they arrived at the drive to Devington House were two individuals: one an Indian female, the other a blond man in an expensive suit running at them, their hands raised with some kind of IDs in them.

'Get down on the ground!' The first car's doors opened up and PS Matthews screamed out the order, pulling his Glock 17 pistol out and aiming it at the woman, purely because she seemed to be in command. The woman turned to him.

'And I said stand down!' she shouted back. 'I'm Detective Sergeant Anjli Kapoor of the City Police! This is Detective Constable William Fitzwarren!' She waved her hand. 'These are our IDs!'

'Where's Baker?' Matthews said, waving for his team to surround the two individuals, taking the IDs from them and examining them.

'He's on the roof,' the male replied. 'One of our team, DI Walsh is up there. There's a gunman.'

'Right then,' Matthews nodded. 'We'll take over from here.'

'You can't!' The woman exclaimed, blocking the way of the team as they moved to the door. 'This is a vital moment in a murder enquiry!'

'The only murder here is going to be you if you don't get out of my way!' Matthews shouted but stopped as an SCO19 truck screeched to a halt beside them. The door opened and three SCO19 officers emerged, all aiming their weapons at the PaDP.

'I suggest you lower your weapons,' a white-haired man emerged from the passenger side, walking over. 'Before something even worse happens.'

'And you are?' Matthews' gun lowered but he didn't holster it.

'DCI Monroe. City Police. It's my man on the roof, and he has a plan to not only save your missing MP, but also catch a killer.'

'And if he fails?' Matthews looked from the armed men aiming their assault rifles at him up to the roof.

'Laddie, the only person who's failed so far is you,' Monroe said. 'How the hell did you let your charge drive away for so long before you realised something was wrong?'

Matthews went to snap back a reply, but the door to Devington House opened and an old man, bleeding from the skull emerged.

'What the bloody hell is going on out here?' Ratcliffe asked.

Monroe was about to reply when the gunshot was heard.

THE GUN FIRED. THE NOISE WAS LOUD, ECHOING AROUND THE roof, but Declan just stood there.

'Well, that didn't work,' he said calmly. 'Try again.'

Francine fired the gun a second time; the gunshot once more echoing in the morning air. She looked down at the gun in a mixture of silent realisation and horror as Declan walked over to the door, unbarring the handle and opening it up. In the distance steps could be heard; those of the police, running up the stairs.

'I don't think your gun works,' he said as he did this. 'Maybe that means that Shaun's not dead either?'

Taking this as his cue and with a smile, Shaun Donnal climbed back to his feet, facing Francine as he revealed the phone in his hand.

Charles Baker's phone.

Set to *voice record*.

'I don't understand,' Charles said. 'How did you know it was firing blanks?'

'I didn't,' Declan replied honestly. 'But even though Shaun's not been the most rational of people recently, he did say one thing on the phone. He mentioned *BFA*. That's shorthand for blank firing adaptor, something we spoke about last night. The moment he said that I knew he'd done something to ensure the gun wouldn't fire. And, when Francine shot him, I knew it was blanks.'

Monroe, Billy and a PaDP officer all ran through the door at the same time.

'You okay?' Monroe asked.

'I'm good,' Declan said. 'Francine admitted to everything on tape.'

'How?' Charles Baker asked now as Billy passed him to cuff Francine. 'How did you know they were blanks?'

Declan pointed to the floor. 'Two shots, close range, no blood.' He looked back at Francine. 'We've got Trix's testimony too, so adding that to the taped confession you just made, oh and the attempted murder of a police officer, I'd say you're not going to have a very good week.' He turned to speak to Susan, to tell her that finally she'd be paying the price for her sister's murder but stopped.

Susan had moved behind Charles Baker, grabbing him by the throat as she backed towards the edge of the roof.

'Don't,' Declan said. 'It's not worth it.'

Everyone paused on the roof, as if scared that a single movement would set her off, but Susan's mind was already made. Now at the edge of the roof, only the parapet wall keeping her from falling, she smiled at Declan.

'You really should have joined me,' she said. 'We could have had a lot of fun together.'

'Please, Susan,' Charles whimpered. 'I don't want to die.'

Susan was now crouching on the parapet; Charles still held close.

'This is the same wall that I pushed my sister off,' she said. 'I never lost a moment's sleep over it. Bitch deserved everything she got.'

'That doesn't mean you have to join her,' Declan said, moving slowly towards Susan. 'We can work something out.'

'Oh honey, I don't play well with others,' Susan said as she pushed Charles to the side, sending him stumbling to the floor, launching herself backwards off the parapet and falling to the ground with a sickening crunch, five storeys below.

Declan had moved forward at this, leaping out with his arms extended, but Monroe had grabbed him, holding him back.

'No point taking you with her,' he said. 'There was no way you could have stopped that.'

Declan walked to the edge, peering down. Susan Devington's mangled body was sprawled on top of one of the PaDP vehicles, her eyes vacant and staring back up at him. Declan shuddered and turned back to the roof, where Charles Baker was being helped up by officers.

'I'm a victim here!' he exclaimed. 'That madman brought me here by gunpoint! I have no recollection of any of this!'

Declan nodded. 'He can go free,' he said to the police officer. 'He's implicated in a lot of things, but he didn't kill anyone.'

Charles nodded, straightening his jacket as if even in gym kit he could look Prime Ministerial.

'There'll be an inquest,' Monroe said. 'Questions will be asked. You might want to table your attempt for power right now, eh?'

Charles ignored him as, with his Protection Officers

finally reunited with him, he followed the police escorting Francine through the door. Declan looked to Monroe.

'You know, the worst thing about this is that he'll come out of it smelling of roses,' Monroe sighed. 'He'll turn this into some kind of narrative where he helped us.'

'I'm not sure about that,' Declan replied. 'Francine will probably have some nice, juicy titbits put aside for when she needs to plea bargain. And there's always Michael Davies's treasure trove of lies and deals, wherever that is.'

'Aye, that's not the last we've heard of Baker to be sure,' Monroe said, looking at Shaun, now being arrested himself by a policeman. 'We'll take him, laddie. You can take the cuffs off.'

'But he had a gun—'

'It was all part of a police sting,' Monroe tapped his nose. 'Be a good lad and go get that thug in the gym. He can join his boss.'

Now free from handcuffs, Shaun walked over to Declan and Monroe.

'How do you feel?' Declan asked. Shaun shrugged.

'I need a drink. Like really need a drink,' he said honestly. 'I don't think I've been this long without one for years.' He looked to the wall where Susan had jumped, shuddering. 'So, what now?'

'Well, now we'll be arresting you,' Monroe said, 'but not with cuffs. You still need to be charged with grievous bodily harm in Soho.'

He waved around the roof.

'But that said, I think all of this, and the fact you've been in a state of fear for the last four or five years is enough to get you a little bit of community service there. As long as you let us help you beat the drink and get you on your feet.'

Shaun nodded as Anjli walked over to take him down the stairs.

'Oh, your wife called again,' she said to Declan. 'Main office. Didn't leave a message.'

'Problems?' Monroe looked concerned. Declan forced a smile.

'I was supposed to see Jess today. But with all this, and the reports—'

'Och, to hell with the reports,' Monroe said. 'We'll cover that. It's what teams do. Go and see your bairn. Tell her hi from her Uncle Monroe.'

Declan grinned. 'I don't think you've ever been "Uncle Monroe", Guv,' he said.

'Well now's as good a time as any to start,' Monroe replied, already pushing Declan to the door. 'Go on, get out of here before I change my mind.'

Declan looked to Anjli and Billy and both officers nodded.

'I'll repay the favour,' Declan said.

'You're damn right you will,' Anjli muttered. 'You're not the one about to scrape an aristocrat off a car roof.'

And with that, before anyone could change their mind, Declan left the roof and made his way out of the building. As he reached the entrance, he saw Ratcliffe at the door, staring at the body of Susan Devington. He had an ice pack to his head.

'What happened to you?' Declan asked.

'The mad tramp hit me with his gun,' Ratcliffe complained. 'Still, it could have been worse. I could have ended up like her.'

'What will you do now?' Declan looked around the

grounds. Ratcliffe had looked after this land for several decades. It seemed cruel to have him removed now.

'I'll be staying here,' Ratcliffe smiled. 'House will always need a good groundsman.'

'Well, good luck to you,' Declan said before walking over to his Audi, stunned that in all of the confusion it hadn't been blocked in by police cars. Pulling out his phone, he dialled Lizzie.

'Where the hell are you?' she said. 'Jess has been waiting for hours!'

'Just caught a murderer,' Declan said. 'I'll be with you within the hour.'

'Well good,' Lizzie grudgingly accepted this. 'Where are you taking her?'

'I thought I'd show her dad's house, maybe take a walk around Hurley, if that's okay?' Declan said, climbing into the car.

'Most dads take their kids to the cinema,' Lizzie suggested.

Declan grinned. 'I'm not like most dads,' he said, disconnecting the call. There was an unread text on his phone; the number he'd asked for in the car. The burner that Sebastian had sent his final message to.

Pressing it, he dialled the number. After three rings, it answered.

'Hi Declan,' the voice of Kendis Taylor spoke through the car's system.

'I thought you might answer my call,' Declan replied. 'I don't seem to have this number for you.'

There was a long pause.

'I didn't mean for him to get killed,' she eventually said.

'He came to me through a friend. He wanted to get Andy; wanted to bring him down.'

'And why did you want to bring him down?'

'There're a few things he did that are good enough reasons. And he insulted you on his show.' Kendis was angry as she spoke. 'If it wasn't me, it would have been someone else. Sebastian called me and said he might have some photos. I said great, send them to me. And then he never replied. I didn't know how he was doing it.'

Declan leaned back in the seat. 'You need to walk away from this,' he said. 'Andy Mac's dead. Susan Devington's dead. Sebastian Payne too. There're too many deaths here.'

'I will, Declan,' Kendis replied. 'But you need to walk away from this too.'

'Already doing that,' Declan finished. 'Throw away this phone.'

And with that he disconnected the call, started the engine and drove out of the driveway of Devington House.

EPILOGUE

His Protection Officers had brought Charles Baker directly to Whitehall. He knew that it was a matter of time before news of this came out and he wanted to start damage limitation before he was overrun with paparazzi. Walsh was right; Charles was about to be implicated in several things, but the fact of the matter was that both Susan Devington and Andrew MacIntyre were dead, and he could use this to throw a lot of the problems onto them.

He smiled, a small one of relief. *He hadn't killed Victoria Davies after all.* Ever since they'd shown him the necklace all those years ago, he'd wondered how truthful they had been but was too scared to actively investigate it. He had too much running on his political career and with his marriage to Donna, to risk anything coming out.

Now he had to write the narrative before someone else did.

As he reached his offices, though, he saw Will Harrison standing at the doorway waiting, running his hand nervously through his stupid haircut. As Charles left the car, Will ran over.

'Th-they're in your office,' he stammered.

'Let's pretend for a moment that I'm not bloody psychic,' Charles replied, walking through the main door. 'Who's in my office?'

'Symonds and Gladwell.'

Charles almost stumbled to a stop. He wanted to swear loudly, but he knew that they'd hear, even in an office a floor away. There was only one reason why Malcolm bloody Gladwell would be here on a Saturday. And there was definitely a small amount of reasons why Walter Symonds would miss his morning brunch.

They were about to tell Charles he wasn't in the running for Prime Minister.

Damn Susan Devington. Damn Francine Pearce. Damn Shaun and Andy and Damn DI bloody Walsh for kicking the stone over in the first place.

Stopping at a mirror, Charles used his fingers to tame his hair back into place. He took a deep breath, holding it for a couple of seconds before releasing it.

'Okay then, he said, turning and walking towards his office. 'Let's go chat with my executioners.' It wasn't all bad. Nigel Dickinson was a terrible bloody choice and Tamara Banks was a toxic Thatcherite. With those two as their choices, the 1922 Committee would probably suggest holding off for a year before ramming the knife in.

Charles Baker was fine with that.

A year was a long time in politics.

MONROE SAT IN HIS OFFICE, WORKING ON HIS LAPTOP.

He was the only one in; Billy and Anjli had left for the day and Doctor Marcos was at an abattoir, smacking pig bodies with some kind of stick to prove Sherlock Holmes wrong about something. He hadn't bothered to ask what.

Leaning back, he moved his head around, letting the muscles in his neck crick and crunch as he tried to loosen up his shoulders. Looking to his bookshelf, he spied a small photo on it.

Walking over, he picked it up, looking down at it.

It was a photo of Monroe, around ten years ago, standing beside Patrick Walsh.

It was the day that Patrick had been promoted to Chief Superintendent. It was probably the last time Monroe had worn his police uniform, too. It was a photo of happier times.

'Ah, you soft wee bastard,' he muttered to himself. 'You would have been proud of the boy. He did good. Fixed your mistake.'

He looked from the photo, his gaze flitting around the office.

'He's going to find out,' he said. 'He knows something happened. It'll get him killed.'

Placing the photo back on the shelf, Monroe returned to the desk, sitting back down. Patrick Walsh was dead, so Alexander Monroe was going to have to be a father-figure now.

He only hoped that Declan would listen to him before he fell too far into the rabbit hole.

Billy sat in *Cecconi's*, at the same table as he had the previous night watching the door, waiting. After a few minutes it opened and a familiar figure entered, walking over to the table and sitting down opposite him.

'Well, I must admit I didn't expect this call,' Rufus Harrington said.

Billy shrugged. 'Blood calls to blood,' he replied. 'Try the wine. It's divine.'

'Rather not,' Rufus looked around. 'Don't really want to be seen with the police, you know?'

'Rufus,' Billy said, leaning in. 'You know why my family don't like me?'

'I've heard rumours.'

'And you understand that this stops certain avenues being opened for me?'

Rufus looked around again, as if scared that the conversation was being observed. It wasn't.

'You want to come in from the cold?' he asked.

Billy shrugged. 'I want a contact, an inside source to my parents,' he said. 'I thought we could make a deal.'

Rufus laughed. 'And what could you possibly give me?' he asked.

Billy smiled. It wasn't a happy one. 'You mentioned Devington Industries,' he said. 'When we spoke last. Do you hold shares?'

'Quite a few,' Rufus replied cautiously. 'All above board.'

'Sell them,' Billy said. 'Sell them right now. Devington shares are about to tank.'

He pulled out his wallet, pulling out enough money to pay for the bill. He felt Rufus staring at him but he didn't say anything. Billy rose from the seat, walking past Rufus.

'Seriously, try the wine. It's glorious, and it's paid for.'

'Why would you tell me about Devington?' Rufus asked. 'Even if it's true?'

'Ask around, you'll see it is.' Billy patted Rufus on the shoulder. 'When you're willing to talk, call me.'

And with that he left the restaurant as Rufus Harrington desperately tried to call his broker on his phone.

———

ANJLI SAT ON THE PARK BENCH PULLING HER COLLAR UP AGAINST the wind. It was cold, and she'd spent half of the day up on a roof. There was a chill deep inside her right now that was unlikely to go away for a while.

She also hated this place too; Meath Gardens had once been a cemetery. When it was changed into a park in the late nineteenth century, all they did was remove the headstones and landscape over the grass.

'There's a hundred thousand bodies under us,' a voice said from behind her. 'Three quarters of which were children; poor little buggers.'

Anjli didn't look away from the ground as Johnny Lucas sat down beside her.

'You got my message then,' he said.

'What do you want, Mister Lucas?' Anjli asked. 'I'm no longer Mile End plod.'

'No, but you're still plod,' Johnny smiled. 'And you're still Mile End born and bred.'

'I was born and bred in Bradford.'

'Ah, that's where you were dug out,' Johnny replied. 'Mile End is where you were forged in fire.'

There was a silence as the two of them watched a child play with a ball.

'Do you think he knows?' Johnny asked. 'That beneath

him are thousands of kiddies the same age?' He turned to Anjli. 'Don't worry, I'm not asking much.'

'That's what you said to Ford.'

'She owed me gambling money,' Johnny nodded. 'Her debt was greater. Yours? Minimal.'

'What do you want?'

Johnny thought for a moment. 'News,' he said. 'That's all. I want news on Declan Walsh. What he's doing, where he's going, who he's friends with, what he's working on.'

'That's it?' Anjli asked. 'Just updates on Walsh. Why?'

'He fascinates me,' Johnny said rising from the bench and walking off. 'That's all.'

And with that Anjli Kapoor stared down at the grass, imagining the thousands of bodies under the ground. *How many bodies had the twins put under the same ground?*

Shaking the gruesome thought off, Anjli rose from the bench and started towards Mile End and a hot coffee.

THEY'D SPENT AN HOUR WALKING ALONG THE THAMES, DOING their usual father and daughter tradition of Declan telling Jessica every detail of the case he'd just finished.

It may have seemed a little gruesome to the fishermen they passed, but Jessica Walsh was cut from the same cloth as her father, her grandfather and the generations of police before them; Declan knew that by the time she was his age, she'd be DCI at minimum.

She was quick, eager to learn and she had also helped him on several cases in the past. All she had to do was dye her hair back to normal and stop wearing fake glasses because all the cool people on Instagram were doing it.

Arriving back at his father's, no, *his* house, Declan brought Jessica upstairs.

'There's something I wanted to show you,' he said.

'Dad, I've spent years coming here,' Jessica replied. 'I think I know everything there is to know about the place.'

Declan walked to the bookshelf in the study, pushing it to the side and exposing the secret room.

'Did you know about this?' he asked.

'No ...' Jessica walked into the small, secret office in wonderment. She examined the pictures on the whiteboard and, when done she opened up the filing cabinet, peering through the cases. 'Was granddad a spy?'

'Granddad was a lot of things, but I don't think he was that.' Declan turned on the desk lamp. 'But there seems to be a lot about him that neither of us knew about.'

He turned his daughter to face him. 'Listen, Jess, you can't tell anyone about this. Not even mum. This is big.'

Jessica nodded, already realising this as she looked across the room at the wall of string-linked faces. 'Did one of these people kill granddad?' she asked.

Declan looked down at her. 'Why would you think something like that?' he asked.

'Cut the crap, dad. I know you,' Jessica said. 'You don't think it was an accident.'

Declan shrugged. 'I don't know what to think,' he admitted. 'But I'm going to investigate all angles until I know for sure.'

'Good,' Jessica said, sitting at the desk. 'So where do we start?'

Declan picked up a sheaf of papers that he'd brought up from downstairs. *Patrick Walsh's memoirs.* 'Every suspect is in here,' he said. 'So first? We read this.'

Declan Walsh sat on the edge of the desk that his father once worked at and, with his daughter beside him, started to read his father's memoirs, looking for suspects in a *murder*.

———————

DI Walsh and the team of the *Last Chance
Saloon* will return in their next thriller

MURDER OF ANGELS

Order Now at Amazon:

http://mybook.to/murderofangels

And read on for a sneak preview...

PROLOGUE

THE MORNINGS ALWAYS STARTED WITH A COUGHING FIT.

Derek Salmon leaned over the side of his bed, violently coughing into a small clear Tupperware container that he'd left there for such situations. He'd found out the hard way that coughing blood onto a carpet first thing in the morning destroyed the weave in it, and as he'd spent a lot of money on having the entire house re-carpeted a few years back, this wasn't on. Now Derek started his mornings leaning to the side and racking up phlegm and blood into a small plastic box; one that used to hold his packed lunch back in the days when he used to have a job.

Cancer was a bastard.

Getting to his feet, Derek stretched his arms and opened out his chest, trying to shake away the morning sluggishness. This was an important day. He needed to be at the top of his game today, although he had been nowhere near the top of anything in quite a while.

After a quick shower, Derek stared at himself in the bathroom mirror. The chemotherapy had turned his once dark brown hair white, but it hadn't fully fallen out yet, and this now made it nothing more than a collection of random white threads of hair that damply flattened out over his scalp.

This wouldn't do.

Grabbing a cordless shaver, Derek ran it over his head, allowing the shaver to remove the wispy white hair, leaving the scalp with nothing more than a small amount of stubble. This done, he used the shaver on his beard scruff; he needed a full shave for the day ahead.

Now, with a closely cropped head and a clean jawline, Derek felt he looked a little more respectable. He pulled at his skin as he stared in the mirror; his face was drawn and haggard, the skin from his rapid weight loss gathering around his jowls. But he expected this, and there was nothing that he could do about it.

Not even makeup would hide the fact that he was dying.

Next was dressing. For the last month he'd worn jogging bottoms and an old tee shirt as his daily clothing, with maybe a hoodie placed over it when he got a little colder, which was increasingly more common these days. He wasn't going out anywhere, and it seemed churlish and vain to tidy himself up, to wear his better clothes for pottering around the house. But today was a day that he needed to be taken seriously. And so it was a shirt, tie, and suit day for Derek Salmon. It was the first time he'd worn such a sartorial combination in months.

He didn't have any breakfast as he didn't know when he'd eat next, and he also knew that there was a very strong chance that he'd throw it back up anyway, most likely in a holding cell. No, it was better to risk hunger than shame. And, if he was finding himself peckish later, he was sure that some old friends would help him out, maybe with a few biscuits or a sandwich.

Pulling his scarf on, Derek looked over to the sideboard in his living room. On it were photos of two women, both in their own respective frames. The older of the two was his ex-wife, Amanda. They'd separated for over ten years now and barely spoke these days, but he liked the photo and had kept it up. As far as Derek knew, Amanda didn't know about his illness and the terminal diagnosis; that was unless the woman in the second photo, his daughter Evie, nineteen years old and starting her second year in University right now had told her. Derek had decided early on that no matter what happened with Amanda, Evie had to be a part of this, had to be *aware* of this, if only to cope with the administration nightmare that would occur once he died.

Now ready for the day ahead, opening his front door and walking out into the brisk North London air, Derek smiled to himself. For the first time in a long while he had a purpose, a reason to do something. It might not be something that he wanted or even expected to do, but he could still do it. The doors were closing on him, but this door was still wide open and beckoning.

He didn't have a car anymore, but the walk to the Tottenham North Command Unit where he once worked wasn't that far a stroll. That said, by the time he reached the entrance he was already woefully out of breath, forced to lean against the door to gain his breath before entering.

The reception to the Unit was the same as any other London Police Station; the floor was a strange linoleum swash of lines and squares; the walls were a mixture of salmon and cream, as if they had one been lighter but years of constant crime passing through the doors had darkened them, while the doors themselves were a pale blue. And, at the front was a glass window above a while counter where the Desk Sergeant sat, waiting for people to come in and most likely ruin her day. Today, it was empty, and the Desk Sergeant looked up as Derek entered the Command Unit, her face paling as she saw the horrific changes to the once Detective Inspector. She hid it well with a fake smile, though. Derek knew it was a fake smile. He'd seen so many of them over the last six months.

'DI Salmon!' she exclaimed. 'Good to see you up on your feet.'

'It's just Derek these days, Maisie.'

'You'll always be DI here, sir.'

Derek smiled back. Unlike the Desk Sergeant's nervous one, his was genuine. Derek genuinely appreciated the sentiment, even if he was going to destroy every piece of goodwill that he'd built up there over years in the next few minutes.

'Did you want to go through?' the Desk Sergeant continued, indicating one of the pale blue doors to the side. 'I can call ahead, let them know?'

'It's not really that sort of visit today,' Derek replied. 'I need you to call DCI Farrow down. Or, if he's not about, call for anyone in serious crimes.'

The Desk Sergeant's face broke into a frown. 'Are you alright?' she asked, the concern obvious in her voice.

And it was the concern that finally broke ex-DI Derek Salmon's patience.

'*Of course I'm not bloody well alright!*' he snapped. Then, composing himself, he continued. 'Look, Maisie, we've known each other for years, and you're a lovely person, but I have terminal pancreatic cancer. I'm absolutely riddled with the bloody thing. I've been told I have weeks left to live. Every pain-ridden moment is now important to me, and I can't waste the minimal time I have left.'

He leaned closer to the screen now, his voice rising.

'So if I say I need to speak to DCI Farrow or the serious crimes unit, I suggest that rather than having a nice little chat about it, you *do your bloody job and call them down here!*' The last part of this was shouted, and Derek felt light-headed, his legs giving way.

No, goddammit.

Forcing himself to straighten, he looked to the Desk Sergeant, already on the phone. After a moment, she looked back to him, the warm, sympathetic smile now gone.

'DCI Farrow will be down in a bit, *sir*,' she said, her tone now cold and expressionless. Derek nodded at this. He understood why she'd feel that way. At the same time though, after he'd said to Farrow what he was there to say, nobody would smile at him again, so she was ahead of the curve there.

A minute later, DCI Farrow opened the pale blue door beside the counter, emerging cautiously into the reception area, already aware of Derek's outburst. With his wire-rimmed glasses and tufty hair sticking out to the sides, Farrow was often likened to a rather irritated owl by the detectives who worked under him. He'd transferred into Tottenham North around six months before Derek had started his treatments, so Derek hadn't really worked with Farrow much in the time they'd both been in the Crime Unit, and he had known little about the man except for Declan's occasional updates.

But he'd known enough to know that DCI Farrow was a jobsworth.

'Derek,' Farrow said, holding out his hand. Derek didn't shake it, so Farrow let it fall back to his side. 'What can we do for you?'

'I need to speak to DI Walsh,' Derek replied.

'You need to keep up a little,' Farrow smiled. 'Declan Walsh no longer works here. He was transferred—'

'I know, to Alex Monroe's team,' Derek nodded. 'But I need you to bring him here. He needs to lead this case.'

Farrow frowned at this, as if worried that Derek was having some kind of episode, one where he thought he was still a DI himself.

'Case?' he asked.

'Yes,' Derek said. 'And yeah, I know you're thinking *what's the old bugger playing at now*, but it's important to me.' He pointed to the Desk Sergeant. 'Promise me, in front of this witness, that after I've explained, you'll bring Declan Walsh in to run the case.'

Farrow sighed. 'Or you could just toddle off down to Temple Inn, find him there and leave us out of whatever this is.'

'I can't,' Derek shook his head. 'I have to confess here. It's part of the agreement.'

'Fine,' DCI Farrow held up his hands. 'You do whatever it is, explain what it is you need to explain, I'll get Walsh and his friends to come here and play with you, and you can bugger off with them, okay?'

Derek thought about this for a moment.

'I needed a legal witness,' he explained. 'You might change your mind. I wanted to ensure you can't. If you don't bring Walsh in now, a court can take my confession as under duress. I could call for a mistrial.'

'What bloody confession?' Farrow was getting exasperated at the theatrics now.

'You know I'm terminal, right?' Derek asked.

'Of course.'

'Then you'll understand that because of this, I've gone beyond the British personality disorder of caring what people think about me,' Derek continued. 'You're an obnoxious little shit, Farrow, and I've hated you since you took over. And yes, I know, I stepped down because of all this,' he pointed to his white stubble, 'but there's something just wrong with you. I can't pinpoint it. I know it's like my cancer, but this time it's affecting everyone here.'

'Is this the explanation?' Farrow asked, bored now. 'Because I really need to—'

'For one bloody second just listen!'

The reception area was silent.

Stone faced, and silent now, Farrow motioned for Derek to continue.

'You remember the Angela Martin case?' Derek asked. 'Was right before I stepped down fully from duties.'

Farrow nodded, now all business, as if the mention of actual police work had brought his interest back. 'Of course. Seventeen years old. Went missing while out with her boyfriend in Walthamstow.'

'That's the one,' Derek said. 'Never found a body, never found a witness. She could be out there under another name as far as we know.'

'So what's this got to do with this minor scene you're making?' Farrow asked. Derek shrugged.

'I killed her,' he replied. 'I killed her, and I hid the body in Epping Forest.'

Neither Farrow nor the Desk Sergeant spoke for a good few seconds.

'That's not funny,' Farrow's tone had grown dark now. 'I'll give you the benefit of the doubt, that your condition has given you a gallows humour...'

'*Do I look like a damned comedian?*' Derek screamed. '*I killed her! I confess! And when Declan Walsh takes over the case, I'll take you to where the body's buried!*'

He paused, a smile now on his lips, the anger fading.

'But until then, how about a cuppa for old times?' he asked. 'I'm gasping.'

MURDER OF ANGELS

Order Now at Amazon:

http://mybook.to/murderofangels

ACKNOWLEDGEMENTS

Although I've been writing for three decades under my real name, these Declan Walsh novels are a first for me; a new name, a new medium and a new lead character.

There are people I need to thank, and they know who they are. To the ones who started me on this path over a coffee during a pandemic to the ones who zoom-called me and gave me advice, the ones on various Facebook groups who encouraged me when I didn't know if I could even do this, who gave advice on cover design and on book formatting all the way to my friends and family, who saw what I was doing not as mad folly, but as something good. Also, I couldn't have done this without my growing army of ARC readers who not only show me where I falter, but also raise awareness of me in the social media world, ensuring that other people learn of my books, and editors and problem catchers like Maureen Webb, Chris Lee, Edwina Townsend, Maryam Paulsen and Jacqueline Beard MBE, the latter of whom has copyedited both books so far (including the prequel), line by line for me.

But mainly, I tip my hat and thank you. *The reader.* Who took a chance on an unknown author in a pile of Kindle books, and thought you'd give them a chance, whether it was with this book or with my first one.

I write Declan Walsh for you. He (and his team) solves crimes for you. And with luck, he'll keep on solving them for a very long time.

Jack Gatland / Tony Lee,
London, November 2020

ABOUT THE AUTHOR

Jack Gatland is the pen name of *#1 New York Times Bestselling Author* Tony Lee, who has been writing in all medias for over thirty years, including comics, graphic novels, middle grade books, audio drama, TV and film for *DC Comics, Marvel, BBC, ITV, Random House, Penguin USA, Hachette* and a ton of other publishers and broadcasters.

These have included licenses such as *Doctor Who, Spider Man, X-Men, Star Trek, Battlestar Galactica, MacGyver, Doctors, Wallace and Gromit* and *Shrek*.

As Tony, he's toured the world talking to reluctant readers with his 'Change The Channel' school tours, and lectures on screenwriting and comic scripting for *Raindance* in London.

An introvert West Londoner by heart, he lives with his wife Tracy and dog Fosco, just outside London.

Locations In The Book

The locations that I use in my books are real, if altered slightly for dramatic intent.

The Boxing Club near Meath Gardens that Johnny Lucas meets Monroe in doesn't exist, and neither do the Twins - but the location used is the current **Globe Town Social Club**, within **Green Lens Studios**, a community centre formerly known as Eastbourne House, that I would pass occasionally in my 20s. In addition, Meath Gardens (where Anjli meets Johnny) is a real location; formerly Victoria Cemetery, it was changed from a burial ground to a park in the 1890s. The 100,000+ bodies buried beneath it are still there.

Hurley-Upon-Thames is a real village, and one that I visited many times from the age of 8 until 16, as my parents and I would spend our spring and summer weekends at the local campsite. It's a location that means a lot to me, my second home throughout my childhood, and so I've decided that this should be the 'home base' for Declan. And by the time book four comes out, I'll have completely destroyed its reputation!

Teddington Lock was indeed a television studios, but is now a series of apartments and small business sites. There is no YouTube studio there, but there easily could be...

The Houses of Parliament are real (obviously) and everything that both Charles and Anjli say about it is real as well. I've even attended the *Sherlock Holmes Society of London* dinners there. In addition, I've also attended SHSL meetings at the **National Liberal Club**; deciding that Anjli was a member of the society wasn't a decision that I took lightly, and it meant I'd use both locations.

Savernake Forest is also a real location, although not a place that bodies are buried in (as far as I know!). The first mention of a woodland *"Safernoc"* was made in AD 934 in the written records of the King Athelstan, but the land passed into Norman ownership soon after the Norman invasion of 1066. The royal forest was established in the 12th Century, and Henry VIII enjoyed deer hunting there. It also homes some of the oldest trees in England, with the 'Big Belly Oak' reported to be 1,100 years old.

The 2011 Radiohead album *The King of Limbs* is named after the ancient King of Limbs tree in the forest near Tottenham House, where the band recorded part of their previous album, *In Rainbows*.

On the subject of houses, **Devington House** doesn't exist. That said, the basis of it does; **Wollaton Hall** in Nottingham, designed by Robert Smythson was my inspiration. To my knowledge it doesn't have any priest holes in it - that was fictional, although Nicholas Owen and his designs are very much factual.

If you're interested in seeing what the *real* locations look like, I intend to post 'behind the scenes' location images on my Instagram feed. This will continue through all the books, and I suggest you follow it.

In fact, feel free to follow me on all my social media, by following the links below. They're new, as *I'm* new - but over time it can be a place where we can engage, discuss Declan and put the world to rights.

www.jackgatland.com

Subscribe to my Readers List:

https://bit.ly/jackgatlandVIP

Want more books by Jack Gatland? Turn the page...

THE THEFT OF A **PRICELESS** PAINTING...
A GANGSTER WITH A **CRIPPLING DEBT**...
A **BODY COUNT** RISING BY THE HOUR...

AND ELLIE RECKLESS IS CAUGHT IN THE MIDDLE.

JACK GATLAND

PAINT
— THE —
DEAD

A 'COP FOR CRIMINALS' ELLIE RECKLESS NOVEL

A NEW PROCEDURAL CRIME SERIES WITH
A TWIST - FROM THE CREATOR OF THE
BESTSELLING 'DI DECLAN WALSH' SERIES

AVAILABLE ON AMAZON / KINDLE UNLIMITED

EIGHT PEOPLE. EIGHT SECRETS.
ONE SNIPER.

THE
B⊕ARD
ROOM

HOW FAR WOULD YOU GO TO GAIN JUSTICE?

NEW YORK TIMES #1 BESTSELLER TONY LEE WRITING AS

JACK GATLAND

A NEW STANDALONE THRILLER WITH
A TWIST - FROM THE CREATOR OF THE
BESTSELLING 'DI DECLAN WALSH' SERIES

AVAILABLE ON AMAZON / KINDLE UNLIMITED

THEY TRIED TO KILL HIM...
NOW HE'S OUT FOR **REVENGE.**

NEW YORK TIMES #1 BESTSELLER **TONY LEE** WRITING AS

JACK GATLAND

THE MURDER OF AN **MI5 AGENT**...
A BURNED SPY **ON THE RUN** FROM HIS OWN PEOPLE...
AN ENEMY OUT TO **STOP HIM** AT ANY COST...
AND A **PRESIDENT** ABOUT TO BE **ASSASSINATED**...

SLEEPING
SOLDIERS

A **TOM MARLOWE** THRILLER

BOOK 1 IN A NEW SERIES OF THRILLERS IN THE STYLE OF
JASON BOURNE, JOHN MILTON OR **BURN NOTICE,** AND
SPINNING OUT OF THE **DECLAN WALSH** SERIES OF BOOKS

AVAILABLE ON AMAZON / KINDLE UNLIMITED

JACK GATLAND

THE LIONHEART CURSE

HUNT THE GREATEST TREASURES
PAY THE GREATEST PRICE

BOOK 1 IN A NEW SERIES OF ADVENTURES
IN THE STYLE OF 'THE DA VINCI CODE'
FROM THE CREATOR OF DECLAN WALSH

Made in United States
North Haven, CT
17 March 2024